ASHE

ASHE

Book 1 of the Storyteller Trilogy

———————

pHil Rittenhouse

Written Books

*

Book Cover design by the Author

First edition 2025

ISBN: 978-1-970322-03-3

*

Written Books

www.writtenbooks.com

For Lorena, of whose hazel eyes I drink.
She told me I must fulfill my dream.

For Heather, who agreed to the
challenge of writing.
She told me we should both
chase our dreams.

For Conner and Ethan and Archer.
I tell them they can achieve theirs.

And for Elizabeth Louise.
Mom, who gave me a love of
stories and storytelling.
She regaled me as both child and adult
with tales of heroes past.

PREFACE

EVERY LIFE TELLS a story. Some tell many.

Once upon a time, the primary medium for conveying stories and history was a verbal recounting around a fire. By the simple fact that I'm publishing this book in 2025, it's patently obvious that I grew up in a time where that core tradition had long since passed.

Except it hadn't.

I was raised in a home that valued reading, in every form. But it was also a home that valued the verbal retelling of the stories read to others. I learned early on that if you retold a story well enough, in just the right way, you could inspire others to read the book themselves. I learned that first by being the recipient of such retellings, but eventually grew into sharing stories I read with others.

And I grew to enjoy the analysis of the various and sundry components of a narrative, and how they interrelated with one another. The natural progression of this was a desire to write a book.

And it sparked a question. How would I infuse a story with that love of storytelling I was given as a child? What if I wrote a book where a large part of the action was built from storytelling itself? Up to a point, of course. It might work. It might.

I built this novel up from nothing. When I started here, all it was, was swamp. Everyone said I was daft to write a novel on a swamp, but I wrote it all the same, just to show 'em. It sank into the swamp. So I wrote a second one. That sank into the swamp. So I wrote a third one. That burned down, fell over, then sank into the swamp. But the fourth one stayed up. And that's what you're gonna get.

Apologies and thanks to Michael Palin in Monty Python and the Holy Grail for that bit, but you get the idea. Decades of early attempts yielded little more than rubbish. Hopefully this fourth book is better.

I'm calling it Book One, just in case.

Welcome to the Storyteller trilogy.

I hope you enjoy meeting Ashe.

This page intentionally left blank.

THE STORYTELLER TRILOGY BOOK 1

Chapter 1 : DESERT

THE OLD MAN couldn't remember the last time he'd died.

He was generally pretty good about remembering such things, but the most recent time still escaped him. No matter; it was the next one that he needed to think about.

He looked across the cave at the small basin that served as his water source, then to the wall above it. For years, water had seeped into the cave via the intricate network of channels he'd carved into the cliffside above. Droplets then trickled down the cave wall to gather in the small cistern he'd hollowed from the rock. The arrangement never produced a great deal of water, but he didn't need much. It had been enough to keep him hydrated most of the time and partially clean on days when it occurred to him to care. Sometimes, when there was enough water and he tired of fire-roasted cave lizard, he'd boil up a rabbit stew.

None of that would happen today, though, nor had it for the past week. This had been the hottest, driest summer he could remember (he could remember many) and the sky offered no promise of relief. Even the cave lizards had left him, searching for cooler sections of the cliff wall or some elusive puddle of water hiding in the crevice of a rock.

The old man licked his cracked lips. There was only one thing to do. He'd have to do it; there was no other way. If he didn't want to die of thirst (and who did, really?), he would have to leave the cave.

Groaning, the old man rose slowly to his feet. His ancient bones protested, crackling audibly. He ran a hand through his hair. It became only slightly less gray as clouds of dust sifted out of it to the cave floor, revealing streaks of black mixed in with his disheveled silver mane.

He shambled to the mouth of the cave and squinted into the colorless afternoon sun. The rocky hillside fell away from his little hideaway thirty feet up the cliff wall and dashed itself to pieces along the deserted access road. He lifted his gaze to the distant chain-link fence which separated his home from the area beyond. At this distance, he could only just make out that one of the warning signs had almost rusted itself free of the fence. He'd have to fix that, of course. Those signs (along with whatever passed for common sense these days) ensured that everyone with at least half a brain knew they'd best come no closer.

Past that fence and the arid buffer zone, the outer fence was but a faint gray line waving to him across the sunbaked expanse. On the far side of that second fence squatted the tangled mass of highways and byways and roads, offices and homes and stores, people and pets and puke that was the city writhing under a dingy orange shroud of its own pollution.

The old man despised the city. Most of its residents, too, although he'd never met most of them. It wasn't the individuals, but the collective, that he resented. He loathed the teeming mass of people that were at best indifferent to him and, at worst, openly hostile.

He had tried to live in the city some time ago. He had become part of its tapestry, its patterns and rhythms. He had even felt a level of kinship to some there. A shared goal will do that, make strangers into something else, if only for a time. Not brothers, but colleagues. Such times pass, though. Things change.

The old man set his jaw. He looked back at the dry stone basin. Things change. This had been a good place. It had been a place where he could watch the passage of time in peace.

Peace. The old man grunted at the thought. He paused a moment to appreciate the irony. Things change.

The old man shook his head. There was no sense in wasting energy with philosophy or reflection. Despite all his best attempts throughout this drought, thinking wasn't going to fill that basin.

He needed water, and he'd have to go to the city to get it. Worse, this wasn't going to be some quick foraging trip. The only way to get what he needed for the remaining days of summer and weeks of autumn and months of winter was to spend time in the city. To walk again among its people, breathe its polluted air, blend into its days and nights.

He'd also need a job.

Chapter 2 : ENCOUNTERS

"COME ON LUV, I'm dying here!"

Amber contemplated that possibility and decided it might not be so bad. Still, she did have a job to do, and the night would only be longer if she got in trouble for not doing it. "Of course, sir, I'm sorry," she told the bigger of the two men at the table. She turned briefly to face him, balancing four plates in her hands and atop her forearms. "It's just, I'm the only server tonight." *I'm the only server every night*, she thought to herself, turning back to the table across the room. "I'll be right back here in a moment to get your drinks and take your order."

By the time she reached the elderly couple near the window, she had calmed down. The smile she flashed for them was genuine. "I've got the Belgian Waffle Platter with bacon, eggs over easy and grits for the gentleman, and an egg-white omelet with fruit for the lady." She distributed the array of plates in front of the couple, both of whom warmly returned her smile. Seeing their cups empty, she added, "And I'll be right back with a warmup for that coffee."

"Thank you, darling," said the silver-haired woman, who then focused her attention on arranging her husband's plates just so on the table.

Amber wove through the empty tables between the couple and the drink station. Along the way, she risked a glance in the direction of the diner's other two patrons, the large obnoxious man and his much smaller, much quieter, associate. They were still both engaged with their respective menus, so Amber stayed on course for her original destination. She snatched a round glass carafe of black coffee, taking pride in its rich aroma. She'd been told by more than one regular customer that they often came to breakfast early so that they could have her coffee rather than the weak mud they brewed on the day shift. As an afterthought, she spun and grabbed a bottle of syrup from the gummy shelf above the coffee pots.

Back at the elderly couple's table, Amber refilled their cups with the rich black liquid, relishing the looks they both gave their steaming cups. She left a little extra room in the elderly man's cup for the generous amounts of creamer she knew he favored. Amber spun away and he thanked her, pausing as he noticed there were only two small pods of creamer at the table. He had not quite formed the words of his request when Amber turned back, depositing another small ceramic bowl brimming with a fresh supply of miniature cups of non-dairy hazelnut and French Vanilla.

"Not to worry, Mr. Sotterbach; I've got you covered. And," she winked at his wife, "extra syrup, 'cause I have a feeling you're gonna be sharing, sweetie."

"Oh, thank you, Amber," said the woman, smiling. Her bright eyes nearly vanished in a scramble of crow's feet. "You are such a doll. Tell me, darling, how is that book of yours coming along?"

"Book, Mrs. Sotterbach? What book?"

"That book you're working on, silly! I always see you writing in those notebooks of yours."

Mr. Sotterbach took a bite of bacon and pointed half the strip at his wife. "And if you manage to make this one's life story remotely interesting, you know I'll be first in line to buy a copy," said the man around a chewy mouthful.

"Oh, Henry, stop it." She slapped her husband's hand playfully. Looking back up, she smiled, "And you know we'll buy a copy no matter what. But I'm sure you have better things to write about than those silly interviews we did for you."

Amber brushed an errant red curl away from her forehead and tucked it back under her green scarf. Only then did she realize her fingers were sticky with syrup. She scrubbed her hand on the apron over her uniform's black polyester skirt. "No real progress to report, I'm afraid, Mrs. Sotterbach. I guess you can dip a horse in butter, but you can't make him sink."

The old woman looked confused. Her husband dipped his bacon into the steaming grits.

Sensing confusion, Amber explained, "It's basic physics, really."

"You're writing a physics book?" asked Mr. Sotterbach around a mouthful of bacon and grits.

"No, it's still... Well, I'm still looking for the right idea, I'm afraid."

"Oh, now you're being silly." Mrs. Sotterbach was glad to be back on the topic of Amber's writing, despite sensing that the topic maybe hadn't changed in the first place. "I'm sure—"

"Oi!" the harsh single syllable of the call sliced through the moment, interrupting Mrs. Sotterbach's assurance before it could be voiced. Amber looked up, seeing that both men at the other table were staring expectantly in her direction.

Amber cringed inside, but smiled at the elderly couple warmly and lifted the coffee pot from the table. Bending sideways at the hips, Amber pantomimed a cartoonish exit and rushed across the restaurant.

Arriving at the men's table, Amber noticed the larger man had flipped his white ceramic cup upright atop its mismatched saucer. The younger man was watching her every move like a second-rate predator.

She looked at the older man. "Coffee, sir?"

The man bared his teeth in an expression he doubtless mistook for a smile and shifted in his seat. The bench groaned under the effort to support his bulk. He ran a ham-like hand over his greased hair and then smoothed the collar of his garish floral shirt, a large diamond glittering on his pinky. *Great,* Amber thought, *trying to impress the poor little waitress.*

Amber genuinely enjoyed the graveyard shift. She liked working in relative solitude and found a strange sense of accomplishment in straightening the place up for the morning shift, though they'd never once thanked her. Amber's friend, Fry, often made fun of her for that, rightly observing that she kept the diner far tidier than her own apartment.

More importantly, working the night shift afforded her the privilege of writing during slow times and engaging in long conversations with certain of her customers, both occasional and regular. Amber believed that people's lives held every detail necessary to compose a best-selling novel, if she could just assemble the right combination of ideas from the right combination of people. And this place, the diner at night, was the perfect backdrop for her research, with its slow pace and comfortable, unassuming presence.

Except on nights like this. Nights like this reminded her that, when it was all said and done, the place was a dive. The only people who ate here were those that couldn't afford nicer places or couldn't find a decent establishment open at such ungodly hours of the morning. And of course, guys like these two in the shiny track suits, determined they had something to show off.

Amber regarded the pair. The first, Pinky Ring, was a behemoth of a man with a protruding belly that strained the buttons of his brightly-colored Hawaiian shirt. His face, half-covered by a huge mustache, reminded her of a colossal walrus as he huffed about the indignities of her service. A perpetual sneer peeked through the bristles of that massive whiskbroom to declare the man's entitlement to whatever caught his eye.

Across the table was the thinner man. Amber realized he wasn't as much younger than Pinky Ring as she had originally thought. Immaturity oozed from every pore as he snickered at a joke the bigger man had told upon Amber's approach. His spiky hair, gelled into what he perceived as a monument to his coolness, broadcast a "rebellious teenager" stage that looked to be in the twilight of its second decade. Stuck in this perpetual state of adolescence, he sported a garish neon green tracksuit trimmed with a gold chain that he must have lifted from the set of a rap music video. He was trying so hard that Amber felt a little sorry for the man:

the little boy with an irreverence that bordered on the absurd.

The Sotterbachs, the diner's only other patrons, exchanged sympathetic glances with Amber as she was drawn into the gravitational well surrounding the two men. Amber was keenly aware of the constrained space as the dining room, not large when empty, had been reduced into a stage for the impending drama.

The man poked a fat finger at his cup. *Big and round as a greasy sausage,* Amber thought. *You're in the right place.* "Coffee?" the big man drawled with a British accent that he probably thought earned him something, "That's what's wrong with your country, innit? Tea, darlin'. Tea. Go and get me some tea is what you can do."

Amber turned and bit her bottom lip as she walked back toward the bussing station. *I need this job; I need this job.* She repeated the words in her head as a healing mantra.

She'd find some way to get through the next hour, then these two would leave, and she could enjoy taking some notes until shift close. Amber couldn't afford to lose this job. She took a deep breath and set the carafe of coffee on the heating plate, trading it for one of scalding hot water and a blue ceramic caddy holding a variety of tea bags.

Eight steps took her back to the men's table. The big man leered up at her. Not quite far enough up, though.

Amber smiled sweetly at the man in an attempt to draw his inappropriately-located attention to her face. "You asked for tea, sir?"

"Sure thing, luv. My cup's right over here." Pinky Ring slid the ceramic cup on its saucer across the table away from Amber until it tapped the wall on the table's edge farthest from her.

Amber knew at once what the man was after, and that she would now have to lean across the entire table to fill his cup. *Okay, whatever, you jerk,* she fumed silently. *Anything to get you fed and outta here.* She sighed quietly. *Not like there's anything much to see down there, anyway.*

Stretching across the table, Amber strained to avoid contact with either man as she spanned the distance separating her from his cup. Right on cue, gravity acted on her uniform blouse and parts beneath, and the big man ogled in appreciation. Amber's jaw locked and the muscles bulged at her temples. *I need this job; I need this job.* She froze suddenly as she felt a clammy hand at the small of her back.

The man grinned, "Thanks, luv! Mind if I get a couple of creamers to go with that?"

"You chuffing nonce!" hooted Track Suit. The boy-man found his fat partner's antics hilariously entertaining.

You can get anything you want, just not from me, you disgusting pig. "Sir, I'll have to ask you to move your hand. It's very distracting," Amber said through her teeth. *And if you move it south, I'll rip your arm off,* she added mentally.

"Oh, sorry, luv. Is this more or less distracting?" His hand dropped lower.

He squeezed.

ॐ • ॐ

"NO, I DIDN'T," Amber spoke into her cell phone. "I mean, I sure wanted to, though. I need this job; I'd get canned for sure if I 'accidentally' poured hot water on a customer again. Best I could do was complain to Keith, and he's not gonna do anything. He thinks he's headed for corporate, so he's not about to risk a customer complaint. Anyway, it'll make a great journal entry. Maybe I can make a story out of it."

Amber crossed the street at a jog, stepping up onto the crumbling curb on the far side just as white walky guy turned into red blinky guy. She could see her apartment building two blocks away.

"What did you call them?" she asked, momentarily holding the phone between cheek and shoulder as she tightened up her headscarf in an attempt to re-imprison some escaped locks of hair. "Well, okay, yeah, that fits. But it's not very catchy, is it? 'Fat Man and Little Boy.' I mean," she mused, "Seems a bit on the nose, dontcha think?"

Amber listened intently for a moment. Confusion marched across her face. "Sure, they totally nuked my evening. I told you that. But I don't get—"

She frowned. "And where would I have read that? You know I don't like reading. No, I find other ways to fill my break time. I write."

Amber waved a dismissive hand at her half of the conversation. She stepped out across the next intersection, jumping the light. A shiny black hatchback whipped by so closely she could feel the breeze of its passing against her stockingless legs. Amber saw the Uber light in the back window as the car rounded the corner. The driver laid on his horn and tossed her an unkind salute out his open window as he drove off.

"Yeah, well, I hope you lose your tip!" she shouted at the departing car. "No, not you. Wait, do you get tips?" Amber joked, knowing the answer. "Maybe I want your job."

A pause.

"Not a lot, that's for sure. Haven't counted it yet," she replied. The other voice spoke for a moment as Amber approached the final leg of her after-work journey. "Sure, but if every day is crap, at what point do crappy days just become normal?" Amber grinned at the response as she turned the corner. "Wow! I totally did not mean to open Pandora's can of worms, Small Fry. Take it easy."

Amber's eyebrows jumped close to each other, causing several of her freckles to jockey for position in the suddenly crowded space. "No, it's 'Pandora's can of worms.' I'm pretty sure."

She paused again to listen to the reply while looking at the construction site she was approaching. Several day laborers were starting their day at the site, pulling toolboxes, ladders, and chainsaws from a battered white Ford pickup truck. The work crew shouted to each other in barrio Spanish, making it hard for Amber to hear the other voice on the phone.

"Geez! You're always correcting me! Yes, I'll look it up, for sure, yeah," Amber promised without meaning it. "Listen, Fry, I gotta go. Coming up on my apartment, and I don't wanna have to shout over the construction guys again. Maybe we can meet up and have some of that mixed metaphor word salad you keep fussing about for lunch." One more grin. "Okaylaterbye." She tapped her phone, ending the call.

The workers were not as boisterous as they typically were, which was a relief. Amber wondered if it had something to do with the heat. Or maybe it was because the chubby guy with the jam box didn't appear to be working today. Either way, she was thankful. Relative peace and quiet on a day like this were better than no peace and quiet at all.

She approached the uneven bench that squatted across from the work area. Amber had come to enjoy sitting on the old bench for a few moments each day before heading inside to her apartment to count her tips and shower after a long night shift. She found inspiration in watching the men work, much like she did in vicariously observing the lives of her late-night patrons at the diner. Amber was fascinated by the everyday lives of common people. She had filled notebook after notebook with snippets and scenes of their conflicts and struggles, some real but many more imagined.

On mornings like this, Amber cherished the hot sun. As a child, she would have been kept inside on a day like this, being told at great length how the sun's rays would darken her freckles and increase their number as her mother would direct her to a stack of books with which she was expected to entertain herself. She had never cared about the freckles or the books, and often found ways to sneak out and bask in the sunlight she craved. It helped her think; it cleared her mind.

Amber often let the sun's heat bake a new collection of purloined stories stolen overnight from the lives of her customers. She pictured the sun as a forge, burning off the dross and refining those ideas. Or maybe an oven, baking all her thoughts together into a concept worthy of the next great American novel. And if not that, then maybe a concept for a hack article some rag website might actually publish.

The sun consoled her today. It embraced her through the black polyester uniform, as if to assure her that her dreams would eventually come true. Conversely, her disheveled hair would have none of it. A bright cascade of unruly ginger waves, her springy curls fought for refuge under the loose green scarf. Some of the outlying curls which most frequently lost that daily battle for shelter had faded to a paler shade of orange.

Amber's apron, crisp just twelve hours ago, hung askew. It testified of the dozens of trays balanced and hundreds of hurried steps she had taken throughout the wee hours of the morning. Approaching the bench, Amber straightened her uniform. She wondered how long it would be until they tore out the old bench to clear space for the new building. The bench was almost always empty, the bus route having moved over to Sixty-Third and Oak the winter before.

Today an old man sat on the far end of her bench. The man's clothes screamed "thrift store" and then muttered "utility" as an optimistic footnote. Dusty jeans and a lightweight gray and blue flannel faded into the weathered and chipped blue paint of the bench. The shirt had started life as a button-down but both collar buttons had long since departed. The wrinkled collar tips now each had a different opinion of which way they should point.

The man sat still as a stone. There was no breeze, but his silver and black hair was disheveled, as if having been blown about on its way here. Amber thought that each irregular-sized lock of hair must have been cut to its own unique length, and not recently. His hooded eyes regarded the day workers from beneath shaggy, untamed brows. He appeared oblivious to Amber's arrival on scene.

Deep lines furrowed the old man's face even at rest, hinting at long years of experience and exposure to decades of sunlight just like this. His shoulders were slumped, and his forearms rested upon his thighs. Amber was unsure if it was sadness he projected, or simply resignation.

Amber stood watching the old man for a moment, curious, her head tilted. She thought she might place him somewhere in his upper sixties. No sooner had she determined this than she questioned that conclusion. Somehow, he appeared both younger and far older than that.

Something about the old man piqued her interest. She could almost hear her notebooks mewling like hungry kittens, wanting her to fill their pages with morsels of his story.

Amber sat on the bench.

She stole a furtive, sidelong glance at the old man. He showed no sign of noticing her.

"I don't mind if you sit here," she said aloud. "I don't charge rent on Mondays."

"Today is Tuesday." The old man's voice was deep and gravelly, flat and unburdened by inflection.

"Nah, every day is Monday 'round here. I'm Amber. How was your weekend?"

Without moving his head, the man slid his eyes to glance at Amber, then away. He said nothing.

"I live in that building there." Amber gestured toward the soot-stained high-rise apartment building to their right. She looked at the large, wooded lot directly in front of them. "I hear they're going to build a 7-Eleven here, once they get all the trees cleared. One with a gas station."

The man grunted.

Amber took his response as progress. "That'll be pretty cool," she continued. "I like Slurpees."

Nothing.

"This used to be a little park, but that was before I moved here. Last few years, it's just been an overgrown haven for junkies. The city stopped taking care of it and I guess it went downhill pretty fast."

The old man inhaled deeply and let out a long sigh. Amber saw his eyes close, and his head dipped slightly.

"You probably came here to sit by the park, didn't you? I'm sorry you missed it." Amber leaned back, crossing her ankles. She regarded her scuffed shoes resting on the dry grass. "That's why I'm not charging you rent; not when there's no park, after you came all this way."

Amber was disappointed to realize she had elicited no further reaction. She regarded the workers in the dying park, watching them prepare for their day of labor.

"At least you still get to watch people. Don't you think people just make it all worthwhile? Each one of them has a story."

She turned to face the old man. "I'll bet you've got a story or two, don't you?"

The old man turned to look at Amber. Their eyes locked for a moment. Amber felt a shiver at the small of her back, despite the baking heat. She imagined for a moment that she could see the first and last pages of her own story at once in those silver-gray eyes. Her mother had once mentioned feeling like someone had just walked over her grave. As a child, Amber had never understood this, since her mother was still alive. She understood now.

The old man broke eye contact and the feeling passed. He rose and walked off.

Chapter 3 : TRANSIT

"I CAN'T SEE it! Gimme your phone." Amber grabbed the device from the other girl's hand as she dropped into an empty seat. The bus lurched into motion, causing Amber's friend to stumble before righting her balance. She swiveled down next to Amber on the padded bench seat.

"Your boss, Cameron Task, has been widely criticized recently for his breakup and transformation of Wisper since his acquisition of the company three months ago. How do you feel his plans for the social media giant relate to his larger goals of, say, space exploration?"

The camera angle on the small screen shifted from the shapely news reporter to a bookish-looking brunette in a white lab coat with thick glasses and a simple coif. Amber's eyes flew wide, and her head pivoted to look at her friend. The girl seated next to her waved Amber back to the screen.

"I'm afraid I can't speak to his work in space, and I really don't know much about social media in general, let alone Wisper in specific."

"Omigosh!" squealed Amber, pausing the video. She vibrated in her seat. "That's you! My little Small Fry is on the news!" She shot up a hand to roughly pinch her friend's cheek.

Fry shoved Amber's hand away and straightened her glasses. "Quiet down already!" she growled at Amber, aware of the unwelcome attention coming their way from the other bus passengers. "That's why I didn't want to show you," she hissed.

Amber grinned, revealing a deep-set dimple in each cheek. A red strand of hair fell free and swung across her face to tap her nose. She jammed the offending lock back into place in her messy bun and thumbed the play icon in the middle of the video. "You quiet down. I wanna watch this."

A small banner slid into the lower left third of the phone screen. It displayed Fry's name and position as Frymet Cieślak, Associate Medical Researcher, Task Life Sciences International. The newswoman continued as the banner retracted.

"We understand you work on Mr. Task's Human Existence Longevity Project, or HELP. Is that correct, Ms. Cieślak?"

"Yes, that's correct."

"Many say that Cameron Task shouldn't be allowed to play God with the human genome, and that his efforts in this arena are nothing more than a very powerful man trying to extend the reach and duration of his already too-extensive power. Do you have an opinion on that?"

The picture shifted again; now Frymet appeared in a different camera angle standing in front of her interrogator. This view emphasized the fact that the attractive reporter towered over her friend's diminutive frame. Amber mused that the network was pulling out all the stops trying to shape public opinion. It was rare that a "man/woman on the street" interview like this featured multiple cameras. Amber concluded the interview had been an ambush. Color crept into Fry's cheeks, both on the video and in real life, confirming Amber's assessment.

"Every bit as much as you do, evidently. I guess I just don't share your opinion. Who says that?"

"Excuse me?" said the reporter.

"You said, 'many say Task shouldn't be allowed to play God.' I was asking you who says that."

"Well... many do. Several prominent talk show hosts, politicians, and—"

"Any real scientists? Peer-reviewed articles? People who've lost loved ones to one of the debilitating diseases

Cameron Task has vowed to stamp out in our lifetime? Any of them say that?"

The bus slowed to a stop and let off some passengers to make room for new additions. Among the new riders were three rough-looking young men. They laughed and pushed each other as they swaggered down the aisle in search of seats.

First in line, the tallest of the three was the apparent leader of the group. He sported a vast array of tattoos that spread across the canvas of his forearms, chest, and neck like a tapestry. A ragged denim jacket hung on his broad shoulders despite the heat which lingered into the evening. He wore each patch and tear in the jacket like a badge of honor. The waistband of his jeans, low-slung in defiance, exposed a riotously colored pair of paisley jockey shorts that broadcast what he had convinced himself was his rebellious spirit.

Following close behind him, a thug that Amber guessed to be the lieutenant adorned himself with an ostentatious display of gold. Though tall, he was a few inches shorter than the group's leader. What he lacked in height, he more than made up for in body mass. He walked like a fighter and was built like someone who took that role seriously. Chains of varying lengths circled the cord-like sinews of his thick neck, the links reflecting the sterile glow of the overhead lights. A ribbed white tank top stretched over his muscular frame, in stark contrast to the tribal-style symbols decorating his arms with dark ink. His gaze, sharp and penetrating, conveyed the weight of responsibility that came with his evident position as the group's enforcer.

Rounding out the group, the third member opted for a different aesthetic, best illustrated by his flat-brimmed baseball cap tilted at a cocky angle. Even if his low station had not been made clear by his place in line, the sheer silliness of his appearance and clear lack of experience and confidence marked him as the afterthought of the group, the newbie. His baggy jeans, like his comrades', rode low on his hips. At least his choice of an oversized graphic-laden hoodie spared Amber an immediate view of his underwear.

Amber marveled at their collective ability to somehow keep their pants from falling off. Tattoo Boss caught Amber's eye on him and leered at her as the bus moved away from the stop.

Amber's eyes darted back to the phone in her hand. The reporter had appeared initially imbalanced by Frymet's question but recovered quickly. She flashed a flawless set of pearly-white teeth at the camera before sliding her focus back to Fry.

"Well, I'm afraid some of that's probably more in your area of expertise than mine. Tell me, though, Ms. Cieślak, what would be your specific response to Cameron Task's detractors?"

"I'd tell them that they should wait for the history books like the rest of us. History is full of great men who seemed mad at the time but were proven out by the greatness of their vision or achievements. Often both. I'd

tell them that the only sure way to achieve greatness is to consistently reach for goals that are just a little beyond your grasp."

"And yet, Ms. Cieślak, I'd have thought that your ethnic background as a Polish immigrant would alert you to the dangers of madmen whose reach exceeded their grasp. Or did your history book not have 1939 in it like mine did?"

The clip ended.

Amber's eyes shot to her friend's ruddy face. "Girl, she owned you! That was a setup if ever I saw one. I can't believe they call that journalism."

Fry took her phone back from Amber and locked the screen before slipping it into her purse. "Yeah, in retrospect it was obvious that they'd researched me and my background. She did a great job of making it feel random, though. I didn't even see it coming."

The bus slowed again, its brakes hissing as it rolled into its next stop. Fry rose and flipped out her lanyard to extract her bus pass. "Look, I'll catch you later, Amber. I'm gonna go home, eat a couple pints of Rocky Road, and see if I can't figure a way to keep my job after Mr. Task sees that interview."

"If anybody can, you can, Small Fry. Catch you later."

Several people exited the bus with Frymet, leaving most of the seats empty. Fry's was a popular stop. Amber saw that the trio of hoodlums had stayed on board. Her jaw clenched when she caught the one wearing all the gold staring at her. Only a single person had boarded at the stop before the doors closed and the vehicle lurched back into motion. She looked out her window rather than back up the aisle, intently observing nothing.

About a mile down the road, the bus hit a rough bump and caused Amber to hit her forehead against the glass with a muted thump. As she sat back, the reflection in the window caught her attention as Ball Cap stood and hitched up his falling jeans. The punk rubbed his nose with two sharp swipes of his thumb and sauntered down the aisle, past Amber's seat. He kept hold of his belt buckle and waistband as he strolled by, taking wide steps to help his jeans stay in place; it seemed he had not yet mastered the fine art of sagging after all. He dropped into an empty seat three rows behind and across the aisle from Amber with a muffled "whump" sound. She closed her eyes and tried to control her breathing.

The bus rumbled past the Whole Foods on 49th, and Amber did her best to conjure a grocery list in an attempt to calm her nerves. She was not sure if it was the three thugs or Fry's interview that made her so agitated, but making mental lists always seemed to help. Not that she would go to Whole Foods, of course. Fry could afford that, but her friend had a decent job, at least for now. Amber decided she would hit the Food Giant on the way to her apartment. Rocky Road?

No. Chunky Monkey.

THE BUS LET Amber off at her usual stop at Sixty-Third and Oak. The walk was not quite a mile, but the evening was made unpleasant by the hot, stagnant air and insufficient lighting. Lengthening shadows snatched at her feet as she walked. Every muscle was tight, her gait rigid. Amber's eyes flitted left, right, left in a desperate dance, trying to locate a doorway that might offer shelter should she require a place of refuge.

She'd made this walk countless times. Many of those had been at night. She had never been nervous like this before, but she'd never had cause to be. She had wished many times that the city had never moved the neighborhood stop; she wished it more fervently now. A bus stop two-thirds of a block away from her apartment would be a welcome thing tonight.

On the approach to Amber's neighborhood, the three gangbangers had joked constantly and smiled to each other. With one member behind her on the bus and the other two in front, they delighted in her discomfort at being caught in the geographic middle of their loud conversation. More than one lewd gesture had been offered her during the trip, and Tattoo Boss had grabbed at her when she passed up the aisle toward the front of the bus. The others had thought this hilarious, and the burly one Amber had taken to calling Goldy had punched the leader's arm for letting her slip from his grasp.

Amber had sighed audibly as her feet touched the pavement. She was relieved to have escaped what could have been an ugly situation.

And then the bus doors had reopened behind her.

ટ • ૡ

FOR TWO BLOCKS, the three of them followed Amber, matching her turn for turn. She focused on the sounds around her. Crickets chided her foolishness from positions of cover in scrubby alleyway bushes. Over the din of their reproach, she could still make out three distinct sets of footfalls behind her. She rubbed her ramrod-stiff neck and wished all the more the city had never relocated that bus stop.

Another corner approached. Amber risked a quick glance over her shoulder. Her eyes widened when she saw only two of the thugs. *"Where is the other one?"* she asked herself. *"The one with all the gold—"*

Amber was still looking over her shoulder when she rammed into Goldy's chest. She felt as if she'd plowed into him hard enough to have a ribbed imprint of his tank top on her cheek. The two tussled in a sudden flurry of arms, hers frantic to evade his grasp and his grasp confident, hungry. Eager.

Amber realized that the thug must have slipped down the alley and sprinted to get ahead of her while she fretted about his two companions. The young man held her by the upper arms. Her only mobility was from the elbows down, but Amber did her best to flail at his chest with open palms. He was too wary to allow her enough range to reach his face with her fingernails. The fingers of her left hand entwined with the massive tangle of gold chains around his neck. One of them broke as she tried in vain to pull back against the man's greater strength. The gold necklace flew free and landed on the dirty sidewalk.

"Skank! You gonna pay for that!"

Amber strained against her captor. She saw that the leader of the pack had caught up with them. He took in the scene.

"Hey, now, now. Ain't no reason for words, now." Tattoo Boss smiled, exposing a collection of gold-capped teeth. "We all friendly 'round here, right?"

Goldy shoved Amber toward his boss in the frayed denim jacket. The gang's leader grabbed her by the arm and slipped his own arm around her neck.

"Yeah, we all friends. We gonna get to know each other, ain't that right?" He leered at Amber. Despite the thug's attempt to advertise his elite status with the pricey dental modifications, his breath reeked of liquor, cigarettes, and poor hygiene. His second in command bent down to retrieve his fallen necklace.

Amber's silence appeared to displease the man. His arm snatched tight around her neck, jerking her head. "Maybe you didn't hear me. I said, ain't that right?"

"No, it ain't."

Barely a low growl, the new voice behind Amber carried the promise of menace like nothing she had ever heard before.

Chapter 4 : CONFLICT

THE LEADER OF the group whirled to face the newcomer. Amber stumbled as Tattoo Boss pulled her along with him in a wide arc. A wavy, thick lock of red hair fell free of her loose bun and partially obstructed her vision, but through it she recognized the form of the old man she had met that morning on the bench by her apartment.

He was built like a fireplug. Amber had heard that phrase somewhere, but never knew what it meant until now. The old man had to look up at Amber's attackers yet still managed to dominate the scene. Stout legs and battered work boots connected him to the pavement as if he were an element of the earth itself, a living extension of the rough and cracked concrete.

The dim light of a streetlamp flickering a block away marched shadows among the deep, craggy furrows that lined his face. His grizzled jaw clenched, and Amber could see the silvered hair at his temples bristling as the muscles tensed.

"Let her go," the old man snarled.

The thug clutching Amber took a step backward to give his mate room to join the party. Goldy rose, his broken necklace forgotten. Amber looked down the street looking for Ball Cap, the third member of the group. He stood a block away, having taken up a position at the far corner of the block. Amber realized that his role as a lookout was all part of a routine the young predators had developed. She wondered how many times they had done this. A chill coursed through her at the thought.

"Now, who gonna make us, old man? You?" Goldy's grating voice yanked Amber's attention back to her immediate predicament. The old man's interruption was no doubt a diversion from their usual pattern, but one they appeared eager and ready to deal with.

The tall, muscular punk circled the old man. His hands balled into fists and then released. Amber heard soft crackling from the younger man's knuckles. "You some kind of five-O? That it? Well, you best call you some backup, old man. Ima lay you out."

Goldy burst into motion. His right fist sailed unimpeded through the space occupied by the old man's head a scant moment before.

"Oh, he fast!" The young man smiled back in the direction of Amber and the gang leader, excited for this bit of sport.

Knowing she was the prize at the end of the contest, Amber struggled against the hand restraining her. She sent a futile kick toward the leader's shin. Tattoo Boss tightened his grip on her neck.

Goldy lunged again. The old man's hand shot out to grab the punk's wrist. Locking his other hand against the younger man's elbow, the old man used his assailant's momentum to throw him against the cinder block wall next to them.

"You boys can walk away, you know. Nobody's done anything they'll regret yet."

The younger fighter's face reddened as he spun back toward the old man. "Only person gonna regret anything tonight is you, gringo. You dyin' tonight!" Goldy leapt across the intervening space at the old man.

Again, the shorter man twisted out of the path of his attacker. This time, though, he grabbed a handful of belt, buckle, and trousers in his right fist. His left hand snaked through the punk's right arm to grip the front of his tank top and a handful of gold necklaces. The younger man found his arm's movement completely restricted by the grapple. He struggled but found the old man's grip to be like an iron vise. His angle prevented Goldy from reaching or striking the old man, and Amber thought he resembled a fish flopping when pulled from the water.

"Lemme go, old man! You over now. You over!" The punk shouted. Amber could see droplets of spittle sparkling as they flew from the younger man's mouth in rage. "You gonna wish you was dead, time I'm done with you!"

Amber was not positioned to see the old man's face, but she saw his shoulders slump and his head shake ever so slightly left to right. He muttered something Amber couldn't make out and placed a foot against the side of Goldy's right knee.

৵ • ৶

THE SOUND THE thug's knee made as it came apart was something Amber was sure she'd never forget. Goldy shrieked, his cry a high-pitched wail of equal parts agony and comprehension.

The old man released his hold of the younger man's belt and Goldy's center of mass slumped downward, finishing the violation of bone and cartilage with a sickening wet crackle. The knee bent sideways at an unnatural angle, with the lower leg rotated slightly outward.

A second incoherent shriek split the night. Goldy flailed at the old man, waving his hands in terror as if to shoo away some marauding ghost. The old man retained his grip on the thug's shirt and the gold circling his neck.

That grip was the only thing keeping the younger man from crashing to the sidewalk.

The old man's right fist hurtled forth like a pile driver. He released his grasp on the younger man and the punk slid unconscious to the cracked pavement.

"What you do, man? What you do?" Tattoo Boss took a half step backward, still holding Amber. She renewed her struggle against him.

The old man turned to face the two of them.

The punk seemed to realize Amber was straining against him for the first time. He shook his head and shoved her roughly away. Stumbling sideways, she fell to the ground.

"What you do?" the gang leader repeated. "Denny my bro', man. What you do? You trash his knee like that? Five-O can't just do that!"

"What, Your friend? He's young; he might walk again. He'll remember me when he does, though." The old man's mouth tightened into a tense line, then he shook his head and appeared to reconsider. "Look, kid, I don't know what gave you guys the idea that I was the police. I just wanted—"

"You not? Then what are you?"

"I'm a concerned citizen looking out for your welfare. Telling you that you can still walk away from all this." The old man shifted his gaze from Tattoo Boss to Amber, sitting on the ground. "Run," he growled at her.

Amber remained immobile. Her eyes stayed fastened to the scene in rapt attention.

The punk stepped forward. The height difference was more pronounced in this fight than the last. Amber estimated Tattoo Boss had well over a foot in advantage over her surprise benefactor, with a reach to match, and he was armed. A knife had appeared in the gang leader's hand.

The knife looked evil; it had been designed for mayhem. Brass knuckles built into the hilt enveloped the thug's fingers below a curved crossguard. A sturdy blade, sharpened on both sides, extended a full six inches from the guard. Each rounded knuckle of the hilt bore a spike and a half-inch spiked pommel protruded from the weapon at the bottom of Tattoo Boss's clenched fist. The knife was neither new nor shiny. Even in the poor light, Amber could tell it had seen much use.

The thug advanced in a crouch, his arms extended. "Yeah, well, I don't care who you are, old man," he said. "You gonna bleed for that, believe me."

Amber watched the softness that had visited the old man's face fade in an instant. He took two steps to his left. This move gave him room to maneuver as needed in the impending clash, Amber realized. It also had the side benefit of taking her out of the gang leader's line of vision.

"Run," the old man repeated to her. He paused, then scowled when she ignored his directive. His eyes returned to his new opponent.

Tattoo Boss moved toward the old man, his attention similarly focused. "Only one runnin' should be you, old man. Not like you could get away, short little legs like those. You can try to run—"

The thug burst forward mid-sentence, expecting to have surprised his foe. The extended knife blade rocketed in and up in an arc intended for the older man's midsection. Tattoo Boss stumbled in an attempt to regain his balance after the knife encountered nothing but empty space where the old man had been.

Righting himself, the punk whirled back to face his opponent who had pivoted out of the way. The gang leader abandoned his crouch and stood to his full height. "Aight, you fast. I forgot," he sneered at the old man. "Don't matter none. You still getting' cut tonight, believe me."

The thug darted forward a second time. The old man stepped inside the range of the thug's knife and sidestepped. Amber realized that it wasn't so much that the old man was fast, but rather that he was efficient. Tattoo Boss hurtled past, carried along by his own momentum. As he passed, the old man landed a solid jab to his opponent's lower ribs.

The younger man tumbled to the ground in a heap but recovered quickly. He rose, clutching his bruised ribs. His knife hand was still extended.

"I'm telling you, bub," said the old man. "It doesn't have to go like this. Put up the knife and go your way, let us go ours. Nobody else gets hurt."

The gang leader bellowed in response. "No way, old man! It's on, now. Ain't no leavin' for you, 'cept on a stretcher!" Saliva sprayed from Tattoo Boss's lips. Veins stood out on his neck, his forehead. Amber was unsure whether the punk's amplified rage stemmed from the fact that the old man had landed the first blow or due to his attempts at reason, but she could see the younger man becoming more unhinged by stages.

"That's it, old man. Playtime's over!" he continued. "It is over! Ima cut you now, believe me!"

The gang leader exploded in the direction of the old man. He closed the distance in a single broad step. His knife hand thrust out in a stabbing lunge—

—And came to a sudden stop against the old man's right palm.

"I believe you," the old man growled through clenched teeth.

Amber's jaw went slack. The old man's right hand was wrapped solidly around his assailant's knife hand. The blade, now red with blood, jutted from the back of the old man's hand. He had neutralized the threat of the blade by impaling his own hand upon it.

The gang leader recognized this fact about the same time that Amber did. He tried to jerk back his hand without success. His hand could not open to release the knife; the old man's iron grip held his fingers captive.

The thug remembered that he had a second hand that had yet to enter the fray. His left fist reared back in readiness to strike. As the blow started forward, the old man spun away to Tattoo Boss's right, raising their entwined hands up and over his head and shoving backward. Air left the younger man's lungs in an audible rush as he slammed against the cement wall, pinned between it and the old man.

"I tried," said the old man. He whipped his right hand in a twisting motion, his hand a blur. A sound like several chicken legs being twisted free of the carcass at once assailed Amber's ears. The old man stepped away from the wall and the gang leader crumpled to the ground, staring at his mangled hand in horror.

"You can't do that, man; you can't do that," he wheezed. "You can't do stuff like that, man, I got rights. I got rights."

The older man yanked the bent blade free of his hand and dropped it clattering down the sewer grate. He looked away toward the corner where the lone streetlight still flickered. Ball Cap, the third punk, raised his hands briefly and then turned and ran in the opposite direction. The old man turned back to the gang leader.

"I got rights," Tattoo Boss was still muttering.

"Yeah, you got rights," replied the old man. "I think about 'em sometimes, when I wanna get myself all riled up."

His left fist flew out and dropped the punk to the ground.

Chapter 5 : BINDING

AMBER'S FINGER STABBED the elevator button a third time. A fourth. "Come on! Not now. Not now!"

"What's the problem?" The old man cradled his right hand. His flannel shirt tangled upon itself where he had wadded it around his wound. Most of the muted gray and blue fabric had turned a deep crimson during the speed-walk to Amber's apartment building.

"The problem is, the stupid elevator is out again. Our cheapskate landlord took seven weeks to get to it, and three days later, it's out again! We're going to need to get you to a hospital."

"Told you on the way here. I'm not going to a hospital." The old man's deep-set eyes were locked on Amber's. She found his unblinking stare slightly unnerving, but attributed his oddness to the pain he was feeling.

"Look," she said, "I don't see what the problem is. You're bleeding like crazy, and you need stitches."

"You said you could fix me up at your apartment. We're at your apartment."

"I only said that because you said you wouldn't go to a hospital," Amber hissed. "I'm not a doctor! The best I can do is clean you up and wrap something around your hand."

"That'll be enough. All I need."

Amber threw her hands in the air. "It's not all you need!" The words burst from her lips. She gathered her composure and forced herself to speak in a level voice. "You had a knife through your hand," she said slowly, each word separated with a pause for clarity. "You *put* a knife through your hand! What kind of crazy person does that?"

"The kind of crazy person that saved your ungrateful butt from those three lowlifes."

"Ungrateful?" Amber's eyes opened wide. "I'm super grateful! I just want you to get some decent medical care," she implored. "Listen, if it's a money thing..."

"It's not a money thing. It's an 'I'm not going to a hospital' thing."

"But the elevator—"

"Stairs are right there."

"Stairs?" Amber's eyes were circles. "I live on the eighth floor!"

"I'll make it. Go."

დ • ლ

"I THOUGHT YOU said you had a lot of alcohol up here. 'The good stuff,' you said."

Amber set the square plastic bottle on the table in front of the old man. "This is the good stuff. Ninety-one percent. I bought five of these big bottles during Covid and still have four of 'em left." She gently pulled the old man's injured hand over a large plastic bowl she had retrieved from the cupboard.

The old man had removed his flannel to staunch his bleeding as they departed the fight scene. Amber regarded his weathered skin, now exposed beneath the short sleeves of his stained undershirt. The old man's arms and hands resembled ancient leather. Scars ranging from white to pink sketched out a map before her to places and hardships she could scarcely imagine. Tracing those scars with her gaze, Amber could easily picture the old man wandering through the harsh crucible of existence for more years than she could count. She raised her eyes to his face and tried to guess his age but found she still could not.

"What's Covid?"

Amber blinked. She looked at the old man. She blinked again. "Are you joking? How do you not know Covid-19?"

The man stared back at her. She'd seen that same look on his face during the street fight. Eyes rounded; their whites visible on all sides but the top. The top lids were drawn down to the periphery of each gray iris. Upper lip tight, his mouth drooping open slightly. Amber was unsure how someone could clench their jaw and let their cheeks and chin go slack at the same time. It seemed to her a feral look, the look of an old wolf finding itself cornered. It was as if the old man had disengaged his face to allow his brain the extra energy it needed to race through every possible outcome to a threatening situation. A master tactician, calculating his next move.

"Just kidding," the old man said after a pause.

Amber blinked a third time and decided not to pursue it. Her thumb popped open the plastic lid. The scent of the rubbing alcohol transformed her kitchen into a hospital ward. "This is gonna hurt," she told the old man, refocusing on the task at hand.

"Already hurts," he replied.

The old man stiffened as the first splash of disinfectant poured from the bottle onto his open palm.

"I'm sorry!" exclaimed Amber. She repeated those words eight more times as she finished cleaning his wound and wrapped the injured hand in gauze and a light bandage.

The old man regarded her work as she secured the outer wrap with a pair of clawed aluminum bandage clips. He turned his wrist over and winced from the pain.

"Easy!" cried Amber. "That's not gonna hold real well. You need a proper dressing. And stitches."

"This will do fine. You do good work. You've had training?"

"No," replied Amber. "Just had a lot of experience. I was just a clumsy kid. I did a lot of research into field medicine when I was a teenager, though. I used to fantasize about becoming a war correspondent."

"Read a lot of books on the subject? Field medicine?"

"No, not really. Mostly the Internet. I don't really like to read."

"Okay, that explains it."

"Explains what?" Amber asked.

"The alcohol. Tip for the future: never clean a deep puncture wound with alcohol."

"What? Are you serious?"

"Go to the library and look it up."

Amber's eyes narrowed at the older man. She called his bluff and reached for her phone.

Amber dismissed the lock screen and opened a web browser. She typed the words "puncture," "wounds," and "alcohol" into the text box and tapped the search button. A curious look flashed on the old man's face as he watched her scroll through and read the top AI-driven returns of her search.

A moment passed and the color drained from Amber's face.

"Omigosh! I am so sorry!" she cried, looking up. "Why didn't you say something?"

The spell of curiosity broken, the old man looked away from the smartphone in Amber's hand. "You were so proud of your alcohol stash. Didn't have the heart."

Amber huffed in exasperation and dropped her phone on the table. She shook her head. "Well, that just proves that we should go to a hospital and have it done right."

"We've been through that. Not gonna happen."

Amber closed her eyes for a moment. She opened them to find the old man staring at her again. Amber had long considered herself a skilled people-watcher, but she again found herself unable to classify his expression. Feeling heat rising in her cheeks, she stood and made an absent-minded attempt to organize her meager medical supplies.

"You never told me your name," she stated.

"You never asked."

"Geez! Does everything gotta be the hard way?" She plastered on a sarcastic smile and sing-songed, "What's your name, sir?"

"Ashe."

"Was that so hard? Nice to meet you. I'm Amber."

"I know."

"You know? Wow! You've got that punctured palm thing going on and you're all-knowing..." A wry grin twitched at the corners of Amber's lips.

Ashe's eyes narrowed to slits. "That's not funny," he told her. Amber felt a shiver at the old man's shift in tone. Previously, she had heard that tone only when he was responding to a threat. She blanched.

"What? I was just saying, you know, your hand was pierced, and—"

"I know what you were saying. But don't ever compare me, or any one of us, to him," growled Ashe. "He came here for all of us and how do we thank him? We treat him to the worst death imaginable. Then, once he's dead, we heap more abuse on his body before it's even taken down to be buried. Not something to joke about."

Amber's cheeks blossomed like a fresh rose. Her face was starting to feel like a blinking Christmas light. "You're right, I'm sorry," she told the old man. She realized she'd touched a nerve.

She pivoted her approach to the subject. "How'd you know my name?"

"You told me this morning. On the bench."

"That's right! I forgot about that. So, did you move into the building or something? I've never seen you around until today."

"I was looking for work at the construction site."

"With the day workers down there? Not what I'd expect for a..." Amber's voice trailed off. She realized there was no way to finish the sentence without being offensive. Still, she imagined the old man's age would keep him from wanting that kind of work. On the other hand, finding decent work these days wasn't easy and she had just watched Ashe dispatch two gangbangers before climbing eight flights of stairs more easily than she did.

"Did you get a job?"

"No. The day work had already been hired for the day. Since I was a gringo, they told me to come back and speak to the foreman after eight o'clock."

Amber realized the old man's arrival in time to rescue her from the three gang members had hinged on nothing but pure dumb luck. She shivered.

"How'd it go? The interview?" she asked, returning to the conversation. She sat down again across from Ashe.

"Foreman took one look at me and said, 'thanks, but no thanks.' Wasn't about to take a chance on somebody my age, like he even knows how old I am," Ashe grumbled. "All the stuff I've built in my lifetime, now I can't even get a job clearing a work site."

"You worked in construction?" Amber asked.

"I was an engineer, of sorts."

"An engineer? Here, I thought you were an MMA fighter or something!"

"Been a fighter, too, of sorts. Been a lot of things."

"Of sorts," Amber added.

"Of sorts."

୭ • ୭

"SO, THE FOREMAN said no job." Amber nodded at the old man. "I get it. I totally understand rejection."

"Boyfriend leave you?"

"Hah! I'd have to have one first. No, I'm a writer. Well, I want to be a writer. Not as easy as it used to be to get started anymore. Artificial Intelligence is taking over all the bit-writing work. Wish they'd told us AI was coming while I was in journalism school. The ones that really hurt are the rejection letters that you can tell were auto-generated by bots. Yep! Rejection is my middle name."

"Parents must've really loved you."

"Ha. A comedian. Anyway, if you're looking for work, why not go for a real job? Well, more real, at least. I'm waiting tables till I get a break, but even working in a fast-food joint or something would have to beat day labor, out in the sun all day. Leave that kind of stuff for the undocumented guys."

"I am undocumented."

"You're what?"

"Just what I said: undocumented. No birth certificate, no ID. Undocumented."

Ashe slid further into his seat and rested his head against the back of the chair.

"You lost your birth certificate? You can get a copy. Just go to the—"

"It's not that easy; trust me. Forget about it. Not your problem to solve. You got aspirin or anything?"

Amber got up and took four steps to a small cupboard by the sink. She stepped back to the table with a white plastic bottle of ibuprofen and a glass of water. "You said you used to be an engineer?"

"Of sorts."

"Of sorts," Amber grinned.

Ashe grunted in reply. He shook out the dozen or so pills remaining in the bottle and downed them with the entire glass of water, seemingly draining it in a single gulp. He set his glass down next to the empty bottle of painkillers.

Amber decided not to broach the subject of correct dosages of over-the-counter medications. "Yeah, so... engineer. What kind of things did you build?"

"At one point, I was Army Corps of Engineers. Built a lot of bridges."

"Really? That's cool. Any bridges I've seen?"

"No, these were temporary, in theater. Used for moving equipment." Ashe lifted his arm from the table and twisted the wrist. He flexed the hand and winced.

"Easy!" Amber admonished him. "It's going to start bleeding again if you're not careful. You really need stitches." Her mind raced back to the encounter from earlier that evening. "What were you thinking?"

"I was thinking you needed help. What were you thinking? I told you to run. Twice."

"I wanted to watch. I've never seen a street fight."

"Great," Ashe grunted. "One of those."

"No, it's not like that, whatever 'that' is. I'm a writer; I need experiences. Plus, I was worried about you: I mean, you kinda stabbed yourself! Didn't you even think about consequences?"

"Fiat justitia ruat caelum."

"What?"

"It's Latin. 'Let justice be done though the heavens fall.'" He looked at her. "You want to be a writer, and you don't speak Latin?"

"Are you kidding? Nobody speaks Latin. Where's that come from? The quote?"

"You want to be a writer and you don't know history?"

"Well, I clearly haven't lived through most of it like you have," she snarked. Her face softened. "Also, I told you. I don't like to read a lot."

"You want to be a writer and you don't like to read?"

"Geez! Can we drop it already? Anyway, listen; I've got an idea."

Amber leaned forward in her chair. "I'm thinking, if you need work, maybe we can work something out. This dump is rent-controlled." She waved at the apartment walls. "My slumlord's too cheap to hire a maintenance guy. We've got all sorts of little jobs that could use some skilled hands. I bet lots of us residents would pay under the table here and there for an occasional handyman. And..."

Ashe stared at her. His face remained impassive.

She continued. "And, until your hand heals up some, you can educate me on history! Well, yours, anyway." Amber was having difficulty cataloging her feelings. Something about the old man, Ashe, intrigued her. He was by turns infuriating, bewildering, and frightening. At the very least, he was interesting, and the perfect source for her pet research project. "You can be my muse."

"Muse." Ashe's expression remained inscrutable. "I don't think you know how that works."

"Seriously, though," cajoled Amber. "I've always wanted to write this series of articles about the lives lived by people in their... sunset years."

"If I told you my history, your brain would melt."

"Come on. All you have to do is tell me about your life."

"Place like this, you don't have old people of your own?"

"Well, yeah, of course. Duh. I've interviewed some of them, but it's all kinda... average. You're interesting."

"Huh. Interesting."

"Come on, what do you say?" pleaded Amber. "You need the money, right?"

"I don't mind helping folks out that need stuff fixed. But you're paying double."

"Double?"

"Double. I get paid to fix your broken crap, and extra for the life story." His eyes narrowed. "And you don't get to question anything. I can tell you any story I want, any way I want. Up to you to decide if I'm lying or not."

"Doesn't matter. Tell me lies all day if you want to. I just want something worth writing about."

"And I get paid in cash."

Amber scoffed. "Nobody uses cash anymore!"

"Wrong. I do. Can you get cash or not?"

"Of course I can get it."

"Then I'll be back." Ashe rose from his chair, shoving it under the table with his good hand. "Tell your friends."

Chapter 6 : ANOTHER BRICK

"HEY! YOU CAME. I wasn't sure you were going to show up today. Come on in." Amber shut the door behind the old man.

"Said I'd be here. What's broken?"

"Well, Okay," Amber shook her head a little. "Good morning to you, too. Um... I... haven't had my coffee yet." She grabbed a green cup from the table and walked the three steps to the nearest part of the kitchen counter. "You want a cup?"

Ashe stood near the doorway. He fidgeted with the bandage on his hand, looking around the apartment. He seemed to pay special attention to the windows in the living room area and the kitchen, both visible from his vantage point.

"No."

Coffee splashed into Amber's cup from a stained little pot. The steaming liquid was dark and thick. She brewed it from beans ground for espresso, at double strength. Triple, on some days. It was actually her third cup of the day, but she decided against sharing that fact, having just lied about it. "Can I at least get you a glass of water or something? I have some flat Mountain Dew, and maybe half a Red Bull...?"

"Water. Thanks."

Amber filled a glass from the tap and handed it to him. Returning to her coffee, she stirred in three heaping spoonfuls of dollar store buttercream frosting and sampled her work. Wrinkling her nose, Amber scooped in a final dollop and stirred the cup vigorously until a faux crema formed and the heady aroma of buttery vanilla filled the kitchen. Amber turned around.

Ashe had already guzzled down his water and stood awkwardly holding the empty glass.

Setting her cup back down on one end of the small table, she took his glass and refilled it. Instead of handing him the glass, she set it on the other end of her improperly assembled IKEA table, trying to avoid the uneven spots where condensation or spills from previous beverages had swollen the glued fibers of engineered wood.

She pulled the second chair out from the table for Ashe before seating herself and grabbing her coffee with both hands. "Sit with me for a minute. Unless you're in a rush to get somewhere?"

"No." The old man sat across from her. He lifted his glass and drained it a second time.

Amber's eyes widened. She raised her coffee cup, loudly slurping her first sips so as to cool the creamy hot liquid. "You want some more?" she asked, pointing at his glass.

"No. Later. So, what's broken?" he repeated, his eyes marching around her apartment. "I can get started."

"You can't work yet! You just got stabbed." Amber pulled a notepad over across the small table. "Tell me a story."

"I'd rather work."

Amber's eyes narrowed. "Fine. Fix my garbage disposal. I bought it used some time back, and I don't think the guy who put it in did it right. I mean, it works, but it gets clogged up pretty bad. Give me a couple minutes though. Let me finish my coffee and I'll run the grounds down to show you what it does."

"You ever consider maybe it doesn't work because you're running coffee grounds down it?"

Amber took another gurgling sip of her coffee. It had cooled past the risk of burning her tongue, but she was amused by the squinty look the old man made in response to the slurping noise. "Everybody's a critic," she stated. "I'm the one paying so you can fix my bad machine, not my bad habits, thank you very much."

Ashe frowned. The old man's eyebrows bristled like a pair of disgruntled gray caterpillars.

Amber was pleased to have gotten a reaction from the old man. "Hey! I know," she said with an exaggerated lilt. "You're supposed to tell me stories, too. Why don't you earn that part of your wage while I finish my coffee?"

The old man scowled. "What do you want to hear about?"

"I don't know…" She thought for a moment. "Oh, I know! You said you built some bridges, right?"

"Yeah, some."

"So, what other kind of things did you build?"

"Aqueducts. Lot of water treatment stuff, back in the day. Roads, too. Worked on a big wall project."

"Big wall project? You mean like Trump's wall? Where were you? Texas? Arizona?"

Ashe's eyebrows furrowed together, competing for space in the middle of the man's forehead.

"What? No. No, I was in northern England."

"Ooh, nice! Tell me about that, then."

"It was a stupid project. There wasn't even a real need for it. Cost the guy building it a fortune, and not a small one. At one point, there were more of us there to build the thing than there were residents in the nearby town."

"Wow, I bet the townies loved that."

"Most really didn't, and they let us know about it." The old man's surly expression softened, surprising Amber. Ashe continued. "There were a few that were okay with our being there, though, at least on some level..."

Ashe's voice trailed off slightly and Amber detected a wistful twinkle in the old man's eye. "And she let you know about it, didn't she?" asked Amber, raising her cup with a sly grin. She was delighted to see the old man thrown suddenly off his guard.

"Who? No. That's not..." he stammered.

Amber grinned. "I know, I'm sorry. I'm just yanking your chain. Come on, though." She sensed a deeper story. "Tell me about it. I don't really care about the wall; you said it was dumb, it was dumb. I'll take your word for that. I wanna hear about the people side of it. Who was she, this English girl?"

"Scottish." Ashe sighed, his body seeming to deflate as his lungs emptied. "She was Scottish. We met not long after I arrived in Newcastle upon Tyne to work on the wall. Her family passed through, headed south. Her father was a... merchant, and she caught my eye. Caught the eye of a lot of us. But when our eyes met..." The old man's face softened. Amber got the sense that she was gazing at another time and place through his eyes. Amber could almost see the old man fast-forwarding his internal narrative, looking for the correct parts of the story to convey. "She was my first wife."

"You loved her."

"Deeply. We married in the spring, against her father's wishes. Gave up my commission to stay with her."

"What was her name?"

"Magdaia. Maggie."

"What did you do? You gave up your commission? Did you keep working on the wall?"

"No, we moved south into the countryside near Gloucester. Lots of us went there when we retired from the service. We farmed, Maggie and I."

"Farmers! Okay, now we're getting somewhere." Amber noticed her now-cold coffee and took a gulp. "What kind of crops did you farm? Or did you have chickens or something?"

"Everybody had chickens. We mostly grew barley. Some oats."

"Barley. Fascinating."

"Really?" Ashe seemed surprised.

"No. I'm not even sure what barley is. Kids?"

"Three. My daughter, Aurelia, and the twins, boys. They..."

Amber waited, but Ashe stopped as if he had reached the end of the tale. The old man's face hardened, and his eyes lost their luster.

"What happened?" she whispered.

"They all died, even their..." Ashe swallowed. "They all died. Contingent of infantry transferred in from Rome to the garrison there in Gloucester. Brought the sickness along with 'em. It spread so... so fast. I was in town with the oldest of the twins, visiting an old comrade who had fallen ill. I guess we brought it home."

"But... not you. They all died but you?"

"No, not me. Doctors figured I must've had the sickness as a child or something; it never even touched me."

Ashe exploded upward, startling Amber. He slid his vacated chair back to its place under the table.

"Thank you for the water. I have to go." He moved toward the door. Amber watched him grab the doorknob and then pause.

Without turning back, Ashe growled, "Throw your stupid coffee grounds in the trash," and left, shutting the door behind him without a sound.

Chapter 7 : BONNY ANNE

"NO WAY."

Ashe scowled back at Amber for a minute before replying. "You don't believe me?"

"That's kind of implied by me saying, 'no way,' isn't it?"

"What do you think they did, then? Just went out and bought a new one like this Task character buys a new yacht?"

Ashe gestured with the pair of channel-lock pliers in his left hand across the open floor plan of the small studio apartment. Mrs. Wilson sat in a battered recliner in the living room watching the television. It was more an area than a separate room. No sound was audible to Ashe and Amber; Mrs. Wilson wore a pair of wireless headphones and dozed as the news played on without her. The screen depicted a large white craft overlaid with a banner reading, "Cameron Task's New Luxury Yacht."

The yacht was shown from the viewpoint of a circling drone. Its hull reflected the sun's rays like a floating palace. Most of the immense craft's rear deck was occupied by a large helipad. A sleek white helicopter sporting the Task Industries logo approached and touched down as lightly as a goose-down feather would drift to the floor. As the helicopter blades slowed, three tiny figures could be seen exiting the aircraft and walking toward the yacht's sundeck. Floor-to-ceiling windows along the length of the boat reflected the azure blue expanse of the open ocean.

Amber continued the discussion with half of her attention fixed on the silent television. "Well, all that pirate booty had to go somewhere, right? I figured they'd save up, then when they had enough for a new ship, they'd trade up."

"Like buying a new car."

"Something like that, yeah."

The picture on the television shifted to show the yacht's owner, leaning against a mahogany and brass rail on the gleaming main deck of the yacht. Amber envied the news crew who'd been lucky enough to snag such an interview with Cameron Task.

Task straddled the line between tech entrepreneur and Hollywood personality and was a consistent media magnet. In his late forties, he projected an air of quiet confidence, wearing an expensively tailored cream-colored suit jacket over a black silk t-shirt. His blue eyes moved from his reporter guest to the vast ocean horizon, his gaze taking full advantage of the camera angle to convey deep intellect with just the right hint of playfulness. Subtle crow's feet materialized as he smiled. He appeared to be describing his yacht: the most recent fruit of a life well-lived, a road paved with challenges and just as many triumphs. His salt-and-pepper hair blew in a light ocean breeze, giving a sense of rugged perseverance. The camera's soft lens captured the multibillionaire's enigmatic smile in just the right light. Amber felt that trademark feature was a little overdone, portraying his ambition as well as a solid understanding of the public eye.

Ashe shook his head. "Not even close." He set a metal bracket in place in Mrs. Wilson's open window and began fastening it to the wall. He turned the head of the first lag bolt with the pliers, gripping them tightly to compensate for the lack of an appropriate tool. Sweat beaded and broke the cover of his unruly sideburns to run downhill toward his chin. The back of his neck glistened with rivulets of moisture as well. Three fingers of his still-bandaged right hand steadied the bracket throughout the operation.

Amber glanced back at the television as the screen moved on to the next item in the daily news cycle. The mayor had announced a clean energy initiative aimed at reducing the city's carbon footprint, assisted by Cameron Task. Since the footage being used was of City Hall and various industrial sites, she lost interest.

She sat down on the floor by a large cardboard box and leafed through an instruction manual without bothering to focus on any of the pages. She realized she was looking at the French section of the book. She flipped the booklet closed and looked up at Ashe.

"What'd they do with all that gold, then?"

Ashe reached to grab a second lag bolt. "You mean, aside from trying to drink all the rum in the western hemisphere? Any fool thing they felt like."

Amber began fanning herself with the instruction booklet. Hair clung to her face in crinkly orange curls, plastered there with sweat. "Hurry up, will you? This heat is ridiculous."

Ashe put a final turn on the second bolt. He tested the first half of his work, judging it sturdy enough. He reached into the air conditioner box to retrieve the second bracket and two more lag bolts. He straightened his back and stood for a moment looking at Amber, who was surprised to see a smile on the old man's face.

"What?" she asked.

"You remind me of Annie. Same drippy red hair and all. She hated the heat, too. Never could figure out what she was doing in the Bahamas."

"Little Orphan Annie? What *was* she doing in the Bahamas?"

Ashe squinted at her strangely, as if she was the one not making sense. "No, not Little Orphan Annie." He shook his head as he spoke.

"So, what then? Another... wife?"

Ashe actually laughed, causing Amber's eyes to widen. "No! No, I'm good at handling pain, but I'm not crazy," the old man smiled. "I wasn't Cap'n Annie's type, anyhow. Not flashy enough."

"Captain Annie? As in Anne Bonny?"

"You've heard of her?" asked Ashe. "I thought you didn't like to read." He positioned the second bracket and started affixing it to the wall.

"Of course I've heard of her, smart guy," Amber declared. "She was a non-player character in a video game we used to play in college." Amber suspected Ashe was feeling playful. Although what she really wanted to hear about was the old man's personal history, she hated to deter him from talking if he was in the mood. Anything to pass the time and keep her mind off the heat while he worked on installing Mrs. Wilson's window unit.

"Alright, Ashe. Tell me a pirate story."

"RACKHAM WAS AN idiot. I guess he was a decent quartermaster, but he just never knew when he'd bitten off more than he could chew."

"Rackham. You mean Calico Jack Rackham?"

"The same."

"Okay, so why'd he choose the name 'Calico Jack,' anyway? Why 'Calico?' Did he have a cat or something?"

Ashe shook his head. "No, 'Calico' came from the clothes he liked to wear. Lots of pirates loved their silks and satins, but that wasn't showy enough for Jack. No, Jack, he loved the patterns. Always wore these fancy patterned fabrics from India. Stuff was called calico. That was one smart thing the guy did, I guess. Calico was this loose-weave cotton; tended to be pretty comfortable in hot climates."

"You don't seem to think much of poor Calico Jack. He made it to being captain, didn't he?"

"He did, but not on merit. Our captain in the early days, Charles Vane, he was a right bas—" Ashe stopped mid-word and then continued. "He was a real jerk."

Amber rolled her eyes. "I've heard cuss words before, you know."

"Not from my mouth, you ain't. Anyway, none of us liked Vane, and he could be fearsome harsh. But despite all that, the man was something of a strategic genius. We spent a lot of time in old Nassau, but Vane knew exactly when to set to sea and strike sail. Every time we did, and I mean *every* time, another ship surrendered their coffers to the crew of the *Ranger* or wished to heaven they had."

Amber leaned forward in enjoyment. She found herself getting into the story. She was astounded at Ashe's peculiar ability to spout pure fiction and make it sound like it was just another slice of his personal experience. "If this Vane guy was so good at his job," she asked, "how did Calico Jack take over?"

Ashe paused before answering to test the solidity of the second half of the bracket. Satisfied, he continued. "Jack was a smarmy sort, always working some angle. He was born in the wrong time, I think. If he were around today, he'd be a good politician, and I don't mean good for the people."

"President Calico Jack Rackham," exclaimed Amber, smiling.

"Saints preserve us!" Ashe shook his head to clear the thought. "So, old Jack, he was quartermaster on the *Ranger*. You know what the quartermaster does?"

Amber shook her head.

"One of the quartermaster's duties is administering the captain's judgment on the crew. Dealing out punishment when it's needed. Or at least making arrangements for it to be done. Jack was never the sort to dish it out himself."

Ashe pulled an insert from the large box and set it aside. "Well, Jack, see, he wanted more. It wasn't enough to be the captain's right hand; he wanted it all to himself." The old man brushed off several little balls of

Styrofoam that had clung to his hands after crumbling off the edges of the insert. "Thought he could helm the ship better than Charlie Vane. So, he started his plan in motion. Captain wanted a crewman punished for something, usually dereliction or laziness or something like that, and Calico Jack made it known to the poor guy what the captain had ordered. Told the guy in full-color detail what was supposed to happen to him, and for what offense. Thing is, when the punishment went down, it wasn't as severe as the guy had been told. Jack gave the guy a break."

"This goes on a while. Most of the crew find themselves one time or another on the wrong end of Vane's wrath but on the right side of Rackham's mercy."

"You, too?" Amber asked Ashe.

He looked at her. "Most of the crew. Most. Not all."

"Calico Jack was never merciful to you?"

"I was never punished," Ashe stated. Straightening, he freed the air conditioner from its box. "I know how to get a job done."

  •

"YOU VOTED?" AMBER was incredulous.

"How else would you elect a new captain?"

"I don't know. I just figured they'd have had a duel to the death or something."

"We were pirates, not barbarians," Ashe explained. "The whole point of being free from the king was to control our own destiny. Democracy was a critical part of that process."

Ashe continued. "Jack's politicking had paid off. Some of us voted to keep things the way they were, but overwhelming support from the majority got Jack his captain's chair at last."

"What happened then?" asked Amber.

"Well, Vane took the King's Pardon and gave it all up. Left the life. I'm certain he'd set aside some stockpile of gold somewhere, so he used the crown's proclamation to get himself out while he could."

"The King's Pardon?"

Ashe slid the air conditioning unit into the window along the brackets he had installed. Aside from a brief screeching sound, the unit slid into place without difficulty and stopped against the backstop of the metal brackets.

The old man stood back, resting one hand on the air conditioner. "King George's Proclamation for Suppressing Pirates. Any pirate that wanted to give up the life simply had to declare and swear loyalty to the crown, and he got off scot-free."

"You mean 'Scotch-free,'" Amber corrected him.

"No, I mean 'scot-free.' What the heck is Scotch-free?"

"You know - just like you said. Scotch-free. Like they escaped so clean and smooth that even tape wouldn't stick to them."

"Seriously?" Ashe stared at Amber. "Where'd you read that?"

Amber stared back.

"Right," Ashe said after a long pause. "I forgot. Scotch-free it is. The King's Pardon. No punishment, no nothing. Vane marches right up to Rogers' face and takes the pardon, and Rogers has to let him do it."

"Rogers," asked Amber. "Who's Rogers?"

"Woodes Rogers, former privateer. Commissioned by the King as Governor of the new, civilized Nassau. He hated pirates in general, but he flat out despised Charles Vane in specific."

"Why's that?"

Ashe flashed a mischievous grin. "Well, it's... possible when Rogers' ship was arriving in the Bahamas for the first time to take up the governorship, Vane... might have arranged for us on the *Ranger* and another ship to be waiting for him. I guess we... maybe boxed Rogers in from two sides and opened up the broadsides. Could be we fired every cannon we had at him, but it wasn't enough. Rogers broke through the gauntlet and made port. Never forgave Vane for trying to kill him, and it irked him sore to have to let Vane off without so much as a tongue lashing."

"Ha!" Amber smiled. "Sounds like Vane caught a pretty good break. What about the rest of you?"

Ashe shrugged. "We kept at it. Kept terrorizing small fishing vessels and smaller merchant ships. Turned out

Calico Jack wasn't so good at lining up big scores like Vane could."

"Why didn't you take over as captain?" asked Amber.

"Me? No, I'm no leader. Not like that."

"What did you do? On the ship. What was your job?"

"I was the shantyman," replied Ashe. The old man looked embarrassed.

"The what, now?"

"I was the chanter. When we needed to pull in a rope or hoist the sails or something that required cooperation from a bunch of men, we'd sing songs. Short ones for short jobs, longer ones for big hauls and such."

"You sang?" Amber's face lit up.

"We all did. I was the chanter. Most of the songs were call-and-response. I'd call out a line, and the other men would echo or sing out the response. It kept us all on the same timing and coordinated our efforts. Thousand-pound anchor on a soaking wet rope isn't coming up if you don't all work together on the windlass and lines."

Amber clasped her hands in delight. "That's awesome! Sing me something! Mrs. Wilson's got her headphones on; you won't even wake her."

Ashe scowled at her. "This story isn't about me. I thought you wanted to hear about Annie."

"Come on, just one song. A little one!"

"No chance."

"Okay, fine," Amber sulked. "Tell me about Anne. Where's Anne Bonny in all this?"

"You sure ask a lot of questions."

"Tell me!" exclaimed Amber, bouncing on the floor like a petulant child.

"Alright," said Ashe, "I'll tell you. But no more interruptions, and at the end, you only get a single question. One." He held up an index finger like an admonishment. "Ask anything more than one question, and I answer none."

Ashe waited for but got no response from Amber. He glared at her, and she finally mimed zipping her lips and locking them with a key.

"Okay. Calico Jack and a few of his men were on shore, drinking at the main inn in Nassau. In walked this little redhead, and the first thing she did is mouth off to the innkeeper. Turned out the innkeeper was her husband."

"Anne Bonny was married?"

"What did I tell you about the questions?"

"Sorry!" grinned Amber. "Sorry... Begging the King's Pardon!"

Ashe scowled and went on. "Anne was married. Man name of James Bonny. Failed pirate, had taken the pardon himself and set up shop at the inn. Jimmy had married Anne when she was thirteen, and he'd never been all that great a catch, if you know what I mean. That, along with him giving up his life of adventure, made him even more hateful and made Anne even less respecting of him. Anne's fiery spirit was more than enough to capture the fancy of our own Calico Jack Rackham.

"And little Annie takes a fancy right back. Less than a week, and they're a right thing, making all manner of plans for a grand future together."

Ashe pulled a half-dozen sheet metal screws from a small bag in the box and traded the pliers for a screwdriver. He began securing the air conditioner to the mounting bracket, struggling only slightly to be driving screws with his left hand.

"Only thing between them and this glorious future is the husband. They entreat him for divorce, but James refuses. He may not love Anne, but he's not about to give her up. Anne petitions Governor Rogers to intervene, but he's less than helpful, still fuming over having had to let Vane get away.

"Finally, Calico Jack approaches James Bonny, man-to-man. He knows there's only one way to handle this situation. Jack offers the man twelve pounds sterling, cash-in-hand."

Ashe's brows furrowed suddenly, and he leveled his index finger at Amber. "No questions!" He ordered. Amber closed her mouth, having opened it to speak.

"The husband, though, isn't granting a divorce regardless of the price offered. Ultimately, Jack and Anne have only one way out of their dilemma.

"Two days after the King's Pardon period expired, we sailed away from Nassau, Calico Jack taking his new-found love with him."

Ashe finished putting in the last screw and tried to jiggle the air conditioner. The unit held fast, and he pulled the open window down atop the device. Spreading the shroud panels to each side, he completed the installation.

The old man leaned against the wall and slid down to seat himself on the floor. "Plug it in," he directed Amber.

∾ • ∿

"THE NEXT SEVERAL months passed in a blur. One ship fell before us, then another. Our luck started to shift. Anne was not only a fierce addition to the crew, but she made up for a lot of what Jack lacked. We stirred up so much trouble that Governor Rogers hired a pair of pirate hunters, Barnett and Bonadvis, to track us down. But that just added to the thrill of it all.

"Good times couldn't last, though. We'd stopped on an island off of Cuba for resupply and some shore time. Next thing we knew, the guard crew we'd left on board came crashing through the foliage to tell Captain Jack that a French man-o'-war had sailed up and made to capture the *Ranger*, which of course they did, since our brave guard crew had deserted the ship."

Ashe paused a moment, breathing deeply of the rapidly cooling air blowing from the window unit. Amber brushed some hair back from her face, also enjoying the coolness. Mrs. Wilson snored lightly in the other room.

Ashe continued. "Well, we got to the beach, and we could see the French ship. She was a monster; we'd never have stood a chance in open battle. But—" the old man grinned, "She already had another ship in tow. A sloop, and a snappy one from the look of her. Two-masted with a snow rig, eighteen guns. She wasn't big, but she was fast and pretty. Calico Jack was in love all over again.

"We waited till nightfall, watching the French take possession of the *Ranger*. Their crew was spread pretty thin, so Jack hatched this plan. Moon was but a sliver that night, so we waited till it was darkest before we took the skiff and rowed out to the sloop. It was only too easy to subdue the half dozen guards they'd left aboard and take the ship. Anne wanted to kill them, but Jack just tied them up.

"An hour later, we'd ferried our crew aboard and weighed anchor. We left the guards gagged in the skiff and by dawn we were so far gone the French barely had a memory of us."

Ashe noticed he was still holding the screwdriver and set the tool on the floor. He rubbed his right hand, wincing. "Jack named the new ship the *William*, and we continued our reign of terror through the Caribbean.

"Jack was in his glory on the *William*. It was all a party to him, his best girl by his side, plunder to be had a-plenty. He took to inviting his conquests aboard to drink with him to celebrate their own downfall. A few of those conquests even left their ships to join our crew, he made it sound so grand.

"Things were going well. Until one of our new crew members, taken aboard from a Dutch merchant, caught Annie's eye. She began showing an interest in the new addition. Days went on, they'd spend more and more time together, not doing anything but walking the deck and talking. Any of us ever came close, and the talking would stop. But just talking. Talking and laughing.

"Needless to say, old Calico Jack Rackham was beside himself with jealousy. One day, he flew into a rage as Anne was walking with her new friend and started to challenge the newcomer to a duel. I'm not sure if Jack realized that he was rubbish with a sword or it just dawned on him that he was captain and could do whatever he wanted, but he ordered Anne's friend restrained. Some of the crew grabbed him, but he was a fierce one and there was a horrific tussle. At the end of it, three of our crew lay sleeping on the deck, Jack himself had a black eye, and the newcomer's clothes were pretty torn up. At that point, we all saw what our new crewmate's secret was."

Ashe paused. He looked at Amber, almost daring her to pose a question. She refrained, surprising even herself.

"Her name was Mary Read," Ashe continued at last. "She'd been at sea for years, passing as a man, with no one the wiser. No one until Anne, that is. They'd hit it off immediately, the two of them, both relieved to have found a kindred spirit.

"Far as Jack was concerned, though, the damage was done. He'd been embarrassed, beat half silly by a girl, and worst of all, he felt left out since Anne had found a new confidante."

"Anne and Mary fought side by side over the next few weeks. Absolutely fearless. They were the best of us, those two, and our coffers filled to overflowing. The tide had turned. Murmurs started amongst the crew that Jack was washed up, that Anne should be captain. Of course, that only added fuel to the fire.

"Jack, he hatched a plan to rid himself of the girls. He sends them ashore in Jamaica with a few other crew members, myself among them, under the pretense of filling casks with water. After getting the water, we return to the coast to find that Jack and the *William* are gone.

"I've never seen anyone so angry as Anne was that day. She was frightening. Mary Read was hardly a moderating influence herself. We spent the next two weeks rowing up and down the coast. We heard many a tale of the *William* and the exploits of the crew nearby but saw nary a sign of the ship.

"We kept looking. Finally, late one night, we saw a distant light dancing out on the water. See, Anne knew that in putting us ashore with more than half the *William's* water casks, Jack was limiting his operating range. She knew he would have to stay near land, at least until he got more barrels.

"Rowing out to the light, we found her at anchor. The *William*. I got hold of the cathead and was able to work my way onto deck and lower a rope for the others.

"The *William* might as well have been a ghost ship. We looked fore and aft but couldn't find a soul on deck. Had the pirate hunters gotten them? Some sickness? Were they all taken by the Flying Dutchman? We ventured below and found our answer."

Ashe looked at Amber. Her eyes were fixed on him in attentive silence. The old man grinned.

"Drunk, to the last man. Every one of them drunk as can be, empty rum bottles strewn everywhere and rolling gently on the swells. And there he was, half-sitting on the floor. Captain Jackanapes himself, head lolled back against a cannon, front of his shirt stained dark with rum."

"Little Annie, she was furious. Her face turned that color it would when she shifted murderous, and we knew to stay out of her way. Sad for old Jack, the cannon he'd picked for a pillow was one that we kept loaded with chain shot, ready for when we came in close upon another ship. Anne throws open the gun port and sets match to tinder from the linstock. She doesn't even bother to run out the cannon; she just primes the touchhole from the quill and lights the thing where it sits.

"The roar was deafening, even to those of us who were ready for it, twelve-pounder setting off in a closed space like that. Well, it woke up Calico Jack, that was sure. The cannon jumped almost a whole foot straight up in the air, not having any run to dress down its recoil. Old Jack, he just lies there on the deck, squeezing his head like he's trying to put his brain back in and wailing like a newborn baby. Anne, she's disgusted, and marches back to the upper deck. Mary Read and me? We just look at each other and shrug before we follow her up.

"We didn't know it at the time, but Barnett and Bonadvis, the hunters, heard the cannon shot across the waters; it was a still night. By the time dawn broke, they were just about upon us; we didn't even see them coming till they were within cannon range. *Their* cannon range.

"We scrambled like we never had before, but there were just five of us on *William* even capable of standing. Everybody else, including our illustrious captain, was still sleeping off their drunken binge. We'd just barely raised the mainsail when the hunter's ranging shots threw up geysers off our starboard bow. Annie hung on the ship's wheel, but *William* was slow to come about without a full sail."

Amber watched Ashe's face lose its color. The old man's eyes stared a hole through Mrs. Wilson's shoddy wallpaper and off across some distant horizon. When he spoke next, his voice had gone flat.

"I'd only just cleated off the halyard when the first volley struck us. Barnett's ship was a frigate, 32 guns on two decks. The second volley followed right behind.

"I didn't even see or hear the cannonball that hit me; I was running for the foremast when it spun me right about, slammed me across and over the gunwale. The shot took my left leg clean off; I didn't even feel it. I only realized it was gone just as I hit the water.

"Next thing I remember, I'm bobbing on the surface clinging to a broken bit of spar. The *William* had pulled away with Barnett's ship having caught up to her. I could see Anne and Mary still fighting alone on the deck. Wasn't long until the deed was done, and Barnett had them both bound.

"All I could do was watch them sail away."

ॐ   •   ॐ

ASHE SHOOK HIS head as if to clear his vision. He turned his head to Amber who found herself unable to speak. Ashe braced his left hand against the now-cool wall behind him and rose to his feet.

"Go on. I'm giving you one question," the old man said. "Let's hear it."

"What... what happened to them?"

"The crew was hanged first, marched up the gallows two-by-two. I was there to watch each one swing and to say goodbye, me with my one leg and my crutch. Calico Jack hanged last, and Rogers ordered his body set on display. The girls, they got temporary stays of execution, both by lying about being pregnant. Poor Mary got sick, though, and died of dysentery while still in prison."

Amber paused for a moment. She tilted her head at Ashe. "Wait a second! You got blown off the ship and left for dead; you only had one leg. How did you swim to shore in shark-infested waters? And what happened to Anne?"

"Nope," said Ashe. "Too many questions. We're done here."

Chapter 8 : QUICK READ

THE FAMILIAR SCENT and bubbling sizzle of potatoes in hot oil lingered in the air, taunting Amber. She regarded the lonely paper-wrapped parcel on her plastic tray and sat down. She slid across the slick red vinyl cushion to wedge herself into the corner of the booth and stretched her feet outward along the seat.

The restaurant buzzed with activity as customers placed lunch orders at newly installed but impersonal kiosks and families who had been served chatted over their shared meals. A few Luddites appeared lost near the counter, hoping in vain to be cared for by another human being. The low murmur of nearby and distant conversations and the occasional clatter of trays overlaid the fainter sizzle of food on the griddle behind the counter. A soft backdrop of music played, blending the lively ambiance into a homogenized, anonymous hum.

Frymet arrived and pulled out one of the aluminum chairs with a grinding squeal along the linoleum floor. She set her tray on the table with a muted clatter and sat facing the half-booth occupied by Amber. Fry wore a demure selection from her typical business casual wardrobe. *At least she remembered to leave her lab coat at work this time,* mused Amber. The ubiquitous lanyard around Fry's neck swung as she slid her chair forward, causing her work badge to strike the edge of the table with a clacking sound.

Amber shifted her attention downward and unwrapped her cheeseburger. The crinkly paper blossom opened to emit a characteristic aroma of seared meat and the metallic tang of ketchup. She took her first doleful bite, wishing she'd thought to order extra everything.

"Where's your drink?" asked her friend. "And your fries? You always get fries."

"Yeah, well, not this time, Small Fry. Couldn't afford it," Amber muttered around a mouthful of food. "Had to buy a magazine this morning."

Frymet glanced over at the magazine. Its glossy front cover was filled with a pensive-looking photo of Fry's boss, Cameron Task. Across the lower area of the dramatic portrait was a statement declaring him the magazine's "Person of the Year" and teasing an internal article about him entitled "Life in the Blood."

"I was going to ask you about that, actually," said Fry. She sipped at her beverage, the dark liquid rushing up the straw and falling back down. "It's not like you to read."

"Everybody's a critic." Amber reached out to snatch one of her friend's french fries.

Frymet acted indignant, then turned the red carton to enable them both to share. "You know I can't get you an interview. I never even met the man."

"What?" Amber was taken aback for a moment until she caught up with Fry's meaning. "No, no, it's not that. I bought the magazine this morning to keep Ashe from beating up the newsstand guy."

"The newsstand guy deserves it," said Frymet. Her eyes widened. "Ashe? You mean that old guy you told me about? The one that saved you last week?"

"Yeah. I ran into him this morning as I was coming back from work. He was standing there at the newsstand reading this," she took another french fry and waved it to indicate the magazine before swiping the fry through the puddle of ketchup Frymet had squeezed onto a napkin between the two girls. "I could see that Ashe was pretty ticked off, but I couldn't tell if it was the article or newsstand guy watching him read it.

"Newsstand guy looked apoplectic; it was kinda comical. Dancing around like he was about to dump his shorts or something. I showed up and the guy just lit into me. Guess he knew I knew Ashe or something. He started screaming that homeless people can't just come up and use his stand as a library, and that somebody had to pay for the magazine. Ashe did his best to ignore the guy, but I could tell it was boiling up. Finally, newsstand guy reached out and grabbed Ashe's arm. I about dumped my shorts."

"Oh, my gosh," said Frymet. "What happened?" Amber had told Fry about the encounter with the three muggers and the short work Ashe had made of the pair of thugs he had dispatched.

"Well, Ashe looked real slow down to the guy's hand on his arm. I swear I could see every single part of Ashe's neck and back and shoulder tensing up. It was like the muscles were physically climbing all over each other, wanting to be the first one to rip into the other guy."

Amber reached for Fry's soda and took a sip. She set it back down. Frymet didn't even react, awaiting the next part of the story as she was.

"I saw the whole thing going down a slippery soap, so I reached out real easy and slid the magazine from Ashe's hands. I pulled out some cash and told newsstand guy I wanted to buy the magazine. He let go of Ashe's arm and took the money."

"That was it?"

"That was it. I think the guy knew he'd almost stepped in it. You never know it until he wants to show you, but Ashe can be pretty scary for an old guy."

"Wow," Frymet stated around a bite of her sandwich. "You'd think he wouldn't take the money, knowing you'd just saved his life."

"Are you kidding? Newsstand guy always takes the money," Amber said, affecting the vendor's thick accent.

"What did Ashe do?" asked Fry.

"Nothing, really. I asked him if he was coming upstairs to work on anything today. I told him old widow Wilson's new air conditioner was doing great. He just kinda growled at me and stomped off."

Amber took a big bite of her cheeseburger. She mopped at her lips with a paper napkin as she chewed and swallowed.

"So, I tried reading the article," she said. "I saw it was about that HELP project you work on, and something about enhancing telomere transfer something-or-others in the blood without telomerase or something or other. And a bunch of other words I can barely pronounce."

Frymet laughed out loud. "Stop, stop! You're going to hurt yourself," she told Amber.

"Okay, so save me from myself. Sum it all up for me." Amber took another bite.

"Well, we're working to isolate the function of telomere-extending extracellular vesicles in the blood. Task has secured the assistance of hospitals, universities, and recently, law enforcement bodies nationwide to cooperate in the establishment of a global anonymized database of blood vectors."

"You don't say," said Amber in a mocking voice. She stole another drink of Frymet's soda.

"Okay, sorry. Let's look at it this way. Imagine your DNA is a shoelace. The plastic tips at the end of the shoelace are telomeres. Telomeres are kinda like protective caps at the ends of your chromosomes. They prevent the DNA from fraying or sticking together, much like the plastic tips prevent a shoelace from unraveling.

"Now, every time a cell in your body divides, the telomeres get a little bit shorter. This is a natural part of the cell division process. As your cells continue to divide over time, the telomeres become shorter and shorter, and that protective cap wears away. When the telomeres become too short to protect the chromosome, eventually you can have a replication error in the chromosome itself. The cell can't divide properly, and it might even stop functioning. This is one of the biggest factors in the aging process."

"So, telomeres are like our biological clock," said Amber, mopping another fry through the ketchup.

"Yeah, kinda," said Frymet. "They play a role in limiting the number of times a cell can divide, so it's associated with the aging of cells. That's tied to the aging of the overall organism. We're working to understand and eventually manipulate telomeres to slow down this aging process. Maybe even reverse it.

"In a healthy organism, telomeres can be maintained and even partially repaired by telomerase. Telomerase is an enzyme that adds DNA sequences back to the ends of the telomeres, rebuilding that protective ferrule on the shoelace. This process is particularly active in cells that divide more frequently, like stem cells."

"Yeah," said Amber. "I saw that about telomerase. Had no idea what it was."

"Telomerase contains both protein and RNA components. The RNA part provides a template for the addition of new DNA sequences. When a cell divides, the DNA is replicated. Like I said, when that happens, the ends of telomeres typically get shorter. Telomerase goes and adds DNA sequences based on that template to the ends of the chromosomes, compensating for the shortening that occurred during cell division."

"So, telomerase helps the telomeres last longer."

"Exactly. While telomerase is active in some cells, like stem cells, most normal body cells don't have much telomerase activity. It's a protective mechanism to prevent uncontrolled cell division, which could lead to conditions like cancer."

"So, telomerase is bad, then."

Fry shook her head. "No, it's not that simple. Uncontrolled telomerase activity would be bad and could lead to cancer and mutations, and who knows what else, but controlled and directed? This is the key to unlocking the mystery of human aging and preventing it."

"You've seen Jurassic Park, right?" quipped Amber. She popped the last bite of her sandwich into her mouth.

"*Daj spokój,* Amber! Not you too," groaned Frymet.

Fry leaned forward. "You know what they didn't have in Jurassic Park? Real computers. They didn't even try to run any simulations, and if they had, what are you going to learn on a 1990s Macintosh? Mr. Task has an entire datacenter in Ashburn dedicated to running simulations on the purification of telomere extracellular vesicles from the blood. We've already shown how adding them to T cells can reverse aging in the immune system of both humans and mice. We're about on the verge of a reliable mechanism that doesn't require telomerase. When his quantum computer comes of age, the pace of our work is going to skyrocket."

"Skyrocket. No pun intended," grinned Amber, referring to Task's other dream of reaching and populating Mars.

"Ha, ha. Anyway, we'll have a 'telomere donor' boosting solution in three to five years. From there, the sky really is the limit."

"What I don't see," mused Amber, "Is why any of that would upset Ashe so much. If he could even understand it."

"Do you think he could?" asked Frymet.

"I dunno. Maybe. He used to be an engineer, so I figure he's smart. He doesn't come across as scientific in any way. Super good at telling stories, though. And as we all know, adept handling of the language is a distinctive marker of advanced intelligence."

"Says someone who frequently uses phrases like, 'a slippery soap.'"

"What? Soap is slippery."

"Slippery *slope*," Fry stressed the second word of the phrase. "We've been over that one."

"Let's grieve to disagree," replied Amber. "I'm just saying, maybe Ashe does understand the article and didn't like it. Or maybe there's something going on behind the scenes that he's freaked out about?" Amber raised one eyebrow, giving her friend a conspiratorial look.

"And exactly how would an old homeless guy know what's going on behind the scenes at Task International?" Fry asked. She ate the last of her sandwich and reached to take her drink from Amber's hand.

"Oh, so there *is* something going on!" exclaimed Amber.

Fry rolled her eyes. "Even the behind-the-scenes coffeepot talk isn't anything that would concern some old man. Sure, there's always rumors circulating around the labs. They say Mr. Task has identified anomalies in some hush-hush sample from the nineties that people in the lab are calling his 'white whale' of telomere reparation. That's all I've heard, just that there's some corrupted super-mutant sample from an old crime scene that even Mr. Task can't pin down with all the computers in Ashburn. It's just the bio-lab equivalent of a ghost story," she laughed.

"Wow," Amber deadpanned. "You nerds have all the fun."

"We do!" Fry sipped at her drink. A girl younger than either of them slipped past their table, balancing a full tray and struggling to keep her three children moving in the same general direction.

Fry lowered her voice. "A lot of what we've learned has other applications as well. Did you know we can take a blood sample and gather enough information from it to pin down where a person sleeps?"

"No way!"

"Yeah, it's experimental, but it looks promising. Your parasympathetic system takes over while you sleep, Cortisol levels go way down during sleep, there's a ton of other changes. Some factor allows occasional new blood cells produced to embed environment-specific markers in those grafted telomeres. We're still working out what that factor is. The replicated cells can actually indicate where the person was during that time. It's not many cells, just a couple per thousand maybe, but when taken in aggregate, it can be moderately reliable. That's how Mr. Task negotiated the use of law enforcement databases in his research."

Amber's eyebrows rose. "Wow, that is some serious Sherlock Holmes stuff, there."

"Sherlock Holmes never had the computing power that Mr. Task has." A dreamy expression came over Frymet's face as she considered the future she was helping create. "He's going to get us there, you know? People are always all over him for trying to play God, but he's doing it for the betterment of mankind. They'll see."

Amber reached for the soda. Fry let her take the cup from her hands.

"Task's work will lead to new forms of prophylactic therapy for immune senescence and age," Fry said. Amber suspected the summary was for Fry's own benefit, based on the vocabulary shift. Fry continued, "It could even eventually lead to aging reversal. You'd think that would be something your old friend would want to happen."

"Yeah, you'd think so," said Amber. She slurped the last of their shared soft drink.

Chapter 9 : PAST AND FUTURE BOTH

ASHE RETURNED TO the building a little over a week later. He had come to collect from Mrs. Wilson, who had asked to defer payment until she received her Social Security check on the third of the month. Amber encountered the old man in the seventh-floor stairwell, where they crossed paths because the elevator was still out. Ashe was headed down when the two of them met.

Amber tried to engage the man in small talk, but he had returned to his usual taciturn self. Whatever strange circumstance had so animated him a week prior appeared to be long gone. Amber asked Ashe to stick around and talk for a while, and he reluctantly accompanied her back upstairs in response to a promise of water.

"Ever seen a summer this hot?" Amber inquired, unlocking her door. She dropped her backpack on the ratty armchair in which she preferred to write and stepped over into the kitchenette. "Lemme get you that water."

"Seen a lot of summers. They're all hot in their way, like the winters are all cold in theirs. Some of each are just more so than others."

Amber's eyes narrowed at the old man. "You doing okay?" she asked.

She extended a hand with the glass of water. Ashe took it from her, moving at a measured pace.

The old man drained the glass in a single pull as she seated herself at the table. Amber wasn't sure she'd ever get used to that. She'd come to refer to the habit jokingly in her notes as his "drinking problem."

"More?"

"No," replied Ashe. "Not right now." He set the empty glass on the table and pulled back the other chair. He followed Amber's lead and sat.

Amber waited as patiently as she was able. Ashe had proven last week that he could be talkative when he wanted to be. She would just have to allow him the opportunity.

Their eyes met for a moment across the table, and it became clear to Amber that Ashe was deep in thought. He caught himself and averted his gaze. Her eyes followed his away from the cheap little table and across the communal area. In her mind, Amber referred to the area with the table as her dining room, while the space with the couch and her off-brand little television was her living room. In her mind, it made sense to separate the two spaces and elevate their status to actual rooms, although the entire center of her apartment was only a single twelve-foot square on a good day.

Amber's eyes scanned the living room and discovered that Ashe's eyes must have moved on out through the smeared window. Her eyes rushed to catch up and found them staring at... nothing.

Ashe filled his lungs and expelled several liters of air in a long sigh.

"It's Mrs. Wilson," he said at last.

"What about her?"

"Does she talk much? Does she go anywhere?"

Amber thought for a moment. Old widow Wilson was either pushing ninety or it was pushing her. Amber had dealt with her on a few occasions, mostly to assist the old woman with a grocery delivery or things like that. "Sure, she talks, I've spoken with her. Not, you know, a lot, but she does talk. As for going out... I can't say I've ever seen her leave the building."

The old man's eyes shambled back into the dining room after a brief trip into the kitchen. His gaze met

Amber's again across the table. His expression was guarded. "Not much of a life, is it?"

"Depends, I guess," Amber said. She knew she was stalling. "I mean, how much of a life do you expect to have at her age?" Again, Amber struggled to guess Ashe's age. He, of all people, had to understand how people and their lives changed as they got older. And since when did someone of his obvious experience ever ask life advice of someone Amber's age?

"Humph," grunted Ashe, breaking eye contact. "How much of a life do any of us expect to have, ever?"

Amber was unsure what the old man meant by that comment. Nor could she tell whether he wanted to talk or not. It was clear to her that he was dealing with some internal struggle, though she had no clue how to get at it.

"Tell me another pirate story," she said after a few moments of silence.

Ashe chuckled, a wry grin on his face. "No, I don't think so," he said. "I've only got the one."

Amber grinned herself. "Okay then. Last we left off, you'd lost your entire leg and your job as a pirate. What happened next?" She made a show of looking underneath the table. "I'm guessing the leg grew back?"

Ashe straightened his left leg. "I guess it did," he replied.

"Good for you!" Amber rocked back in her chair and clapped her hands in delight. "What did you do next? Did you stay in the Bahamas?"

"Not for long. There wasn't anything left for me there after a time. I did some traveling, held different odd jobs."

"Where'd you go?"

"Back to England for a while, then to France. Spent the coldest winter I've ever seen southwest of Smolensk in Russia. After that, I decided I'd had enough of Europe and headed this way. Ended up in Winchester, Virginia, and settled down again."

"Settled down..." Amber spoke slowly. She let her implied question hang in the air between them.

Ashe looked straight at Amber. A tightness at the corners of his mouth gave clear witness that he understood the question. A brief moment passed before he answered. "Yes," he stated, "I got married again."

He paused. Amber figured Ashe was deciding how best to talk about whatever came next. She was filled with admiration for the old man's storytelling skills, and with gratitude that he was willing to share his stories with her.

His face softened as memory flooded back. "Loved her more than anything. I'd just sit and drink of her hazel eyes like they were the very waters of life. I even got a song named after her."

"Seriously?" Amber tried and failed to think of anything more romantic. "Tell me about that!"

"Well, I'd made a trip up toward Zanesville for a couple weeks. Had an acquaintance up there, a former pastor, name of Henry. I was having dinner with Henry one night, and he shows me this poem he'd written about a lost love. It was pretty good, I told him.

"It was so good I mentioned it to another friend of mine, JP. JP had lost his singing voice and was working at being a composer. I told JP about the poem, and suggested they meet. The three of us got together a couple of days later, and JP just sat at the piano and banged out this tune in A major while he read through the poem. Very catchy melody.

"So, I grab a guitar JP had there, and start playing along. I almost have the chords worked out when JP stops playing. He says the girl's name doesn't work. I thought Henry was about to come unglued. 'We can't change the name,' he says. That's how personal it was to him: line in the sand kind of thing. He tells us the full backstory, how he'd been a pastor and had fallen for the prettiest sheep in his flock. So much so that he proposed.

"Well, the girl's family shut down the romance in no time flat. Her family was pretty well-to-do and wanted nothing to do with their girl getting married off to a flat broke preacher. It tore Henry up pretty bad, to the point where he resigned his church altogether.

"Took me and JP the better part of an hour of delicate conversation to finally convince Henry that, despite the origin story, the name 'Emma' just wasn't going to work for this song. JP's music called for a three-syllable name.

"'Please,' JP practically begs Henry, 'just give me another name.' He really wanted to publish the song."

Amber found herself leaning forward on her elbows. "And did he... Henry?" she asked. "Did Henry come up with another name?"

"Yep," replaced Ashe.

"Well, don't keep me in suspense! What was it?"

"Bertha."

Amber's brain took a moment to process. She felt like she'd just tripped over a parking block.

"I know," said Ashe, seeing her confusion. "Me and JP, neither one of us knew what to say either. I mean what do you say? Sure, the guy's distraught and lovesick, but he's a poet and a former pastor. You figure he has a passable command of the language. But he doesn't even know how many syllables are in his lost lover's name!

"JP just starts playing the song's intro again from the top, soft-like, and I join in on the guitar and start singing. Comes time for the girl's name, I just fill in my own wife's name, and it kinda stuck.

"JP publishes the song, and it goes on to be a big hit. But I get to take it home and sing it to my wife, the gal it's named for. She loved it. Not long after that, though, war breaks out and I'm called back up. I never saw JP or Henry again."

"But you were married! And older. Wasn't the draft for young men?"

"Young, old, doesn't matter. That's the thing about war, isn't it? Don't kid yourself. Any war worth its salt will take as many as know how to fight, and still can. We blame the politicians, and we should, but war has a mind and purpose all its own. The politicians are just tools in the killin'.

"But at least I had the song to keep me through the battles and the marches and the long nights. Sang it every single day I was gone." Ashe's face fell. "Then I was injured and sent home, only to find the song was all I had left."

Oh, no, Amber thought. *Not again.* "What happened?"

"There was… a fire. Our house burnt down while I was off to war. While she slept and I wasn't there. She was gone for almost a year, and I never even knew. I lost my way for a long while after that."

"I'm so sorry, Ashe," Amber whispered. In a louder voice, she asked the one question she had to ask. "What was her name?"

Ashe opened his mouth to answer, and a knock came at Amber's door.

☙ • ❧

"SMALL FRY! GET in here! There's somebody I want you to meet."

Amber grabbed Frymet's arm and yanked her friend into the apartment before kicking the door shut. She swept her backpack out of the frayed armchair and pulled it over to the table, where she encouraged Frymet to join them.

"Ashe, this is Fry. Remember, she's the one I showed you the video of."

"The interview you ranted about for three days straight?"

"Well, yeah. That one."

Ashe had risen when the newcomer had arrived. Amber's friend held forth a tentative hand. "Um... Hi, I'm Frymet."

Ashe took the preferred hand in a gentle but confident grip. He looked Frymet directly in the eye. "Dzien dobry, Pani...?" asked Ashe, letting his question hang in the air.

"Pani Cieślak, bardzo dziękuję. Frymet Cieślak. Seriously, though," Frymet released Ashe's hand and switched back to English for Amber's benefit, "Please, just call me Fry."

Once Frymet and Amber were seated, Ashe sat again at the table. "Very well, Fry. It's a pleasure to meet you. I'm Ashe."

"Um..." Amber interjected. She looked from Ashe to Frymet. She looked from Frymet back to Ashe. "What just happened?"

"I introduced myself," Ashe stated.

"You speak Polish?" Amber demanded.

"I speak a few languages."

"How'd you know she was Polish?"

"The interview you ranted about for three days straight."

Amber found herself at a loss as to how to respond. She popped up to her feet. "I know!" she said. "Let's have some water."

Stepping around Frymet's chair, Amber retrieved three glasses, filling each with water from the tap. She set one down in front of Frymet, then at her own seat. The third glass she placed in front of Ashe, close enough to his other glass that the two touched with a clinking sound.

As Amber reclaimed her seat, Frymet raised her glass to her lips. Ashe did the same, draining the glass in less than two seconds. He set the glass back in its place next to his prior empty glass. Clink.

Frymet noticed his behavior and cast a curious look in Amber's direction. Amber, not having touched her glass since setting it on the table, gestured with an outstretched palm to forestall any questions or comments about the water.

Amber asked her friend, "So, how's work?" with a facial expression that was only slightly exaggerated.

"It's good," replied Frymet. "Honestly, I'm relieved to even still have a job after that interview debacle. My manager told me Mr. Task had watched it several times, and I kinda figured it was all over for me. But my boss said Mr. Task felt bad for me. Turns out he was really cool about it, actually."

"Cool enough to let you take a spin on his ship?" asked Amber.

A bewildered look darkened Frymet's face. "How did you know about that? I haven't told anyone yet."

"Told anyone?" Amber was herself confused. "About Task's new yacht? It was all over television. Kinda hard to miss."

"Oh!" exclaimed Frymet. "That ship! I thought you meant M.U.R.P.H.E.," she smiled. She continued on to explain. "I applied for the Mars program this week. I'm waiting to hear back."

Amber's face lit up as well. "Mars! No way! That is so cool! You're going to Mars?"

"No, that's years and years away. Probably decades, and I'll be too old by then. I just want to be part of getting us there."

"Who's Murphy?" asked Ashe. He mimicked Frymet's pronunciation of the acronym.

"M.U.R.P.H.E.," stated Frymet, pronouncing each letter separately. "It stands for the 'Mars Unified Research and Planetary Habitat Endeavor.' It's Mr. Task's long-term program aimed at preparing humans for Mars and Mars for humans."

Ashe's brows furrowed. The old man looked from Frymet to Amber, and back again.

"You're skeptical," observed Frymet.

"Usually," was Ashe's terse reply. "Does this Task guy think we're ready to go to Mars?"

"Well, no, of course not. Not yet. It's a long-term goal, and everything he's doing is in support of that. I work in genetic research at Task Life Sciences International. All of our work on the human genome, telomere engineering, extension of the human lifespan, targeted eradication of disease... it's all centered around his goal of getting us ready to go into space."

"Huh. And he wants to go, why?"

"Well, you know all the work he's done in sustainability."

"Let's presume I don't."

Frymet looked a bit confused but went on. "All his early work at Solar, enhancing the grid with renewable options, his SolarDrive cars, the biodegradable batteries, even his work on carbon-negative data centers... I mean, how important is that?" She paused.

Ashe realized she was expecting an answer. "I'm guessing very," he replied.

"It is!" said Frymet, warming to her topic. "What real impact has all of that made on the environment though? Not as much as it should have, and Mr. Task knows that. He sees that his vision doesn't stand a chance unless everyone, every person in every country, is on board, chasing a common goal. That's why he's leading where no one else wants to lead. Where no one else *can* lead." She took a breath. "That's why he's going to Mars. And if I can't go myself, I want to at least be part of it."

"But it's still people," said Ashe.

It was Frymet's turn to be confused. She frowned. "What do you mean?"

"I've been a lot of places in this world. Almost everywhere. And what you're overlooking is that people are the same everywhere, in every time. People are stupid. They're self-serving. They're evil. The fallen state of mankind is the only constant, no matter how we all try, or how we look at it. Sure, there are occasional, even frequent, flares of good, but they all get stamped out in due time. Why does Task think going into space will change any of that?"

"Mr. Task wouldn't disagree with you!" exclaimed Frymet. Amber, who had taken to scribbling furiously in her notebook, looked up in surprise.

"Sorry," said Frymet in a softer voice. "Mr. Task gets that. That's why he's doing what he's doing, why he's done what he's always done. Great men have to lead."

Ashe frowned at her. His jaw clenched and his lips drew to a thin line. When he spoke, it was with a deep guttural tone, nearly a growl. "In my experience, the biggest names in history, the names everyone knows, those men weren't trying to change the world for the good of mankind. I only see one fool-proof example of that type of goodness. One. The others who've actually changed the world on the scale we're talking about: the ones who 'have to lead'? They all wanted something, and that something usually involved taking rights away from somebody else. Or worse." Ashe's lips curled in remembered disgust. "The men and women in history who were truly great weren't great because they wanted to be. History revealed them to be great when they resisted the tyranny of those making active, usually violent, attempts to recreate the world in their own image."

Frymet was taken aback by all of this. She looked to her friend for assistance. "Amber, what do you think? Where are you in all this?"

Amber bit her lower lip. "Look," she said, "You know me, Fry. I want to form my own opinion, but I'm not qualified to weigh in on something like this. If I could talk to Task in person or something... Maybe research for an article. What do you think? Can you get me an interview with your boss?"

The atmosphere in Amber's small kitchenette had shifted. Though it was warm in the apartment, the air appeared to have chilled in the moment's awkward silence.

"Come on, Amber, we've talked about that," Frymet demurred at last. She scowled. "Hey, I'm late for yoga class or something." Standing up, she walked toward the door. "I gotta go. I'll see you later, Amber."

Amber gazed at the door as it closed behind her friend. She blinked and turned toward Ashe, who was staring intently at the table.

"Well," said Amber, "I'm sure glad you two met."

Chapter 10 : THE BAND PLAYED

"WHAT'S THIS? I thought we were going to the fifth floor to fix Mr. Ling's water heater."

Several days had passed since Ashe's disastrous encounter with Fry, and Amber was eager to get things back to a happier tone.

"We are, but it can wait a little bit. I got these from a guy up on twelve! Well, borrowed them." Amber was glowing, excited about the surprise gift she had arranged for her new friend.

Ashe stood in Amber's apartment looking down at the two instruments. Both were old, both had seen a great deal of use, and neither made any attempt to hide its feelings about those long years of abuse. On the left, leaning against Amber's worn couch, the guitar looked as old as Ashe. The chipped lacquer of the headstock still declared the maker's name as "Yamaki." The headstock and neck may have both started life as a rich full-colored Rosewood but had faded over the years to a sick purplish gray. Two strings were missing, as was one of the tuning pegs.

Next to the guitar, a tired old banjo slumped against Amber's box-like footstool. This instrument's tuning pegs had long ago turned a smoky yellow color; they were no longer white and opalescent. Decades of fingers had marched across the goatskin head, darkening it on both sides of the strings. The banjo was open-backed and lacked a resonator, but Ashe could not tell if that was from intention or neglect.

"Congratulations," Ashe said.

Amber rolled her eyes. "Have a seat," she told Ashe, placing a hand on his elbow. "I got them so you could play me that song of yours. The one you named after your wife."

The old man stood firmly in place, oblivious to Amber's pull on his arm. "I'm not playing that song for you," he stated.

"Oh, come on! You haven't been around for almost a week," she implored him. "Fry said she feels really bad you guys didn't agree on more stuff. And every time you show up, you just want to get right to work! You need to relax a little. I told Fry the same thing. You guys both need to chill out some. I thought it would be good to just have some downtime before you start working today. Please play a song? It'll be fun."

"Um... no."

"You are so difficult!" Amber's face flushed. "I went through all this trouble to borrow these, so you can at least play me a song. Any song."

Ashe stood still for a long moment, glaring at her. A random thought occurred to Amber, and she pictured the old man's unmoving face on Mount Rushmore. His face was impassive like granite, just a lot scruffier. Downright fuzzy around the sideburns. Okay, maybe he wasn't stonelike after all, but still grumpy. She toyed with the idea of commenting on it, but she figured he'd go off on great men and history and honor and all that stuff. Why couldn't the old man just relax a little?

"Any song?"

"Any song," Amber's face broke into a smile. She renewed her pull on the old man's arm. "But—" she added, "It has to tell a story. That's part of our deal. No 'Happy Birthday, I'm done now' tricks. I'll get you a glass of water when you're done."

"Then we can go get busy on Mr. Ling's water heater?"

"What? You got somewhere important to be?"

AMBER SETTLED INTO her threadbare brocade armchair, which she had turned to face Ashe. The old man took a seat on the boxy faux-leather footstool that doubled as a storage container. Deciding it could support his weight, he contemplated the two offerings Amber had brought him. He reached for the banjo, thinking it best to go for an instrument that possessed four strings by design rather than circumstance.

Ashe plucked tentatively on the strings and reached for the tuning pegs. "Do you think your friend will mind if I switch to Irish tuning?" he asked.

"He won't even notice," replied Amber. "He doesn't play, he just collects things."

The old man grunted and spent a few moments tuning the banjo. It was clear to Amber that Ashe had not touched an instrument in some time, but his exploratory picking soon gained confidence. His picking on the dilapidated instrument shifted into a repetitive sequence that rose and fell like waves to provide a consistent backdrop for the opening lines of his song:

"Now when I was a young man, I carried me pack,
And I lived the free life of a rover

From the Murray's green basin to the dusty outback,
Well, I waltzed my Matilda all over.

Then in 1915, my country said 'Son,
It's time you stopped rambling, there's work to be done.'

So they gave me a tin hat, and they gave me a gun,
And they marched me away to the war.

And the band played Waltzing Matilda,
As the ship pulled away from the quay

And amidst all the cheers, the flag-waving and tears,
We sailed off for Gallipoli"

As he reached the last two lines which comprised the refrain, Amber noticed that Ashe's voice had taken on the shadow of a convincing brogue. The word, "Quay" was pronounced "Key". Amber was unsure if this was due to the old man's newly affected accent or the rhyming needs of the song.

"How well I remember that terrible day,
How our blood stained the sand and the water

And of how in that hell that they called Suvla Bay,
We were butchered like lambs at the slaughter.

Johnny Turk he was waiting, he'd primed himself well.
He showered us with bullets, and he rained us with shell

And in five minutes flat, he'd blown us all to hell.
Nearly blew us right back to Australia.

But the band played Waltzing Matilda,
When we stopped to bury our slain.

We buried ours, and the Turks buried theirs,
Then we started all over again."

Ashe stopped playing and looked at Amber. Seeing the look on her face, he asked, "It doesn't get any better. You want me to stop?"

Amber shook her head. "No... The story's not finished, so you're not off the hook. You started this."

Ashe resumed playing. As he began the second verse, the old man kicked a heel back roughly against the box-like footstool in time with the music. The first loud thump was so loud it startled Amber. The repeated rhythm simulated the steady explosions of artillery fire and quickly became an inexorable background, expressing a hopelessness that clawed more deeply into Amber's stomach with each beat of Ashe's makeshift drum.

> *"And those that were left, well we tried to survive,*
> *In that mad world of blood, death and fire.*
>
> *And for ten weary weeks, I kept myself alive,*
> *Though around me the corpses piled higher.*
>
> *Then a big Turkish shell knocked me arse over head,*
> *And when I woke up in my hospital bed,*
>
> *And saw what it had done, well I wished I was dead.*
> *Never knew there was worse things than dyin'.*
>
> *For I'll go no more waltzing Matilda,*
> *All around the green bush far and free.*
>
> *To hump tent and pegs, a man needs both legs.*
> *No more Waltzing Matilda for me."*

By the time he finished the third verse, Ashe had stripped away any patina or pretense of respectability. His voice now bristled with a deep, resonant bitterness that rasped in the back of his throat. The refrain hit Amber like a hammer striking an anvil and she found herself wincing at the end of each new line, dreading the beginning of the next.

Amber was grateful for the instrumental interlude Ashe played as the next portion of the song. She felt she needed a moment to absorb what she had experienced so far. She found herself transported to another time and place, invested in the story being told in verse by the old man.

He resumed:

"So they gathered the crippled, the wounded, the maimed
And they shipped us back home to Australia.

The legless, the armless, the blind, the insane,
Those proud wounded heroes of Suvla.

And as our ship pulled into Circular Quay,
I looked at the place where me legs used to be.

And thanked Christ there was nobody waiting for me
To grieve, to mourn and to pity

But the band played Waltzing Matilda,
As they carried us down the gangway.

But nobody cheered, they just stood and stared,
Then they turned all their faces away."

Amber had never heard such a deeply personal rendition of a song. Any song. She thought that Ashe's voice no longer followed the sad melody so much as coughed it from bloodied lungs. She found herself completely immersed in both the hypnotic tune and the layered complexity of the lyrics. She only reached to wipe her tears when she realized they had run down her cheeks and started falling unbidden from her quivering chin.

> *"And so now every April, I sit on me porch, And I watch the parade pass before me.*
>
> *And I see my old comrades, how proudly they march, Reviving old dreams of past glories.*
>
> *The old men march slowly, old bones stiff and sore. They're tired old heroes from a forgotten war.*
>
> *And the young people ask, what are they marching for? And I ask myself the same question.*
>
> *But the band plays Waltzing Matilda, And the old men still answer the call,*
>
> *But as year follows year, more old men disappear. Someday no one will march there at all."*

The next part took on a different tone. Amber didn't know enough about music to discern if it was a key change or just a slightly different way that Ashe picked at the strings. It was, she guessed, a wistful inclusion or an adaptation of the original tune that Ashe's lyrics had referred to "the band" playing:

> *"Waltzing Matilda, Waltzing Matilda,*
> *who'll come a-waltzing Matilda with me?*
>
> *And their ghosts may be heard*
> *as they march by that billabong,*
>
> *Who'll come a-waltzing Matilda with me?"*

Ashe's playing faded and he held the banjo with reverence, as if the instrument had earned his respect through shared experience. Amber realized she was simply present as a bystander to a recollection of adversity shared between two old warriors.

"Which leg did you lose that time?" Amber asked, hoping to inject some levity into the heaviness of the atmosphere.

Ashe leaned the banjo gently against the sofa next to the guitar. "Both of them, right below the knees."

So much for levity, Amber thought. "Did you write that?"

"Write it? Me? No, that was Eric Bogle. Covered a lot, though. My favorite version was the Pogues'. Shane and the boys made it real."

Amber wiped a final tear. "More real than your version? You made that sound pretty personal."

"It was pretty personal. Can we go now?"

"Yes," Amber whispered.

ASHE

Chapter 11 : DIGGING DEEPER

ASHE HAD THAT look again. He got that way sometimes; more and more often lately. They'd be talking, or delivering groceries to a shut-in resident, or working on someone's dishwasher (Ashe did all the work, of course; she watched and listened to his stories and took notes) and then he'd get that look. At those moments, Amber suspected he was regretting ever meeting her, like she was some horrible complication in his otherwise well-managed life. Sometimes it made Amber angry, other times it was bewildering. Either way, these moments of disapproval always gave her a chill. It was a strange reaction, to be sure, but one she couldn't deny, however quickly his mood passed.

"What's the problem now?" Amber asked the old man. She stole a glance at the couple seated at the next table. She hoped Ashe wouldn't cause a scene. They sat together at a small table in the neighborhood coffee shop that she liked to frequent on her days off. She liked coming here to be surrounded by the tapestry of people, and to watch, wikisurf, and write. They knew her here, and she would be embarrassed if Ashe made a fuss.

In front of Amber sat a colossal white ceramic cup. It bore the shop's logo and held the latter half of her cinnamon roll cappuccino. It was one indulgence she made time and budget for every week. Ashe had emptied his third tall glass of water.

Getting no immediate response, Amber asked again, "What did I say this time?"

Ashe shook his head. "Nothing. I just don't see why anybody would want to research something like that," he grumbled.

"What, the Spear of Destiny? I told you. I want to find some new, unused idea for an article about Cameron Task. If I'm ever gonna get something published, I need an angle that no AI bot will ever come up with. I need a hook."

"Hitler's quest for the Spear of Destiny," Ashe said flatly. "I'd say you found something. Task will be thrilled about the comparison."

"Well, yeah, but..." Amber paused, collecting her thoughts. "Just saying, so many people think Task is a visionary; others think he's a megalomaniac. The guy comes across as kinda obsessed with prolonging the human lifespan, and a lot of people question that. I think an article about it would get noticed. A lot of people are convinced his quest for power isn't going anywhere good."

"Quests for power rarely do."

Silence sat with them at the table for a moment. Amber squirmed under Ashe's withering gaze.

"What do you think about the man?" Ashe asked her.

"Me? I don't have any real opinion. But the article would get read, I bet."

"Shouldn't you focus your writing on something you actually have an opinion about? Why would people care about a topic if you don't?"

Just like that, Amber recovered from the feeling his disdain gave her. It helped her to get frustrated, and she was heading that way now at a rapid pace.

"Okay, yeah, it's a rabbit hole. But check this out." Amber spun her laptop around to show Ashe the web page she was reading. On the screen were several pictures of a spear from different angles. The haft of the spear was an elaborate thing made of iron and some dark wood with engraving and a gold filigree thread winding its way toward the spearhead. Fine red cloth was wrapped around areas of the haft and accented by golden tassels.

The business end of the spear was a delicately wrought blade hammered to a fine edge on both sides. The spearhead seemed to have been broken at some point in history and later repaired. The middle area of the long blade had been replaced with solid gold cast in the shape of the missing piece of the original.

"What's that supposed to be?" grumbled Ashe.

"It says so right there!" cried Amber. "The Spear of Destiny. It's the spear that pierced the side of Christ."

"No, it isn't."

Amber was infuriated at how arbitrarily difficult the old man could be. "Oh, right, I'd forgotten you know everything about everything." She scrolled down the page to show him another image. "Look, here it is right here, on display in the Imperial Treasury in Vienna. This is the actual relic recovered from Hitler's bunker after his death. It's labeled right there as the Lance of Longinus." She stabbed her finger at the laptop's screen.

Ashe regarded the screen, unimpressed. He blinked. "Who's Longinus?"

"Saint Longinus. Says here he was the Roman soldier who stabbed Jesus at the crucifixion."

"And they made him a saint, did they? That makes good sense."

Amber closed her eyes and tried to count to ten. She made it to seven. "Okay, you win," she said. "Why are you so sure this isn't the Spear of Destiny?"

Ashe scooted his chair forward three inches to make room for the barista to slip behind him with a pair of lattes for the next table. "First, there's no such thing as destiny. Second, look at the thing. All that gold? Maybe that was the spear of an emperor; it sure didn't belong to somebody who fought for one."

"Okay, sure," agreed Amber. "But the spear has been around for two thousand years! Plenty of people have sought it out, and I'm sure a lot of them have embellished it to make it look more the part. The church fancied up all kinds of relics in the Middle Ages."

"That spear is not two thousand years old."

"How do you know? Did you carbon date it?"

"Don't have to," said Ashe. "Look at the spearhead. That's eighth century, upper European. Profile is all wrong for Rome. Plus, look at the metalwork. That's not a Centurion's weapon; it's not functional at all. It's obviously ceremonial."

"Oh, is that your story for the day?" sniped Amber. Her tone dripped with more acid than she intended; he'd gotten to her at last. "That's what you want to tell me all about today? How you used to hang out with the soldier who stabbed Jesus?"

And there it was again: the look. Amber shuddered, knowing she'd pushed too far without even knowing what they were really talking about. Silence fell like a lead curtain across the small table between them. The little tabletop stretched into an impassible expanse.

Amber listened for anything in the bustling coffee shop that might distract them, something to help her change the subject. Her efforts were in vain; she couldn't concentrate well enough to distinguish individual words above the general buzz of a half dozen conversations or the repeated chime of the cash register or the constant din of her thoughts.

She glared at Ashe and sipped from her coffee, now lukewarm.

Ashe looked at Amber across the table. His face softened, although his mouth retained its tightness. His eyes slid shut. The old man pulled in a quarter of a bushel of air and slowly expelled it in a long, ghostly sigh.

"Hitler wasn't hunting for the actual spear," said Ashe quietly. "Yes, I'm sure that's the one that was in his bunker," he added, stopping her rebuttal before she could make it. The old man opened his eyes. They were dark, hooded, and they drilled into Amber's soul as he continued. "But the physical artifact was just a by-product of Hitler's real quest. It was never anything but a means to an end; he never ascribed any real power to the spear itself. He used it for bait.

"It was *bait*," Ashe repeated, stressing the last word. "It was a way for him to get what he really wanted. That's all it ever was. And the stupid spear wasn't even from Rome. You'd think an art student might have known that."

Amber was confused but remained silent.

"His quest was never about power, not directly. It wasn't about having an invincible army in battle. They always get that part wrong. It was about eternal life. Immortality."

"Are you talking about Hitler or Task?" Amber asked, frowning.

Ashe rose from the table. "There's your hook," he said. The old man pushed in his chair without making a sound. "I have to go," he said. "Mrs. Wilson's sink is clogged again by now."

Amber looked at Ashe's broad back as he walked to the coffee shop's door. The old man slumped as he retreated, as if he had aged twenty years in the span of their conversation. The little bell on the door jangled when he opened the door to exit.

What just happened? Amber asked herself.

Chapter 12 : ENOUGH

WHEN WOULD IT ever be enough?

Ashe sat on his bed, the only furniture in his abode, and leaned against the cool wall of the cave. Calling it "cool" was generous, to be sure, but at least it was cooler than the stifling air outside the cave. The relative cool was of little help, even though the ancient stone should have provided some level of rest and comfort.

Ashe felt neither rested nor comforted. Why had he ever talked himself into leaving this spot? He knew what going into the city would do to him. He knew from before that first day out of the cave (his home, if only for the reason that no one else would want the place) that he'd get drawn in if he went there.

He always got drawn in. There was always someone he'd encounter that he ended up caring about for some reason. Someone always crept past his defenses and made him start to feel human again. Well, as human as he was allowed to feel. Sometimes it wouldn't last long, other times the relationship would go on for years before souring. The only consistent factor was his inability to learn from the mistake of allowing it to happen in the first place.

Ashe cursed quietly under his breath and fished the last fragments of tuna from the small tin with his fingers. Sliding a fingernail along a tooth to free the last pink bit trapped there, he told himself he'd make one more trip and pick up a fork or something. There were plenty of fast-food places he could just walk into and grab things like that. Maybe he'd snatch some salt or hot sauce, too. Spoil himself. As if he deserved it.

When would he ever learn?

How many times had this scenario played out? He'd lived too long to count. But it was always the same story, the same outcome. He'd get entwined with someone, and either he or they would suffer for it. Often both. And he was always the only one to see it coming, for all the good that his foreknowledge ever did. Every time the cycle had repeated, as far back as he could remember, he'd known how it would end, but somehow failed to make himself walk away from the impending disaster.

Even that very first time so long ago, that was the time that established the pattern and earned him the curse of endless repetition. That seminal event changed him on so fundamental a level that he would never break the cycle.

He had been a soldier, plain and simple. He'd had a job to do, and he'd known what that job was. What that job wasn't, he reminded himself for the billionth time, was developing empathy for a dying man. Especially that one, as his superiors had made abundantly clear. That one was trouble to the established order of things, and it had been decreed that he die, guilty or not.

Had he simply stood by and watched it all happen without getting involved, stood by like a good soldier, he wouldn't have been punished by his superiors for overstepping his bounds. Nor would he have gotten his own personal albatross placed around his neck to carry for eternity.

Ashe tossed the empty tuna can across the cave. It landed cleanly in the rusted bucket that he used for trash with a metallic clatter. He'd empty the bin on his next and final trip into the city. The cave wasn't all that big, and with the heat stretching on, the last thing he wanted was the stench of a tuna can spoiling the delightful ambiance of his home.

He made a quick count and determined that he'd made it almost thirty years this time without something going wrong and causing him to get mixed up with people again. Hardly a record, but not the worst he'd done, either. Ashe drained a bottle of water and crushed the air from the plastic container before screwing the lid back on. The crumpled bottle sailed through the air to join the tuna can. Normally, his inclination to frugality would have had him save the empty bottle and refill it. But now, with no rain in the foreseeable future and having built his stockpile, he felt no pressing need to conserve every empty bottle.

He looked at the wall of water bottles before him, opposite his bed. The count had passed a hundred cases earlier in the week.

It would have to be enough.

If he stayed under a gallon a day, his recently acquired stockpile should provide him enough water for a year and a half. He could stretch that to three years if he was careful. That would be long enough to see the weather change and get back to having nature supply his needs, he was certain.

What he was less sure of was whether it would be long enough to get Amber out of his head. Of all people in the city to run into on day one of his return, what cruel aspect of his curse had mandated it be someone who was the spitting image of Aurelia? All these years later, and the pain of losing Magdaia and the children was still as fresh as it had been when they all died so long ago. But no other memory of that tragedy compared by half to that of his firstborn, Aurelia, wailing in her mother's arms while holding the still body of her own firstborn son.

Magdaia had slipped away next, only a few days after the boy. Within a week, the twins had succumbed as well, along with their own families. Somehow, his daughter had held on through all of it, her body racked with fever and her swollen throat unable to put words behind her accusing gaze as each of her brothers, nephews and nieces joined her mother and her child in death.

Finally, Ashe had held Aurelia as she took her last struggling breath. The unruly red hair that had been his delight her entire life was plastered in sticky tangles to her sallow face with sweat and vomit and pus from the sores that had made her pale skin a battlefield. Aurelia's eyes had accused him silently until the light faded from them. Accused him for not getting sick himself. Accused him for outliving his entire family. All these years, and he had never suffered enough to make her accusation fade.

"God! When will it be enough?" Ashe shouted at the empty cave and heard only silence in response. "I showed mercy because I thought that was what I should do. I didn't let them use their hammers. Me! I didn't care about being punished for it. Fiat justitia ruat caelum, right? I knew I'd bleed for it. But it was *right*," he growled.

Ashe wept then into his folded arms, great heaving sobs racking his entire body. "So why have I had to be punished for it ever since?" he said, his tears subsiding.

"Where's my justice? Huh? When do I get my due for all I've done? Good and bad, let's just get on with it already.

"But no, that's not how you play, is it?"

Ashe wiped snot from his face with the back of a hairy wrist. "When is it ever enough?" he repeated, more quietly.

Why had he had to encounter Amber? It was bad enough that she looked so much like Aurelia, but she had that same knack for making you talk to her, just like she was pulling your life story out of you in a thread, year by year. Until she hadn't wanted to talk any more. Until she couldn't.

Ashe decided he would not return to the city. He had enough water. And the small stockpile of food would get him through the lean times for a few months. When he'd have to eat something but could find nothing. Things would get better; the weather would change. Things would return to the way they were. They had to.

He couldn't go back to the city, and he could no longer just pack up and go somewhere else, like he had in the past. No, technology had seen to that, hadn't it? The world out there had shrunk by orders of magnitude while he slept the years away like some cursed Rip van Winkle. He had no papers, no identity. And if his identity were to be known, he would be hunted down; he'd seen to that. That was part of the cycle too. It had happened before.

This Task character reminded him of the last time. Human longevity research. Just perfect. Just like the last time. All the guy needed was a stupid little mustache. Just like the last guy. And Amber wondered why he got triggered.

Speaking of triggers, Ashe considered his plan for tomorrow. The handyman job Amber had arranged for the morning. Nguyen's bathroom leak. Nguyen. If that doesn't trigger him, he doesn't know what will.

God. Where are you? All the wars, all the fighting. Hunting, being hunted.

"When is it going to be enough?" Ashe shouted into the air. "After all this time, why can't you tell me what you want from me? When is it finally enough? Why can I not be around people without getting tied in with them? It always ends up the same way. Always."

No, it was time to cut ties, before things got any worse, Ashe told himself. Best to just not go back. "Let the dang fool city and all the dang fools in it fend for themselves," he whispered.

Ashe again regarded his water stockpile. It was going to have to be enough.

He wasn't going back.

Chapter 13 : SOUP SANDWICH

"IF YOU HATE this job so much, why do you keep coming back?"

Ashe seized a hand towel from the floor and stopped grumbling long enough to mop water from his face. Once he was partially dry, he turned his attention to the rust-colored puddle in the cabinet beneath the sink. The leak had slowed to a reluctant drip, but the damage had been done. He wadded up the stained cloth and lobbed it into the tub of the corner shower, where it made a slapping noise and fell to cover the drain.

With effort, he turned over, faced the ceiling, and squeezed his upper body into the confined space of the crusty vanity cabinet. Rust flaked from the corroded pipes above him, peppering his shirt as he twisted his broad shoulders into place.

Ashe thrust a rough-knuckled hand from his new vantage point under the bathroom sink. "Are you kidding? I love this job," he growled. "I do it for the perks. Give me my new crescent."

Amber handed the old man a chipped and rusted wrench from the canvas bag. Mr. Nguyen had offered the weathered old satchel full of random tools to Ashe in lieu of payment for fixing a leak and running a new line to his shower.

A grinding sound emanated from under the sink, and the old pipes moaned, protesting Ashe's interference with decades of mineral buildup and corrosion.

He exhaled slowly, a long-suffering sigh as he adjusted his grip. "Maybe I just like fixing things. It's my calling."

Amber snorted. "Right... 'Look! Up in the stairwell! It's a rat. It's a roach. No, it's PlumberMan! Yes, it's PlumberMan! Mysterious drifter from who-knows-where, who arrived at this rundown apartment building with skills and patience far beyond those of your average maintenance guy! PlumberMan: who can unclog the most horrifying of drains, tighten leaky pipes with a single scowl, and lift entire water heaters when the landlord refuses to pay for a dolly!'"

Amber looked under the sink for a reaction. The old man continued his very intent examination of the nasty piping, clearly finding it more interesting than he found her. She continued.

"And who, disguised as Ashe... um..." Amber paused, realizing she had no idea what his last name was. Well, she wasn't a writer for no reason, right?

"And who, disguised as Ashe Malcontent, a permanently grumpy, questionably skilled handyman, fights a never-ending battle against broken fixtures, cheap landlords, and tenants who swear they didn't flush a whole roll of paper towels down the toilet."

Still no reaction. She frowned.

"And now, another thrilling episode of PlumberMan! Will he finally fix the hot water? Will the building stop smelling like mildew and despair? Will he ever tell a decent story for his double-rate fee? Stay tuned!"

Amber frowned. She'd felt sure she'd at least get a chuckle out of that last bit. Of course, he was an old man...

"Wait a minute! Are you asleep?"

"Yes. Yes, I am."

She crossed her arms, leaning against the doorframe, studying him. "I think you like helping people. But you don't want anyone to know you like it. I think it messes with your whole 'miserable old cuss' vibe."

From under the sink, Ashe grumbled, "I fix things because people break things. It's the only predictable constant in the world. People always break things." He wrenched the last fitting free, pulled it from the pipe, and reached around to let it clatter into the sink.

"That's pretty cynical," Amber said.

"That's pretty accurate," Ashe corrected. He wiped rust and grime from his fingers and reached for the replacement part. "People break things. I fix things. End of story."

Amber tilted her head, watching him work. "What about people? Do you fix those too?"

Ashe froze for the briefest second before resuming his work, tightening the new locknut with a slow, deliberate twist.

"No," he said finally. "People don't get fixed."

Amber let the silence stretch between them, considering the meaning of his words.

"Guess that means you're still broken, huh?" she asked.

Ashe didn't answer. But the way his grip tightened on the wrench said enough.

"Anyway. I think you are the grumpiest person I've ever met. You barely speak to anyone but me, and you're really not all that nice to me. If I didn't know better…"

"You don't. Shut up."

"Tell me why."

"Because you talk too much."

Amber kicked his leg. Not hard, but enough to be satisfying.

"No, why are you helping us out here? It's not for the money; hardly anyone you've helped out has even paid you, except me."

"Well, even you haven't paid me double for stories like you promised."

"You haven't told me a story in a week!"

Ashe grunted and Amber winced at the tortured squeal of the next ancient locknut as it gave way to twisting pressure.

ఞ • ఌ

"WAIT A MINUTE," said Amber. "I thought you said way back when that you were in the Army Corps of Engineers?"

"I was," answered Ashe. He scowled at his handiwork and wiped his sweating brow. Despite his best efforts over the past hour, the new pipe connection still leaked. "Way back when."

"You just now said you were Marine Recon."

"Maybe I was both. Whose story is this?"

"Okay, okay."

"As I was saying, me and my unit were humping it overland from the west. We were... well, I still don't know for sure exactly where we were. We'd lost both our map cases and radios, and best guess, we were three days out from our AOR—"

"AOR?"

Ashe fixed Amber with a withering glare from beneath the sink. She raised both hands as if in surrender.

"Lost in enemy territory," Ashe continued. "We were nine men I'd cobbled together from two LRRPs. Down five men altogether, since Ming had gone off the reservation and we'd lost Chisholm 'bout two weeks before, while the other patrol had lost their lead and AL, and radio operator. No supplies, out of water. Slogging through this swampy lake south of the hills, chest deep and covered in leeches…"

Ashe's voice faded slightly in Amber's ears as she struggled with some quick mental math. If nothing else, her association with Ashe had made a ten-fold improvement in her ability to do numbers in her head. Well, maybe nine-fold. Eight, if she was being honest. Timelines were always a little confusing with Ashe. He claimed to have served in at least two branches of the military, with at least one certain re-enlistment in one of those periods of service, maybe both. At the very least, he'd been an officer before marrying his first wife, having mentioned a commission. He'd gone back to war after being married for some time to his second wife. Presuming Ashe was now seventy-five… No, that seemed a ridiculous stretch; most days she wouldn't put him past fifty. But if he was, she concluded he had to be talking now about events in the early nineteen-nineties. The Gulf War. But that would mean…

"Lake?" Amber interjected. "What lake is there in the desert?"

"Desert? Who said anything about a desert?" Ashe asked her.

"The desert! Operation Desert Shield, right? Based on your age, that's where you were, wasn't it?"

"I thought I told you it was your job to figure out what was true and what wasn't. Not tell me about it," growled Ashe. "Besides, if you're so good at figuring out my age, why don't you just write me up a birth certificate so I can get a real job, huh?"

"Okay, okay, sorry! Swampy lake it is."

"Water, water everywhere, nor any drop to drink. One sip of that muck gave a man the squirts worse than death, and we were all of us out of purification tabs. We had to move, so after dark, I called it. We hadn't had comms for a day and a half, so we were on our own."

Ashe finished re-taping the connection and cranked the locknut. He sat upright and reached under the sink before pulling at the new water line to test it. Amber observed that he did so with his still-bandaged right hand. She was pleased that he was healing up so well from the stab wound.

"We made it across the trail south of what looked like a commune without incident. But we knew the darkness working in our favor worked in Charlie's, too. So we took it slow, leapfrogging across the trail, covering each other as we headed north into the low hills. Best we could figure, the Ben Het camp was somewhere under ten klicks east of us. It was almost twenty-two hundred, so we figured to make it in from the cold a little before dawn."

"Cold? I thought this was a jungle story?"

Ashe's jaw tensed. "'In from the cold.' It's a manner of expression. Out of danger. Back home, in a safe place."

"Oh! Okay. Please go on." Amber grinned sheepishly.

"It was anything but cold. Black as night, second of March, and we're all still sweating bullets. Probably more due to not knowing what's over the next hill more than the actual weather, but either way, it wasn't cold.

"We'd crested the second hill north of the trail when we heard the diesel engines start up maybe a klick back to the west of us. Guessing it was coming from the commune, but it didn't sound like the trucks Charlie used to drive produce around. And there were a lot of them. Six, maybe eight vehicles.

"We hunkered down as best we could. The hillside was covered in scrubby brush, so we were able to find some cover at least. Not enough to hide from VC infantry in daylight, but we'd have to worry about that in the morning.

"The engines got closer, drove to reach our location in about ten minutes. Andrews swore it was tanks, but we all knew better. The PAVN didn't have any tanks; that was clear in every mission brief we ever got. I mean, what good would tanks do in the jungle, or the swamps?"

"Did our side have any tanks?"

"You're getting ahead of me. Yeah, we had tanks. But they rarely did us any good either, on account of the terrain. Matty had heard something a couple missions back from a Green Beret that the Army had some

Pattons at Ben Het, where we were headed. I figured we must have been wrong about how far east we were. Maybe we were actually on the far side of Ben Het. Hard to tell when it all looks the same and you got no maps."

"Even for an experienced Recon unit?" Amber couldn't imagine any group led by Ashe not knowing what it was doing.

"Experienced unit? You know what 'experienced' meant over there? It just meant you hadn't died yet. Some of us were lucky, others had nine lives like a cat. Not one of us had it figured out. Nobody was good at it.

"Pitch black in the middle of the night, experience don't help all that much. You know what you can hear on a battlefield in the black of night? Mosquitoes." Ashe's voice was husky. "You know what you can really hear? Tanks."

"Anyway, the machines caught up with us. It was tanks for sure; four of them. The lead machine thundered past us not fifty feet from where we'd dug in.

"Hadn't been that close to a tank in years. First thing you notice when you're on the ground that close is this deep rumbling. You feel it in your chest more than hear it, because what's going on in your ears is too loud to let you think. The clanking like a giant banging all his kettles together at once. By the time he's in close, the vibration of tread links slamming onto the ground is like to shake you right out of your boots." Ashe shook his head as if to clear his vision.

"About shook our teeth right out of our fool heads. The other three flanked us, but far enough out so we'd never get away by going cross-path. We had to just keep our heads down and wait it out. Matty wanted to signal to them, convinced they were our guys, but I told him to shut it. I was not about to jump up and announce our presence till I knew something instead of just thinking it. The tanks moved past our position, still heading east. They kept going for about another ten minutes before they shut down.

"We laid low until about four a.m. We didn't move till we were sure we hadn't heard anything but mosquitoes for a couple hours. I made the call to send Matty and Bellows back west to see if we had somehow circled round and ended up east of Ben Het. Rest of us stayed low and quiet for about an hour before we heard some rustling in the brush. Matty and Bee slipped back into our hide with exactly the news I didn't want."

Amber watched Ashe's face without uttering a word.

The old man continued. "They'd gotten up close to one of the tanks that had stopped farther west of us, not the four in the vanguard that rumbled past our position. It wasn't ours; Bee said he thought it was a PT-76, a Soviet amphibious light tank. Whatever it was, he'd seen Vietnamese characters stenciled on the side of the turret when the driver or somebody had been foolish enough to light up a cigarette. Bee tells Matty, and the two of them hightail it back east to us, but not before almost running smack into a platoon of VC, trying to get themselves dug in before sun-up."

Ashe bent forward to retrieve the dripping towel from under the sink. He reached up from his seated position on the floor and wrung out the fabric into the sink above. This, of course, accelerated the dripping of the pipe beneath the sink. He grumbled and replaced the towel under the vanity. It made a plopping sound on the damp particle board.

"Some Recon unit, huh" Ashe mused. "Charlie coulda had half a battalion wrapped all around us, and we never even knew they were there."

Ashe scratched at his right hand through the bandages. The wrap had gotten wet during his work on the sink and had taken on a two-tone appearance.

"Sun comes up, and all we could do is shelter in place for the day. If the air was hot at night, it was stifling during the day. I'm surprised Charlie couldn't locate us just by watching the clouds of mosquitoes, but I imagine he was doing the same thing and facing the same problems. We spent the entire day without moving more than we needed to."

"The sun went down around eighteen hundred on March third. I told the guys we were going to lay low for a couple hours and then move out east. We had to stay ahead of that VC infantry if we stood any chance at all. Nothing happened before we vacated around twenty hundred hours.

"We picked our way along for the better part of an hour when we heard Charlie open up with recoilless rifles somewhere behind us. A little after that, they started up with mortar fire and regular artillery. They lit up the zones ahead of us to the east; they were giving it to the base pretty good to soften them up."

Amber was silent in rapt attention. Ashe arched his back against the bathroom doorjamb. A series of cracks sounded along his spine.

"We knew we had a small window once Charlie stopped shelling, where he'd move his men closer and into position. We had to be ahead of that wave, so once it started to quiet down, we beat feet. It was still blacker than a witch's soul out there, but we had to just haul it and hope for the best.

"Well, we crested the next hill, and I'm guessing we were still a kilometer from the base when one of the tanks that had passed us a night before started up and jumped forward. Problem was, he rolled right onto an anti-tank mine. Blew his entire right tread clean off and caught the tank on fire. Bellows had been right; it was a PT-76.

"Funny thing about the PT-76? Like I said, they were amphibious. When you try to make a weapon do too many things, it doesn't do any of them great. Just kinda does all the things poorly. The PT-76 was an okay swimmer, not great, but it was a downright pathetic tank. Thin armor, underpowered gun, all that. What it did make, though, was a pretty darn effective torch.

"It lit up the entire hillside, including us, nine fool Marines sprinting three hundred yards down one open hillside and another four hundred up the next." Ashe shook his head.

"It also illuminated the PT-76's friends. Three T-62 medium battle tanks and an armored personnel carrier. The APC was pretty fast and had already started hightailing it out of the area by the time we saw it. For its part, the burning PT-76 managed to get off one round before its crew got out. I think they were trying to fire on our base a kilometer off, but the round fell way short. Gunner was distracted, I guess. We saw them bail a few seconds before the remaining shells inside started cooking off.

"The APC saw us right around that time and skidded to a stop, throwing up great clods of earth. A VC short platoon poured out of the APC and opened up on us with AKs. Six of them dropped and set up a pair of mortars in no time at all.

"You know how in movies, mortar shells whistle, letting you know you've got incoming? It's a myth. They don't do that in real life. One second there's no mortar shell, and the next, there's no... whatever it hit.

"Eddie went down in the first round; most of his middle was just gone. Eddie was our machine gunner. I picked up his pig and draped the belt over my left forearm. I did what I could to lay down cover, but I knew it wouldn't be enough. That PT-76 was still lighting things up. We still had more than half the next hill to hump, and Charlie could see us as well as we could see him.

"Sam and Frito still had rounds for their thumpers, so I had them drop a line of HE as close as they could to the APC and those mortars. It seemed at first that did the trick 'cause Charlie slowed down. We thought we'd backed them off a bit. Turns out they were slowing down on purpose, no thanks to us.

"All three T-62s turned their guns in our direction. You'd think they'd have saved the big guns for the base, or the other tanks. Evidently, Charlie was still new enough at tank warfare to not know you didn't waste the big guns on nine marines. Well, eight now.

"You ever see a T-62 fire its main gun?" Ashe looked over toward the bathroom's toilet. "It's almost comical in a twisted way. Aims its gun and fires. The earth shakes for a half mile around, the recoil pushes the barrel back into the turret. Next thing, and here's the funny part, a little door opens up at the back of the turret and ejects the shell casing out through the air. Just poops it out the back."

Amber had learned by now to just let the old man talk. Even if she had a notebook, these moments were so intimate it would feel like a violation to write anything down.

Ashe's eyes suddenly came back to the present. He looked straight at her. "Do you know what the definition of 'overkill' is?"

She shook her head.

"Three T-62s against eight marines." Ashe paused a moment.

"They opened up the night sky for us. All three of 'em, firing as fast as they could reload, pooping their empty shells out behind them." The distant look returned to his eyes. "Christ, but Charlie brought it that night. It was almost worse than Suvla."

Minutes passed.

"What happened next?" Amber gasped out.

"I woke up in a hospital near Arlington, swaddled head to toe in bandages like a newborn baby."

"What about your men?" Amber whispered. "The rest of your unit?"

"They're still in Arlington."

Chapter 14 : LIVING FOREVER

THE MACHINE WAS enormous and yellow and rusted all over. It fascinated Amber; she'd never seen anything like it. The thick metal skin covering the diesel engine, the gaping maw where it took in its food, the arching chute that spat out its waste: these all bore the dents and scars of long years of heavy use. The machine looked old, but Amber would never dare say it was used up. Its appearance alone would command attention, even if the machine was quiet.

The machine was not quiet.

Thirty feet separated the machine from her bench, but even at that distance Amber suspected she ought to be wearing hearing protection. At idle, the noise was loud but tolerable. The rhythmic thrumming of the engine almost lulled her, like the rumbling purr of some oversized predator resting contently between kills. It wasn't soothing, exactly, but it was steady. Familiar in a way that made her eyelids grow heavier. She decided it was probably because she'd been up all night. Any constant tone would serve as a lullaby right now.

When the workers fed the machine, though? That was a different story.

The men carried their offerings of brush and branches, limbs and logs, to the machine and cast them into its ever-hungry mouth. The noise the machine made then, while it ate, was a horrendous cacophony of truly epic proportion. The trees, dismembered by human aggression, released their final ear-piercing shrieks as they were devoured. The machine took the wood, regardless of size, and turned it to nothing but pulp before vomiting out a stream of chipped and shredded waste. Branches cracked like bones, limbs split with the sharp report of gunfire, and the whole violent symphony ended in a regurgitated geyser of shredded remains spewing from the chute, flung fifteen feet through the open air into a waiting dump truck.

Amber watched the process with a mixture of morbid curiosity and quiet unease. Splinters. At the end, that's all there was left. Mighty oaks and maples, once tall and strong and proud, were fed to this machine because they had been judged useless. Their years of steady, silent existence were erased in moments, reduced to splinters and dust. The finality of it unsettled her, and she shook her head, trying to shake off the creeping weight of thought. Maybe she was just tired.

The workers finished depositing a fresh load of severed limbs into the grinding teeth of the machine, and Amber winced at the wailing of the wood. One of the workers, rounding the front of the trailer, accidentally bumped another, and the second man smacked his knee against the heavy iron ring protruding from the front. He cursed loudly in Spanish and, in a brief surge of frustration, lashed out with a swift kick to the machine's rusted frame.

The machine, of course, felt nothing.

Amber watched it, this massive, deaf and dumb thing, that was led around by the ring in its nose to do the will of its masters, to serve at their whim. A tool taken from one place to another, dealing destruction on behalf of whoever held the reins. A tool they could kick, curse, abuse without consequence. Because it wasn't alive. Because it wasn't supposed to feel anything.

Amber shook her head. She must be more tired than she thought to get so morose and philosophical about a woodchipper.

Amber blinked and realized she was no longer alone.

"What do you call that part of the trailer that you hook up so you can tow it around?" she asked, not turning her head.

"The hitch," replied Ashe. "That's a lunette ring for a pintle hitch; usually means the machine is military surplus."

"Military surplus." Amber mused. She took a sharp breath, letting the words settle. "You know I'm going to have to charge you rent," she told the old man.

"You're not going to charge me rent," replied Ashe. "Not on a Monday."

"Today's Thursday," said Amber, finally looking at him.

Ashe turned his head slightly, as if sizing her up for the first time, then made a show of examining her clothing. His eyes traced the state of her uniform: the black polyester, wrinkled beyond redemption, coffee-stained and streaked with evidence of her shift in the nightmare realm. At least three condiments decorated the fabric in an abstract expressionist tribute to minimum wage, and her name tag still bore a ribbon of dried, rubbery ketchup.

Ashe's lips twitched. "Looks like a Monday to me."

Amber followed his gaze down to her uniform, registering the state of it. The ketchup. The mustard. The grease stains that had somehow migrated from a tray to the front of her apron in ways defying both logic and gravity. She tried to recall how the ketchup had even ended up on her name tag, but the memory refused to materialize. She sighed.

This job costs me more in laundry tokens than it gives me in tips.

She reached into her pocket and pulled out her meager take from the night, counting the small bills and loose change with a practiced hand.

Yep. Definitely less than it gives me in tips.

Amber shoved the cash back into her pocket and turned her attention back to the machine. The workers were picking up another bundle of the dead, preparing the next sacrifice.

"What brings you to the bench on a fine Monday morning such as this?" Amber asked.

"Mrs. Wilson asked me to get her a few things from the Food Giant." Ashe held up a twenty-dollar bill. "Unless we want to skip town with her money?"

∾   •   ∽

"DO YOU THINK she's dead?"

Ashe frowned at Amber. "No, I don't think she's dead," he said. "I think she's old. You just wait till it's your turn." He switched the grocery bags from one hand to the other and pressed the doorbell button a fourth time. "I can hear her moving around in there."

"She's probably getting all dressed up. You know, Ashe, as much time as you spend up here with her, I'm kinda surprised she hasn't given you a key."

"Shut up."

The door opened, stopping after four inches. Hilda Wilson's eyes peered out from the crack of the door just above the taut security chain. Her face wore a mask of wrinkled curiosity for a moment before the light of recognition flared in her eyes. Her silvered head bobbed as the door closed once more. Amber could hear the old woman slide the security chain free with her trembling hands, and the doorknob turned. Mrs. Wilson opened the door for her visitors and stepped away from the door to give them room. Her mismatched fuzzy slippers and walker repeated a distinctive clunk-swish-swish, clunk-swish-swish pattern as she crossed the linoleum floor of the entryway.

"Getting around pretty well today, Mrs. Wilson," remarked Amber.

"Oh, yes! That nice doctor gave me my Heparin this morning." Mrs. Wilson's dentures shone brightly in a wide smile. The old lady gestured toward the small kitchen nook with one gnarled hand, where Amber could see an antiquated IV stand and a few pieces of other equipment. The free clinic two blocks over made house calls to care for shut-ins like Mrs. Wilson. "I always feel a little frisky after that," the old lady finished with a wink.

Amber elbowed Ashe in the ribs. The old man glared at her from beneath his bushy eyebrows.

Mrs. Wilson resumed her journey into the living room. She had been watching the news again. This time, she had not been using her headphones, and the television was loud.

Ashe glanced at the glowing screen. "Is that guy all they ever talk about?"

The program was some sort of expanded news show, the kind that spent an hour on a specific topic, event, or interview. Today, the host was sitting in a casual studio environment having a conversation with Cameron Task. Task was speaking.

"...not just because it can be done. Because it must be done. Pollution, over-population, and over-crowding are some of the biggest obstacles we face as a species."

The interviewer wore a practiced look of equal parts curiosity and rapt attention. *"And I understand all that, from the perspective of your goal of establishing mankind in habitats on Mars, and of creating industry on Earth's moon,"* the host stated. *"But help—pardon the pun—help me understand where you're going with the intent of prolonging and extending the human lifespan?"* A wry grin on the interviewer's face showed that the pun had been intentionally crafted. The grin faded. *"If overpopulation and overcrowding are such problems, why is it so critical to make us all live longer and wipe out disease? Won't that just make the problem worse?"*

"Not at all," replied Task. *"HELP, my Human Existence Longevity Project, is critical to all the other goals. Mars isn't the final objective, and space travel takes a long time. But even before we get to space, even if mankind never leaves its ancestral home, we must increase the human life span. It has been conclusively shown that health, quality and duration of life are inversely linked to population growth. Eradicating disease, improving the quality of life, eliminating poverty, and educating the populace... All of*

these have the end effect of reducing societal pressure situations that lead to unsustainable population growth.

"Lower carbon emissions follow almost immediately. Data indicates that when mortality rates fall, so, too, do birth rates. It's a natural progression to expand my focus from addressing the roots of poverty and unrest to saving people already alive and extending their lives. I am convinced that we will be able to slow or even reverse aging within the next one to two decades."

"Remarkable and admirable goals, Mr. Task. Of course, it's…"

Mrs. Wilson reached the living room and shut off the television. Amber and Ashe finished putting her groceries away by the time she shuffled her walker back to the kitchen.

"Thank you, dear," Mrs. Wilson reached to peck a kiss on Amber's cheek as she and Ashe stepped to her door.

"And Mr. Ashe? If that Cameron Task ever discovers how to turn back aging, you better believe I'm coming for you." The elderly woman grinned with a twinkle in her eye and pinched Ashe's left buttock.

∾ • ⌀

"YOU THINK HE'LL actually do it?"

Ashe looked at Amber without replying to her. The old man placed his empty glass on her table next to her notebook and pen.

Amber continued. "I mean, I'm not sure I can get my head around going to Mars. But I wonder about the other parts. Task has done some really good work in reducing disease and poverty."

"Is that what your friend works on?" Ashe asked. "Vaccines and such?"

"Who, Fry? No, she works in HELP."

"Extending the human lifespan," Ashe said, his voice flat.

"Yeah. Small Fry says she thinks Task is being conservative. About his timeline, I mean. She's never met him, but she's heard him speak at internal events and so on. Says he's absolutely driven."

Amber tilted her head and repeated her earlier question. "Do you think he'll manage it? Prolonging our lives?"

"Why does he want to? That's the question."

Amber appeared confused. "You mean his motives? He's a businessman. Of course, he's motivated for his own reasons, but if the end result benefits humanity isn't that the important thing? Living longer and not having a lot of the terminal illnesses that we fight now. I mean, what could somebody achieve if they lived longer, right? Lived forever?"

Ashe interrupted her. "Who wants to live forever? He's never going to cure everything. People are still going to die. Who wants to see their loved ones wither and die over and over while all they can do is watch? Bigger picture, who wants to watch as mankind does its best to destroy itself over and over again? This clown Task thinks it'd all be so grand but trust me, nobody wants to live forever."

Ashe's voice had taken on that tone again. Amber took a step backward. The old man continued, his voice loud enough to hurt her ears. "Nobody. Ain't no blessing; it's a curse."

Ashe stormed out of Amber's apartment, slamming the door behind him.

Amber stood for a moment. She had some trouble processing what had happened. It seemed that dealing with Ashe could go so smoothly, until it just... didn't. Like she stepped on some unexpected land mine, and it all went up in her face.

Amber knew he was old and had seen some things, but she felt like he was missing the big picture. Like he couldn't see what was directly in front of his face. She'd been exhausted before running into Ashe on the bench earlier, and the trip to the store and the old man's moodiness had emptied her out. She liked the old man well enough, but was the time spent with him trying to help him out more trouble than it was worth?

She decided that was a question best answered after some sleep. Maybe after some corn flakes and some sleep.

Amber stepped to the kitchen and selected one bowl that needed to be washed a little less urgently than its peers. She filled it halfway with the last of a box of cereal, moving the box in a circle to distribute the powdery, sugary residue at the end of the bag. Smelling the milk, she decided it was still non-toxic. There was enough liquid in the quart jug to wet about half the flakes and create a syrupy sludge in the bottom of the bowl. She wandered to the open window, munching on her first bite.

Eight floors down, she saw Ashe step out of the front door of the building. Even from this distance, she could see the agitation in the old man's gait.

Her eyes shifted and time slowed to a crawl. The next several events seemed to play out in slow motion.

Across the street, a small boy chased his red ball. An empty dump truck approached down the street, coming to replace the previous one filled by the day workers.

The red ball bounced into the street. The child darted after it.

The truck driver failed to brake.

Ashe exploded into motion. He moved faster than Amber had ever seen another human move. He was a streak of gray hurtling toward the boy.

Ashe dove the last eight feet. His hand thrust outward with his arm rigid at the elbow. His palm hit the child center mass, and all the remaining events happened at once.

Stopped in his tracks, the boy stumbled backward and fell in the gutter.

The dump truck slammed into Ashe, then finally laid hard on its brakes.

Ashe flew through the air, launched by impact with the truck, and stumbled in a futile attempt to regain his balance.

Ashe fell into the woodchipper.

The ball bounced across the street in arcs of diminishing height.

Amber's bowl of corn flakes shattered on the floor.

❧ • ❦

AMBER BURST THROUGH the entrance of her apartment building onto the street. She had flown down eight flights of stairs, taking two and three steps at a time. Despite her breakneck pace, a crowd had gathered by the time she reached the scene.

The young boy was wailing and sat surrounded by one group of onlookers. A second, larger group clustered around the woodchipper. Amber pushed and shoved her way through that group.

Arriving at the machine, she found it silent. One of the day workers had slammed the big red emergency stop button. He had not done so quickly enough.

The chipped yellow paint and rust of the machine was now dripping with red. The spray pattern emanated outward from the now still blades within the large intake chute. Ashe's blood covered the rear half of the machine. Several in the crowd pointed; others covered their mouths. None looked away; none wanted to miss the spectacle.

Amber saw the blood drip from the mouth of the machine and start to form a small pool on the asphalt. She saw red footprints clustered together nearby and saw them proceed away and fade as they moved off. She saw the day workers huddled together and pointing off in the direction the footprints had taken. She saw all this in a single glance.

What she did not see was Ashe.

Chapter 15 : THE SAMPLE

"SODIUM CITRATE?" AMBER exclaimed. "Where on God's earth am I supposed to find Sodium Citrate?"

Amber was hurtling up the stairs as quickly as she could move without using the banister for assistance. In one hand she held her cell phone. The device was Amber's lifeline. The name of the current call read, "Small Fry" and a highlighted icon on the screen showed that the speakerphone feature was active.

Amber paused on the fifth floor. She could barely afford the time, but she had to catch her breath. She bent over at the waist, pressing the heel of one palm into her side to alleviate a painful muscle spasm. "What *is* Sodium Citrate?" she gasped.

"It's an acid regulator in foods." Frymet's voice came from the phone. It was clear that Amber's friend was working hard to maintain a calm demeanor in hopes of helping Amber do the same. "Also an emulsifier... People use it to make cheese."

"Cheese?" Amber said. "You've seen the people who live in my apartment building, Fry," she growled. "Do we look like a commune of rogue amateur cheese makers? You gotta do better than that!"

"Look I'm on my way now. I'll be there in ten minutes," Frymet told her. "But you have to keep that sample uncoagulated until I get there! Don't agitate it."

"Don't agitate it? I'm sprinting up eight flights of stairs, and you tell me not to agitate it?" Amber looked at the container in her other hand and started up the stairs again, this time at a more measured pace.

Amber crested the sixth-floor landing. "I don't even know why I'm going to my apartment instead of grabbing an Uber and heading your way!"

"I told you. We need to keep that sample from coagulating," Fry's voice strained to remain patient. "If you want me to sequence that sample and try to find your friend, you've got to keep that blood liquid till I can."

Amber looked again at the stainless-steel container. Upon discovering that Ashe had left the scene and gone who knows where, Amber had called Frymet, seeking her assistance in locating the injured old man. Who knew what condition he was in? There was so much blood in the woodchipper Amber could barely imagine how the old man was still alive, let alone able to walk. *He has to be alive*, she thought.

"Can't I just put it in my fridge until you get here?"

"That's not going to be reliable enough, there's a differential curve. It only slows coagulation. And the potassium leakage is an unpredictable factor—"

"English, Fry! Fisher-Price it for me!" Amber stopped on the stairway, gritting her teeth. The pain in her side had passed, but her agitation level continued to rise steadily. "What do I need to do here?"

"I told you! You need to find an anti-coagulant, like Sodium Citrate."

"And I told you, no one here's gonna have Sodium Citrate! What else do you got?"

"I don't know!" Frymet's voice was starting to crumble at the edges; she was being infected by Amber's frantic desperation. "Um, any anticoagulant... maybe Warfarin, or a chelating agent like EDTA, or a post-op med like Heparin, or— "

"Heparin? Mrs. Wilson!" Amber shouted at the phone. She reversed course and headed down to the fourth floor as fast as her shaking legs could carry her.

∾ • ⌇

"YOU PUT IT in a *thermos*?" Frymet's face looked more than a little green. "That is really not okay."

Amber was horrified. "What do you mean, it's not okay? Are you telling me I ruined the sample?"

"No, I'm telling you it's super disgusting."

Amber and Frymet stood just outside the door to Mrs. Wilson's apartment. The old widow had been more than happy to part with her medication when she was told that it could save Ashe's life. Amber had not offered more detail than that on Ashe's situation, not wanting to give the old woman a heart attack despite her blood thinners.

"Where'd you get the thermos? I'm guessing it's not yours."

The stainless-steel canister was half-covered with layers of stickers ranging from the call letters of a local Latin music station to a sneaker brand to a caricature of a mariachi player in a sombrero dabbing while holding a guitar. Over the stickers was smeared a splotchy patina of sticky red fingerprints. The cup-like lid to the thermos was streaked with dried blood in a pattern matching the thigh of Amber's jeans where she had tried to clean the silver canister to a more presentable condition.

"When you told me you could find Ashe if I got you a blood sample, I grabbed the first container I could find and headed for the woodchipper. One of the migrant workers on the crew downstairs had it full of water. I dumped it out. The guy yelled at me and chased me across the sidewalk, but once he saw me start filling it up, I think it grossed him out, and he just let me keep it."

"I can imagine so. Listen, Amber," Frymet's voice dropped a few decibels. "I said I *might* be able to do something if you got me a sample." She continued even more quietly. "The databases that Mr. Task has access to... Genetic information that ties back to personally identifiable information like that is highly restricted. He's probably not even supposed to have access to it, and I'm certainly not supposed to."

Frymet spoke in a level voice that reminded Amber of the time she had been told as a child that there was no Santa Claus. Amber accepted this placating news as well as she had received that earlier disappointment from her mother.

"No!" Amber jabbed a finger at her friend. "You said you could sequence Ashe's DNA or whatever and find out where he lives. You said you could look up his hospital records or vaccinations to something. You are going to find him. He is going to die if you don't find him."

Frymet made one more attempt. "Why don't we just start calling all the hospitals in this part of town? He wouldn't have gone far, if he was hurt as badly as you say."

"As badly as I say? He fell into a giant woodchipper. I filled up a thermos of blood. Do you think I'm exaggerating?"

"No, of course not!"

"What he wouldn't have done is go to a hospital, trust me. It's a long shot that you'll even find him in any hospital records at all, but I don't know what else to do, Fry. You've got to find him," Amber implored her friend.

"I'll do what I can, I promise." Frymet held out her hand for the thermos. Taking it from Amber, she felt the weight of it. A shocked look crossed her face, and she screwed off the top to look inside.

"Amber, that's a lot of blood."

"I know. There was a lot of it in the woodchipper. I did mention he fell into a woodchipper, right? A. Wood. Chipper." Each word was forcefully enunciated through clenched teeth. The strain in Amber's voice indicated she was nearing her breaking point.

"I'll do what I can," repeated Frymet. Amber watched her head quickly down the stairs, thermos in hand.

Chapter 16 : TASK

AMBER PACED A recurring pattern in her apartment. Four steps from the table to the kitchen sink. Two steps to the kitchen window. Five steps back to the table. Four to the living area window. Sit on the brocade love seat. Get up. Return to the table. Repeat.

Frymet had told Amber that she wouldn't be able to do anything with the sample of Ashe's blood until after working hours. Further, she wouldn't be able to start accessing any databases, legally or otherwise, until after gene sequencing the sample. Amber had practically come unglued, but her friend had convinced her that the one thing they couldn't do was rush the results. It was an unfortunate truth that the necessary procedures and the subsequent research would all take as long as they would take.

Amber tried to calm herself by reminding herself Ashe was by far the toughest person she had ever met. The old man endured things that she imagined would break men half his age. Whatever that was. Despite his obvious penchant for inflating his personal history and converting it to extravagant tall tales, if he had lived through even a tenth of the stuff he had embellished on throughout their story-telling sessions, he was no stranger to hardship. Still, none of that did anything to soothe Amber's nerves.

It had been four days.

Four days of waiting. Four days of chewing her nails, then her cuticles. Four days of scrubbing at her fingertips with an emery board to smooth away the splinters and all the rough edges she'd just created. Four days of pacing laps around her five-hundred square foot apartment. Four days of coffee and Red Bull and flat Mountain Dew punctuated by three entire bottles of chewable, berry-flavored antacids. The trash bin in the kitchen to Amber's left and rumpled bedsheets across the studio to her right reminded her that Hot Pockets and ramen and fitful sleep had been sprinkled throughout the schedule somewhere, but she couldn't quite remember when.

Four days of silence from her friend Frymet. Four days of unanswered phone calls to Fry's home and cell and work numbers. Four days with only two semi-cryptic text messages from her friend: "Sequencing complete," late in the evening of the day Ashe had fallen into the woodchipper, and "Routine dbs got nothing. Trying the other stuff," mid-evening the next day. Nothing since then, despite all of Amber's near-constant attempts to contact her friend for more information.

That first night and again yesterday afternoon, Amber had gone out walking the neighborhood, desperate for some clue that might indicate where Ashe had vanished to. The bloody trail had been washed away halfheartedly by someone, but she could still see it move away from the absent woodchipper's former location into the old park and future construction site, where the footprints were soon lost in the dust and dirt. Frustrated by these unsuccessful forays around the neighborhood, she had resigned herself to waiting patiently in her apartment.

Amber looked down at her right hand and was startled to see it holding her phone. When had she picked that up? She couldn't recall. The high levels of caffeine in her recent diet were starting to exact a toll. Amber brushed away any concerns about that and tapped the number atop her speed dial list.

At the end of a voicemail greeting she could now recite backwards, Amber left yet another message. "Fry, it's Amber. I'm guessing you knew that. Anyway, call me back, please. I haven't heard from you since... well, since the last message I left about two hours ago. You gotta give me something here. Callmebackbye."

Amber's head flopped backward against the top of the love seat. She stretched her feet outward across a threadbare Persian floor covering that was more rag than rug. She had picked it up at a stall in an antique and craft market down in the Grove two years ago. She'd paid fifteen dollars for the carpet only to find out the merchant had planned to drop it in a dumpster at the end of the day. The man had refused to return her money, saying that if she'd wanted it for free, she shouldn't have been dumb enough to buy it.

Amber decided she'd wait until the end of the day before calling Fry again. She glanced at her phone, tapping it with a thumb to wake the lock screen. Eleven twenty-three in the morning. She knew there was no way she could wait until the end of the day. She lifted her hand and the phone in a slow arc upward from the brocade cushion.

The phone was halfway to a dialing position when the knock sounded at the door.

ॐ • ॐ

FOUR FIGURES FILLED Amber's doorway. Her heart leapt to see Fry standing there next to a tall man. They were in front of two uniformed police officers. The policemen appeared to be at ease, as if they were there as nothing more than escorts. Amber looked at her friend and noticed that Frymet seemed very guarded. She remained silent but stared intently at Amber. Amber noted that Fry's face, at first just ghostly, had turned a whiter shade of pale.

Ashe would have loved that: she'd made a music reference, and to one of those old songs he liked, no less.

The fourth figure commanded Amber's attention. The man stood between and in front of the uniformed officers. His stance was confident, radiating an air of invincibility. Amber pictured the very universe itself conspiring to ensure his success in whatever he wanted to do. A hand-tailored flax linen suit accented by an impeccably knotted tie clung to his sculpted frame. Not a single hair was out of place on his head; Amber imagined the man's hair product alone costing as much as her little apartment each month.

He extended his hand with an irresistible smile.

"You must be Ms. Olsen. I've heard so much about you," the man said to Amber. He possessed a charismatic charm that would make the smoothest politician wilt with comparative insecurity.

Beneath the polished exterior, Amber sensed shrewdness and determination. She got the feeling that whatever game the man played, he viewed himself as a chessmaster, staying effortlessly several moves ahead of his opponents.

Amber disliked the man immediately.

Since Amber had ignored the man's proffered hand, he withdrew it. Amber detected the slightest hint of tightness around his mouth, though his eyes belied nothing. "Please allow me to introduce myself. My name is Owen Spirit. I'm an associate of your friend, Frymet, here," he said cheerfully. His voice dripped with a certain cockiness, every word spoken through an unbearably self-impressed half-smile.

Amber's eyes flitted out to regard first Fry, then the officers. Returning her gaze to the man's face, she asked, "What can I do for you, Mr. Spirit?"

Spirit's ocean-blue eyes sparkled, reflecting the daylight streaming through her apartment windows. "Well, Ms. Olsen, to put it simply, we need your help." The man shrugged at exactly the right time, his shoulders rising to precisely the correct height. He continued. "I understand a friend of yours was recently injured, perhaps gravely. We may have located him—"

Amber's eyes flew wide. "You found Ashe?"

"Ashe," said Spirit, filing away the new tidbit of information for future use. "Well, we have a direction, a lead, at the very least. As it turns out, we are on our way to follow up on that lead with the assistance of these fine officers here, and we need your help. You see, none of us here have ever seen your friend, and would be hard pressed to identify him should our lead prove fruitful."

Amber was not sure where the conversation was going at this point. Identify Ashe? No one has seen him? Fry had met Ashe not long ago, but... Amber looked at Frymet. Her friend's whole body was stiff, as it had been since they'd arrived. Fry shook her head almost imperceptibly from right to left.

"Um..." Amber said warily. "You need my help? To identify a man who recently fell into a woodchipper. Not very observant, then, I guess?"

The man's face darkened at Amber's sarcasm, but he said nothing in reply. Fry wanted to keep her acquaintance with Ashe from this Owen Spirit for some reason, that much was clear to Amber. She wasn't sure why that should be, but Fry was the smartest person Amber knew. If Fry wanted something kept under wraps, it was a pretty solid bet she had a good reason.

All that was secondary in light of the reason for their visit. Fry's analysis of Ashe's blood and her follow-up investigations must have proven successful.

None of her visitors had moved since she had opened the door, but Amber now practically vibrated with the need to follow her visitor and find Ashe.

స్ • ⤳

THEY EXITED THE apartment building in single file by way of the revolving door. The two police officers bracketed the others and were first and last through the door.

Amber's steps faltered as she looked up and beheld the scene in front of her apartment building. Several vehicles were in evidence, including two police cars with their lights flashing. They were parked front- and rearmost of the vehicles strung out along the street and served to block or redirect traffic. Two additional police cars sat closer in, framing the two vehicles in the middle of the group.

The centerpieces of the collection were not parked so much as just stopped in the middle of the street directly in front of Amber's apartment building. These were a matched pair of imposing sport-utility vehicles, replete with tinted windows and, for all Amber knew, armor plate hidden beneath their flat black exteriors. Amber mused that she had never seen vehicles that tried so hard to be non-reflective, as if the ebony behemoths thought they could go unnoticed if they weren't shiny.

Owen Spirit led the group toward the front-most of these two SUVs. There, between the front SUV and the nearest police car, was a group of men. Police officers in the outer ring of the group made way for the new arrivals. The inner circle of this group was an eclectic mix of business types in pricey suits alongside technicians wearing blue jeans and t-shirts. A couple other men stood off to one side wearing more rugged clothing, fitting in with neither suits nor nerds. The apparent leaders of the group examined a large street map of the city spread across the trunk of the squad car. One man marked on the map's stained dry-erase surface with a grease pencil. Two of the technicians reviewed what looked like traffic camera footage on tablet PCs.

One of these men seemed to have found something of interest in the footage and presented his tablet to the tall man in the center of the group. The man had his back to Amber, but she could tell from the deferential actions of the others in the group that this man was the clear leader of the pack. He took the tablet and regarded it. He used an index finger to scrub the video clip back and forth a few times. As he was doing so, one of the men wearing a business suit noticed that Amber and the others had arrived. This man leaned over to whisper to the man Amber had identified as the boss.

In one fluid motion, the man thrust the tablet at the technician and executed a smooth turn to face Amber and the new arrivals.

Amber gasped. "You! You're... you're..."

"Cameron Task," the man replied.

Chapter 17 : RUBICON

"FRY, WHAT IS going on?" Amber asked in a whisper. She and Frymet stood by the rear corner of the second black SUV. The police were just out of earshot and Task and Spirit were conferring. The rest of Task's entourage folded maps, stowed laptops and dispersed to the police cars which appeared to be serving as their personal limousines.

Frymet looked at Amber, then back to Task and his group. "I sequenced Ashe's blood, but it made no sense," she hissed. "I ran it again twice more and got the same results. Anyway, I dug through every public record database I could once I had the markers, and nothing showed up anywhere.

"That wasn't surprising, really, based on what you told me," she continued. "But it did make me start digging deeper, into some of those sketchier data sources I mentioned. Task was on to me immediately. He must have had alerts in place to notify him."

"How hard did he come down on you?" asked Amber.

"That's what's weird. He didn't. I'm still waiting for the other shoe to drop. Anyway, he took one look at the markers I was tracking, then confiscated my sample and re-ran the sequencing himself. Next thing you know, he gives me unfettered access to every database he has. And he has stuff he shouldn't, stuff no one should have. This morning he says he's leaving to talk to the mayor, and when he comes back with an army of police, we load up and drive over here with the police escort."

"Why didn't you answer my calls, Fry? I've been blowing up your cell and your machine at home. I was worried sick."

"I didn't know there were any calls. I haven't been home since I left you with that sample. Spirit sent someone to get me a bag from my house, and I've been working right next to Task for this whole time."

"Did you find out anything working next to him?"

"I found out that the man doesn't sleep. I knew he was driven, but he's been working at a maniacal pace. I have never seen anyone so motivated. I think—" Fry stopped, seemingly afraid of her next words.

"What?" demanded Amber. "You think what?"

Fry looked at the group of men surrounding Task. "I think Ashe is Mr. Task's 'white whale.' That mysterious blood sample from the nineties he's been so obsessed with tracing. Nothing else makes any sense."

A police officer walked past Amber and Fry with a large dog on a leash. The dog was thick-bodied, with large drooping ears and soulful eyes. Fry fell silent as the man passed by, and Amber paused a moment as well.

"Didn't you have your phone with you?" Amber asked once the cop had passed.

"No. Once he took the sample from me, Task moved us into a secure lab. No outside electronics, no phones, no nothing. All the computers were air-gapped. I'm sorry I couldn't call."

Owen Spirit looked back in their direction.

"What's up with this Owen Spirit guy?" asked Amber.

Before Frymet could answer, three of the more nicely dressed businessmen got into the front Suburban alongside Cameron Task. Owen Spirit walked back over to Amber and Fry.

Spirit clapped his hands together. "Load up, ladies, it's time to go get your friend." This last he directed at Amber as he opened the door for them.

෨ • ෧

AMBER GLANCED OUT the rear window of the SUV. Behind them were two of the squad cars, lights flashing.

The caravan had been moving purposefully through the city toward the outskirts for nearly ten minutes. They weren't speeding, but they moved unimpeded through any traffic stops due to the flashing lights of their police escort. The front and rear police vehicles engaged in a leapfrog dance, with the front-most vehicle rushing ahead to block intersections. At this point, the rear cruiser would move up around the other cars and take the lead position. Once the group was past, the blocking car would rejoin at the end of the line.

Amber turned forward to Spirit, seated in the front seat next to the driver. "What is going on?" she asked the man. "Why all the police? I mean, I really appreciate the help finding my friend, but why all the security? And why does Cameron Task want to help so much? Why is he so interested? Is this something about Ashe's blood?"

"You sure ask a lot of questions, young lady!" Spirit turned her way with a broad smile. "Frymet mentioned to me that you were an aspiring journalist. I think you'll do very well. Unfortunately, I'm not at liberty to answer any of your questions. Almost everything that goes on in Cameron Task's brain is a trade secret, as you can imagine. Not only the how of things, but even the what and why in a lot of cases. This is one of those."

"Is that why you've kept Fry from contacting me?"

Spirit looked shocked. "No one has kept anyone from doing anything, Ms. Olsen! Frymet has been very busy the last few days, working hand-in-hand with Cameron Task. On a project you asked her to undertake, I might add. It's not uncommon for Principal Researchers at Task International to, well, drop off the grid from time to time."

Frymet's head snapped up. "Principal? I'm not a Principal, I'm an Associate Researcher."

"Oh, right!" said Spirit. "Things have been moving so fast." He reached into the breast pocket of his jacket and handed Frymet a paper folded in thirds. The man smiled. "Congratulations on your promotion, Ms. Cieślak."

Amber watched as her friend unfolded the paper. Fry looked bewildered. "This is a five-level jump!"

"Surprise!" said Spirit. "And I'm sure you'll find the five-level jump in compensation a pleasant surprise as well."

Amber's eyes narrowed to slits. "So, correct me if I'm wrong, but it sounds a little like you're trying to bribe her into keeping quiet about something."

"Bribe her? There's no need to bribe her for or about anything. A Principal Researcher at Task International is privileged to vast amounts of sensitive and even compartmentalized information, and a company must both reward its brightest minds as well as protect its trade secrets." Spirit produced a new set of papers from his jacket. "We have a non-disclosure agreement safeguarding such information."

Amber snatched the papers from the man's hand. She looked over the four-page document, barely able to read most of the words, let alone make sense of their meaning.

"You mentioned her being out of contact," Spirit said to Amber. "Let me call your attention to paragraph twelve, clause four, on page three."

Amber flipped the pages to that portion of the document, titled, *"Control of Vehicles of Disbursement of Information."* She squinted at the fine print. "I've never even seen most of these words before!"

Fry reached over and took the agreement from Amber's hand. She read the document, flipped back and forth to previous pages a few times, then back. She referred to the other document, the one detailing her promotion. Her shoulders slumped against the cushioned back of her seat.

"It says any employee of Principal Researcher level or higher is considered to have their interests inextricably linked to the company's for the rest of their life, even if they leave Task Industries. As such, they agree that the company has sole purview and actionably enforceable control over all means of internal and external communication. Whether it's related to any proprietary information or not."

Amber looked at her friend. "Wait a minute! You mean they have complete control over everything you say now?"

"Everything I say, everything I write. Songs I sing. Non-verbal communication. You name it. Forever." Frymet's voice was dull and flat.

"That's ridiculous!" exclaimed Amber. "You're not going to sign that!" She turned to Spirit. The man looked smug. "She's not going to sign that," Amber told him.

"She already did, Ms. Olsen. Standard requirement of employment when she joined the company three years ago. I have to congratulate you, Ms. Cieślak. You are by far the youngest Principal Researcher Task International has ever had."

"That's... That can't be legal," said Amber. "She'll get out of it."

"Better and more experienced people have tried, Ms. Olsen. Lots of them. It's iron-clad. I wrote that NDA myself."

"What, you're a lawyer? Your Task's lawyer?"

"Well, sure, I'm a lawyer. But that's a little like saying the filet from McBride's is a steak." A sly grin tickled the corners of Spirit's mouth. "But," he continued, "I like to let people form their own opinions about me."

Amber leveled her gaze at the man. "Except, you just handed me the only opinion that you think matters."

Owen Spirit laughed out loud. It was an endearing yet manly laugh. Amber could picture the man spending hours in front of a mirror to perfect it.

"Why, so I did," chuckled the lawyer. "You're good, Ms. Olsen. I like you."

His smile vanished.

"We've arrived."

ॐ • ॐ

THE WIND WAS hot and dry. It blew coarse dust into Amber's face. Dust from the other side of the fence. Amber quickly brushed the grit out of her eyes, more than a little concerned. The dust gone, she brushed again wildly at her face, not sure what the dust had left behind. She ran her hands over her blouse and paid special attention to the zipper area of her blue jeans, frantic to brush away any speck of dust that might have adhered itself to her clothing.

Owen Spirit smiled at her. "You can relax a bit, Ms. Olsen. This is a dangerous place, to be sure, but I don't think immediately so." The man closed the front door of the Suburban in which they had driven here and walked away toward Cameron Task and his entourage who stood near the chains and lock securing the gate.

Amber regarded her surroundings. This was a place she'd known about her entire life but had been neither brave nor stupid enough to visit. The east section of the city ended just behind them, bordered along its length by the rusted chain-link fence they now faced. At Amber's feet, scrubby grasses transitioned from the greener lawns of the city. Life in this area, it seemed, continued only with great hardship. By all appearances, that hardship got worse on the other side of the fence, where even the dry brown grasses struggled for purchase. An occasional gnarled tree rose here or there to punctuate the landscape.

Far off in the hazy distance, Amber could make out a second fence line and the shattered foothills beyond, but waves of heat baking the isolated territory obscured any detail she might have sought to pick out. She turned her attention back to the nearer fence and the signs attached to it.

"KEEP OUT," a large sign commanded in bold letters. The once-bright yellow and vibrant red of the sign had faded over years of exposure to a muddy beige and ghostly pink; the black lettering was cracked and chipped. Rust had overcome the galvanized coating of the sign long ago, making the large steel rectangle look like a relic of a forgotten age. A half dozen bullet holes perforated the metal sign, but the words "HAZARDOUS CONTAINMENT AREA" remained legible.

To the right and left of the central warning sign hung two triangular signs, each one similarly faded from their original vibrant yellow. The black ink here was also worn and cracked, but there was no mistaking the easily recognizable icon composed of three curved wedges emanating from a central circle. For those rare individuals unfamiliar with the universally feared symbol, the signs bore the words, "RADIATION HAZARD," in heavy block lettering.

Dust devils swirled around the rusted fence posts and danced teasingly in Amber's direction.

Amber watched Owen Spirit peel away from the larger group and grab a handful of badges from a box that had been taken out of the rear of the lead SUV. The man walked back toward Amber and Frymet. He got the attention of their vehicle's driver, who was standing with arms folded across his chest.

"You'll be waiting here, Oscar. The police aren't allowing any vehicles in, not even theirs. Especially not theirs. They're refusing to go in with us, even with precautions." Spirit handed Amber and Frymet each one of the badges he had grabbed, clipping one to his own lapel.

The badges were robin-egg blue and hexagonal in shape. Gray felt pads at the top and bottom secured an outer layer of acrylic over what looked like a silvery-gray film. The clips themselves were thick and heavy. Amber could tell from the heft of the badges that they were well-made and expensive.

"What is going on?" she demanded. "Is this what I think it is?"

"Do you think it's a dosimeter?" quipped the lawyer. "If so, then you're right. Recent background readings say we should be okay for three to four hours in there, provided we stay on the marked paths. Should be. But who wants to take that chance, am I right?"

Amber was infuriated by the man's arrogant smugness but choked back a snide remark. "What is going on," she repeated. "Is Ashe in there?"

Owen Spirit's eyes opened a little wider and he pulled his head more upright. He shot a smile at Frymet. "Ms. Cieślak!" he admonished. "You haven't filled in your friend? Your non-disclosure doesn't say, 'no talking, ever,'" he said. "Well, most times." The smile faded as he turned his gaze back to Amber.

"Mr. Task was able to use traffic camera and other security footage provided by the boys in blue at the mayor's behest. He tracked your friend, Ashe, from the site of the accident. The trail leads here. Unfortunately, it ends here, too. As you can imagine, there aren't a lot of traffic cameras in there." Spirit jerked a thumb in the direction of the irradiated zone across the fence line. A single dusty road led away into the distance. Its pavement was cracked asunder by years of neglect.

"Our problem is, the police refuse to go in with us, and we can't drive. So we're going to have to hoof it. Unfortunate, but those are the rules of the day. The bigger problem is the dog."

Amber glanced around and noticed for the first time that one of the uniformed officers held the leash of the large dog the girls had seen earlier. The officer knelt down to rub the animal's drooping jowls, then reached to scrub at the loose and wrinkled skin above its front shoulders. The dog let out a delighted warbling howl in response.

"Police chief says his men can't go in. And he doesn't want the metal in any of the cars absorbing any radiation and bringing it out of the containment area," Spirit continued. "And if they can't go in, the dog can't. With eighteen thousand acres, more or less, we'll never find your friend in the time we have without the bloodhound."

"So what do we do now, then?" asked Amber. She was already planning to brave the exclusion zone later on her own after they called off the search. If that happened, she planned to stumble and "drop" her radiation badge under a rock for later retrieval.

Spirit smiled and shoved his hands into his pockets. Arching his back, he put on his most charming self and somehow managed to come across as even more arrogant than before. "What we do now is, we negotiate a solution."

Motion caught Amber's eye within the larger group. One of Task's minions produced a checkbook and wrote in it. Ripping out a slip of paper, he handed it to the officer with whom Cameron Task had been most recently speaking. The policeman looked at the check, then around at his peers. With a shrug, the officer pocketed the check. He then removed his service pistol, still in its Kydex holster, and pulled off his badge. These he handed to the officer to his right. He clipped one of the dosimeter badges into the space recently vacated by his police shield.

"And just like that," said Spirit, "We have a retired police officer on our hiking team, along with..." He paused, letting the last word hang in the air.

The now-ex-officer walked across the group to the man holding the bloodhound's leash. Nearby, another officer took a pair of bolt-cutters to the chain securing the fence, snapping through the links with a single practiced motion.

The former K-9 tracking officer took the dog's leash from the junior patrol officer and rejoined the group clustered around Cameron Task.

Owen Spirit winked at Amber. "...Along with his trusty, also-retired, pet."

Chapter 18 : THE CAVE

AMBER CHECKED HER dosimeter for the fifth time. The badge registered no change. She looked at it again to be certain.

"The badges are cumulative, Amber," said Frymet, walking next to her. "They're ledge detectors, set to trip at 500 milliSieverts. That should give us enough time to hike back out before getting a harmful dose."

"Should?"

"Will," amended Fry. "Is that better?"

"Not much. It was under duress." *Just like this whole situation,* Amber finished silently to herself. She looked ahead to the front of their group.

The former police officer and his bloodhound led the group along the fractured roadway. One of Task's men stayed about a half pace behind the ex-cop at all times, carrying a Geiger counter and presumably ensuring that the path the group followed was not "hotter" than they could handle safely. A second, smaller device was clipped to the man's waistband. Fry had informed her that this was a more intricate form of personal dosimeter, one which provided a continual display of the dosage encountered in a percentage of the targeted danger level. About half of the party, including Task and Spirit, had these devices in addition to their badge dosimeters.

One of the other men in front of Amber and Fry paused to adjust his pack. He was one of two outdoorsmen types in the party and carried a backpack. Amber guessed the packs were full of whatever equipment they thought the group would need to effect Ashe's rescue. The man waited for them to pass and slipped back to confer with Cameron Task about something.

"And why would Ashe even come in here? If he's here, he's been in here for days! How much radiation is he getting?"

"I don't have any answers," said Fry. "This whole thing has gotten out of control faster than I could keep up with."

"I'll say," responded Amber. She cast a furtive glance over her shoulder. Task and Spirit were about twenty feet behind them, talking to the man with the pack and a couple others as they walked along the road. "Still think that guy's the greatest thing since sliced bread?" Amber asked, indicating Task with a tilt of her head.

"I don't know. I'm not even sure who he is anymore." Frymet shook her head, looking down at her feet. She stepped around a large rock. "It's one thing when you know you'll never even meet the man in person. I... the closest I ever got to Task before this was being in the same building once, one floor beneath the conference room he was in. I thought that was pretty cool."

"Not so cool working directly with him, huh?"

Fry looked directly at Amber. The mental anguish was plain on Fry's face. "It's like he's a machine or something. No, that's not it. He has emotions, but he's driven. Like he... like individual people don't matter. Just the big picture, just achieving his goals."

The man with the pack stepped past Amber and Fry again, followed by a second man. While the man with the pack wore clothing suited for a day of hiking and activity, this second man appeared to be some mid-level executive in Task's empire. Amber examined his dark suit and polished shoes, now covered with a fine layer of dust. She guessed that the man had not spent more than a couple hours outside all summer, rather suffering through the drought in a climate-controlled office building.

The suit slipped past Amber and Fry and moved to get around the man directly in front of them, trying to keep up with the man bearing the pack. It seemed suit guy wanted to discuss something with the ex-cop, so he stepped around the man with the pack as well as they crested a small rise.

Suit guy stepped off the edge of the road slightly in order to pass and stumbled. He hit one knee as the crumbled edge of the roadway disintegrated beneath his dress shoe. Off-balance, the man slipped further and soon passed the point where he could correct for his error in footing. He tumbled down a slight grade and into what had once been a water run-off for the road, back when it had been a road and when there had been water.

The group quickly moved up to congregate on the edge of the road, looking on as onlookers do. One of the men started down the embankment but was stopped by the lead man with the Geiger counter. This man waved the device's wand down in the direction suit guy had fallen, and Amber could hear the clicking accelerate.

Suit guy by now was on all fours, scrabbling to gain purchase on the loose rock and gravel and climb back up. The man with the larger of the two backpacks, previously bringing up the rear of the group, had joined them. He dropped one shoulder to remove the strap and spun the large pack around his body. A cloud of dust rose from the roadway as the pack dropped onto the ground.

The man fished a rope out of his pack and tossed one end of the coil down to suit guy. Holding onto the rope, suit guy was able to make his way up to join the rest of the group.

The man with the rope held out his hand to suit guy to help him the last few feet, then indicated suit guy's dosimeter with an extended index finger. Amber could see that suit guy's badge had gone over its own ledge as he tried to get out of the dry culvert. Color drained from the man's face, his skin making him resemble a ghost by its contrast with his dark suit.

Amber stepped to one side as suit guy pushed through the group to speak with his boss. Cameron Task, for his part, was visibly annoyed at the man's incompetence and released a string of invective at his employee.

Task examined his dosimeter and called out for a check of the others. The other men with the percentage dosimeters called out their readings in turn; none was over twenty-five percent.

Suit guy remained as white as a sheet. He reached out to Cameron Task, grabbing his upper arm. Task brushed the man's hand aside roughly, yelling at him and pointing back the way they'd come. Suit guy took off toward the city at a fast pace, and Task waved the party onward toward the craggy foothills.

IN ANOTHER THIRTY minutes, the bloodhound led them to the steps.

The path had grown more treacherous as they neared the cliffside, the ground shifting from dry, brittle grass to hard-packed earth and scattered rocks. Along the way, they'd passed a second chain-link fence, this one in worse condition than the first but still standing. Unlike the outer barrier, this one bristled with warning signs, their bold red lettering half-faded but still legible: RESTRICTED AREA. NO TRESPASSING. VIOLATORS WILL BE PROSECUTED. A few of the signs hung loose, swaying slightly in the breeze, but one caught Amber's attention: a metal plate, cleanly reattached to the rusting fence with fresh wire.

Ten minutes past that inner fence, the terrain grew more harsh. The sparse vegetation gave way to jagged, sun-bleached rock, and the air felt drier, heavier, as if even the atmosphere knew it wasn't meant to linger here. The bloodhound moved with renewed urgency, its snout pressed close to the ground, occasionally jerking its head up to sniff at the air before resuming its relentless pursuit.

Then, finally, they reached the cliffside.

The rock face loomed before them, worn by time and weather, its surface pitted and cracked. Task said a few words to the ex-cop, who gave a curt nod, turned, and began the trek back the way they had come, the bloodhound trotting dutifully at his side. Amber watched them go, noting the stiffness in the man's posture, the way his shoulders seemed to relax just a fraction as he put distance between himself and the cliff.

He didn't want to be here.

Task, however, showed no hesitation. He turned to one of his men, who pulled a cell phone from his pocket, staring at the screen for a long moment before dialing. The man turned slightly away as he spoke, but Amber could still hear the murmured report, the steady recitation of GPS coordinates.

Her attention, however, was drawn upward.

The steps were crude, uneven, as if they'd been hacked into the sloping rock of the cliff's lower portion by hand. The edges were rough, chipped, and weathered, yet still serviceable. They ascended for about ten feet before giving way to a series of natural rock ledges, the kind carved by erosion and time rather than human effort. These narrow, precarious platforms led higher, zigzagging their way up to a dark opening in the cliff face.

A cave.

Amber squinted, trying to gauge its depth from below, but the angle made it impossible. From here, it looked like nothing more than a dark maw, a hole in the rock swallowing the light.

She let her gaze drift downward and froze.

Drops of blood.

Chapter 19 : WATER

THE SMELL HIT Amber first, before her eyes could adjust to the gloom. She stepped off the semi-rigid composite rope ladder, allowing Owen Spirit to hold her elbow and steady her ascent into the cave mouth. She had to breathe slowly through her mouth to cope with the stench.

Task's pair of action-oriented lackeys had scaled the cliff by way of the natural and man-made steps in advance of the rest of the group and secured the rope ladder for the others. The ladder was of a type that cinched tight after being moored at the top so that it became almost as solid as a metal ladder would have been. Once it was in place, Spirit and Task had been next up the cliff face, followed by an additional goon and then Amber herself.

Spirit helped Frymet into the cave entryway next, and Amber felt rather than saw that the available space in the cave was running very short. The men were standing still in a cluster looking deeper into the cave. Spirit stepped around Amber and Fry to inform the men still below and on their way up the ladder that there was no more room in the cave.

Once the lawyer had stepped out of Amber's line of sight, she began to make out details in the darkness. Looking down near her feet, Amber saw a small basin that had been scratched into the rock with some sort of tool. Thin grooves led up the cliff wall above the basin, some up and out toward the cave mouth, others deeper into the cave itself. Past the basin was a newly-stacked row of cases of water bottles. These shrink-wrapped bundles were stacked floor to ceiling, some eight feet in height nearer the front of the cave, less than six farther in. The stack was two deep to the wall in spots; Amber guessed there had to be a hundred cases of water bottles.

Next to the wall of water were a handful of metal food cans, predominantly beans and tuna with a few rectangular tins of processed meat. High-protein, long shelf life goods, heavy on utility without much consideration for flavor.

The dusty floor of the cave was littered with empty bean and tuna cans and a couple dozen bottles of water, all drained. These cans were a clear contributor to the smell in the cave, providing strong notes of stale fish to the musty, earthy odor of ancient rock. It was a peculiar blend of sea and stone with other, less pleasant, odors woven throughout into a rancid tapestry: the strong metallic tang of blood, the acrid stench of human waste, the cloying sweetness of hatching fly larvae. All of these aromas blended into a gut-wrenching olfactory tableau at this nexus where the stifling dry heat outside mixed with the cooler air in the cave.

Amber heard Fry gag behind her as Cameron Task stepped aside to speak with Owen Spirit. As Task moved aside, Amber caught her first glimpse of a low pallet along the wall opposite the water stockpile. A wounded old man lay on the pallet, his chest quivering in pain, his breaths fluttering in the quiet still of the cave.

"Ashe!" Amber cried out. She rushed to the old man's bedside. Without considering his wretched appearance, she shot forth a hand to his ruddy cheek and then pulled it back in horror. Ashe's skin crinkled like parchment, and he felt hotter to the touch than Amber had ever imagined people could get. "He's burning up! Get him some water! What is wrong with you people?"

Amber rocketed away from Ashe's bunk and shoved Cameron Task aside in her urgent rush for the old man's hoarded water. The billionaire stumbled and crashed into Owen Spirit. Task fell to the floor in the tight confines of the cave and his men stepped quickly to avoid tangling up with their boss. Amber grabbed two bottles and dove back to the old man. She fought with the first bottle in her haste, then managed to open it. She poured the water over Ashe's head, chest and left arm, where the ragged flesh showed the most obvious signs of his recent trauma. Water flowed over the dried blood and lacerated flesh, washing away many of the maggots crawling on the old man's wounds. She threw the empty bottle to one side and opened the second. This she held gingerly to the old man's cracked lips and was gratified when he took several sputtering gulps. Recognition and gratitude illuminated the old man's eyes.

This moment was interrupted as Cameron Task grabbed Amber's upper arm and jerked her roughly up off the bed. Amber's hair whipped about her face. Task spun her about, and she rebounded from the shrink-wrapped stacks of water. Amber's vision exploded into a white-hot light as the back of the man's right hand smashed into her left cheekbone and eye socket. Amber collapsed to the cave floor atop the empty cans and plastic bottles.

She felt rather than saw the bolt of lightning smash into Cameron Task from behind with nearly enough force to fold the man in half.

WATER BOTTLES FLEW everywhere as Ashe's tackle drove Task into the stack of hoarded water. Many burst instantly with the impact, showering everyone in the small cave with natural pure spring water or plain old tap water, depending on one's point of view regarding bottling practices. Most of the neatly stacked wall of shrink-wrapped cases collapsed under the onslaught of the two bodies hurtling into it.

Cameron Task was a fit man. He was convinced that a sound and capable mind required a sound and capable physical body to properly support it. He adhered to a number of weekly schedules. An hour in his state-of-the-art gym facility before dawn four times a week, pushing himself to the limits of his physical endurance. Two three-hour kick-boxing sessions across town at Stone's gym, training with professional fighters. A half-century or more on his bike on Sundays when he could make the time. Task held five black belts in three disciplines and was advancing rapidly at the Northside Krav Maga center.

No part of that routine did him the least bit of good at this moment; Cameron Task lay gasping for air on the floor where he had been thrown like a rag doll by the impact. He lay among, atop, and under dozens of burst water bottles. Shattered plastic was all his hands could find as he grabbed desperately for something, anything he might use to defend himself from his unexpected attacker.

Despite his own compromised condition, it took Ashe less than three seconds to right himself after their first collision and launch himself at Task again. Before anyone else in the cave could react, let alone intervene, Ashe was on top of the other man.

Under other conditions, Ashe might have fought with more decorum. Amber had seen the old man do so; she knew he could fight with patience, cunning, and discipline. The Ashe she saw now was severely wounded and no doubt compromised in ways that went beyond mere physical injury. This version of the old man displayed neither planning nor restraint. This Ashe was unbridled fury; a cornered animal defending its home, its pack.

The two men rolled around on the water-slicked stone of the cave floor. Each was soon covered with a patina of silty gray mud. Though only marginally effective, this mud was all the armor Task had from Ashe's pummeling fists and grappling hands. The old man resorted to gouging with fingers tensed into claws. He kicked at Cameron Task as if trying to disembowel him. He tore at Task; he dug fingers into flesh, searching for nerve clusters. He grabbed fistfuls of hair in an attempt to pull back Task's head and expose his vulnerable throat. Soon the gray mud was streaked red with both men's blood: Ashe's from recent and grievously infected wounds reopened by the current struggle, Task's from fresh injuries inflicted by Ashe's hands.

It seemed an eternity had passed, so intense was this savage conflict, but Amber knew it had been only seconds. Task had been taken completely off guard by Ashe's attack, but he began to regain his composure. Ashe had grabbed him around the neck, but the mud and gore coating the two combatants made securing his grip impossible. Task spun in his grasp and thrust upward, breaking the faulty hold. Following up with what he intended to be a solid kick to Ashe's solar plexus, he managed only to grate his heel against Ashe's ribs.

But it was enough for a brief respite, and Task gulped heaving lungfuls of air. Ashe grabbed at his side momentarily. The flesh there, recently torn to shreds by the woodchipper, flapped open to expose the flashing white bone of the old man's ribs. Whatever twinkle of reason or mercy might have been found in Ashe vanished in an instant. With a deafening bellow, he turned back to Cameron Task. The old man took a step to the left, watching for his next opening.

Rising over Ashe's howl, Task's voice rang out in the cave.

"Shoot him!"

Amber had been so intently watching the fight she missed that two of the men in the cave had produced weapons. The first fired while the second man was still clearing his weapon from his pack. He hit Ashe with a taser gun, sending fifty-thousand volts coursing through the old man's body.

The taser did little to slow Ashe, however. He twitched and stumbled, but advanced on Task as if wading through deep water. Every eye beholding the old man widened in disbelief.

The second man had finally brought his weapon to bear, having fished the small metal case of specialized ammunition from his pack and loaded the breech. He aimed the short rifle at Ashe's back.

"Drop him!" shouted Task, "Now!"

The second man's gun produced a sharp, popping cough and a fluffy red dart appeared center mass in Ashe's back. He clawed at the projectile but came on. The man's air gun was either a semi-automatic or he was very skilled at reloading it; two more pops sounded and a second and third dart appeared in Ashe's broad back. Ashe wavered, slowing almost to a stop. With great effort, the old man lifted his right foot and planted it three inches closer to Cameron Task. His teeth clenched with the extreme effort, and saliva dripped from his bared fangs. The shooter fired a fourth dart, and Ashe at last fell heavily to the cave floor.

Cameron Task struggled to his feet, dripping with mud and sweat, streaked with blood. His foot slipped on a crumpled blue and pink metal tin, slipping on the wet cave floor. When Owen Spirit rushed over to offer assistance, Task growled at him and pushed the lawyer away with a curse.

Amber heard the rapid thumping sound of a helicopter moving in their direction. Cameron Task walked nearer the cave's entryway, still working to catch his breath. He pointed at the unconscious old man.

"Get him bound," ordered task, "And get him on a stretcher."

Chapter 20 : DEPARTURES

"WHAT ARE YOU going to do with him?" demanded Amber.

Amber stood with Frymet to one side in the cave. The two girls were informally guarded by one of Task's men. He had loaded a fresh cartridge into the Taser pistol he gripped loosely in one hand. Amber had no illusions that he held it in plain sight by accident. She also had no illusions that she could shake off the effects of being tased the way Ashe had done. The thought was sufficient to keep Amber docile, but not enough to keep her quiet.

"Did you hear me?" she said more loudly, directly at Task. "I said, what are you going to do with Ashe? He needs to be in a hospital."

Cameron Task and Owen Spirit stood together near the mouth of the cave. The man with the tranquilizer gun had been joined by another man crowding in from below. Together the two of them had assembled a collapsible litter from the larger of the two backpacks. They wrangled Ashe's unconscious form onto the litter and cinched straps tightly around the old man.

Amber caught a glimpse of the helicopter descending outside. It was white and blue, sporting a royal blue Task International logo. The pilot flared to land a couple hundred feet from the foot of the cliff before the helicopter dropped too low for her to see. The pilot had to be skilled, as Amber could not recall seeing a flat area out there large enough to handle the aircraft. She presumed Task had called for the helicopter without clearing it with the police; he'd surely have no trouble dealing with whatever censure they handed him for his transgression. Even if Task had to have the aircraft destroyed, it would not even register as a footnote on his annual balance sheet.

"Task!" Amber struggled to be heard over the rhythmic thumping of helicopter blades slicing the air outside. The aircraft's mechanical drumbeat intensified to a crescendo, then started to fade quickly as the pilot dropped the skids onto the ground and started to power down the machine. A high metallic whine pierced the air before a final hum faded to silence.

"Task," Amber repeated, her voice loud in the new silence.

Cameron Task spun about. A look of controlled rage darkened the billionaire's face. Amber could make out livid bruising on his neck through the torn collar of his shirt. Mud and blood stained his shirt in unpleasant splotches.

"What?" Task hissed through clenched teeth.

"Which hospital are we going to?"

Task did not reply. Rather, he stood in place and fixed Amber with a stolid glare.

Owen Spirit spoke up instead. "The girl's not wrong, Cameron. The old guy was in pretty rough shape when we got here, let alone now. Not to mention the drugs. One of those darts would have dropped a horse; he took four. I think the old man probably needs a hospital."

Task stabbed Spirit's chest with an index finger. "*You* will need a hospital if *he*..." Task shifted to point at Ashe, "...is not on that helicopter in fifteen minutes and strapped to a bed in *my* facility within the hour."

Task stepped to the cave mouth and the ladder mounted there. "Get him lowered down," he ordered Spirit and the two other men. "There's limited space in the helicopter with the stretcher. There's a second bird on the way. I want all the men loaded on it and out of this place. They can stop and get the cars at the gate.

Spirit, you're with me on this chopper; bring Cieślak with us. I need her."

"And Ms. Olsen?" asked Spirit.

Cameron Task looked at his lawyer for a long moment before speaking. "Her, I *don't* need. She walks back or stays here. I couldn't care less," he sneered. The man exited the cave and climbed down the ladder.

The two pack-bearers had rigged the gurney in such a way that it could be lowered from the cave without tipping over. This they did, and set about packing their bags. The second helicopter could be heard in the distance.

Owen Spirit gestured for Frymet to accompany him. "Ms. Cieślak, it's time to go."

Fry folded her arms across her chest. "We are not leaving Amber here."

The lawyer looked pained. Amber almost thought the expression was genuine. "We do not have a choice here, Ms. Cieślak. And Ms. Olsen, I am truly sorry. Stay exactly on the path we took coming in, and you should be okay."

"No!" exclaimed Frymet. "She rides on the second helicopter, then."

"You heard the man. Trust me; you do not want to push back on this. *I* do not want to push back on this. We have to go now, please." Spirit's imploring face showed a hint of fear.

Fry stood her ground. Spirit looked out the cave at the helicopter below. Amber could hear the whine of its engine starting to spool up. The other helicopter circled, waiting for the first chopper to free up the landing space it had chosen in the rocky terrain.

Spirit snapped his fingers and gestured to the man kneeling on the floor. He was putting the last few items into his pack. "Leave those for her," Spirit told the man, who set a Geiger counter and one of the belt dosimeters aside, pushing them in Amber's direction.

"It's the best I can do," said Spirit to Amber.

Amber looked at her friend. "It's okay, Fry; go on. I want to tidy this place up a bit for when Ashe comes back. And he *will* come back." This last she directed at Spirit, who looked back at her like a whipped puppy.

Frymet grudgingly joined Spirit. "Don't stay here long," she told Amber as she disappeared down the ladder.

⤙ • ⤚

AMBER WATCHED AS the second helicopter lifted off in a rolling cloud of dust. She checked the belt dosimeter and saw a current reading of thirty-four percent. Emboldened by this, she looked around the cave, now empty save for herself.

Roughly one-fourth of the stacked bundles of bottled water had split open, spilling plastic bottles out to roll everywhere throughout the cave. Many of these had burst in the brief but fierce struggle between Ashe and Cameron Task. The canned goods stacked nearby had been toppled and cans lay tumbled about in the dust and mud.

Amber did what she could with the bottles. She stacked the remaining cases together, then turned her attention to the loose bottles. These were stacked between cases, lying on their side so that they wouldn't go rolling about. The burst bottles and other trash she did her best with as well. Regarding her handiwork, she decided there was little else she could do there and looked around the rest of the cave.

On the other wall, the frame of Ashe's pallet squatted unevenly, one leg having collapsed under some impact that Amber had missed in the chaos. Intrigued, Amber stepped closer for a closer look at the makeshift bed. The frame appeared to have been made from the straightest pieces of wood that the old man could find. It was composed of four legs and a boxed frame of longer rails. All of these looked to have been shaped roughly with a knife and scraped smooth. The joints were the most interesting part to Amber; the intersections of the individual pieces were elaborate hand-carved angles that interlocked without nails or screws. The bed was built to be taken apart easily, but also in a way that its structure was pulled together more tightly when a person lay on the pallet. The sleeping surface was made of military webbing straps woven together, making the bed more hammock than mattress.

One corner of this bed had splintered in the fight, and even if Amber could have understood the nature of

Ashe's engineering, she had no materials with which to attempt a repair.

Near the foot of this bed was a plywood box, painted in chipping olive drab. The box, about three feet in its longest dimension, had been knocked over in the scuffle. To one end of the box was pasted a crumbling lime green label, attesting the box's prepaid shipping status as serviceman's baggage by way of Asiatic Forwarders, Inc. Amber righted the heavy box, noting that the lid bore the stenciled letters, "U. S."

Some items had fallen out of the chest when it had tipped. Amber found a dry spot on the cave floor and began to walk through Ashe's life by way of his keepsakes and memorabilia. She marveled that a man's long life could be reduced to the contents of a three-foot lockbox.

She found a smaller box holding medals from several wars. Evidently Ashe was not only himself a soldier but came from a line of ancestors who had served as well. There were faded color photos that made her think of Vietnam, black-and-white photos from the first and second World Wars. She even found a pair of daguerreotypes from the Civil War, one of a Confederate soldier in uniform and the other of the same man dressed in finery and standing arm-in-arm with a beautiful southern belle. Amber was amazed at how much Ashe's ancestor in these old images resembled Ashe himself.

Deep in the chest Amber discovered a weighty bundle of oiled cloth. Unwrapping it, she gasped. The bundle held a pair of pistols. The first was a five-shot revolver that she imagined Dr. Watson describing as "ancient and weathered, yet serviceable." She'd never read any of Sir Doyle's books, of course, but she thought she'd heard Watson use that phrase in some movie she'd watched. The second captured her attention and made her consider options she'd not previously thought open to her.

Ashe was in trouble. She wanted, needed, to help, but had not thought she had the capability to do so. Looking at the heavy automatic pistol in her hand, her writer's mind could not help but appreciate the poetry of using Ashe's own weapons to wage war on his behalf. She pictured herself walking into Task's building and marching out with Ashe and Fry in tow...

Amber shook her head, making an effort to return to reality. She placed the pistol down on the floor and was surprised to hear a rapid clicking sound. She looked down to see the wand of the Geiger counter sitting near the weapon. Frantic, she grabbed the wand up and the clicking slowed. Waving it back at the pistol, the clicking sped up again.

She scrambled backward away from the footlocker on all fours. *You idiot*, she berated herself. The gun was a hunk of metal. Metal absorbed radiation. The police had not allowed the cars into this area for that very reason. Amber's heart raced as she realized how much time she had spent in this place, playing with items that had been here for who knows how many years, absorbing who knows how much radiation.

She dove three paces to the dosimeter and held its readout where she could see it. Sixty-three percent.

Amber picked up the pistol at arm's length, holding it gingerly by the trigger guard with two fingertips. She dropped it in the footlocker. The gun made a loud thumping sound as it fell to the lowest corner of the chest. The writer in Amber wondered what Chekhov would think of her leaving it behind.

She paused, wheels turning in her head. Amber realized she might not be able to take the gun, but she was by no means unarmed in this fight. She was a writer.

Amber glanced again at the dosimeter. Sixty-four percent.

Maybe she was a writer, but she really had to get going.

Chapter 21 : TAKEN TO TASK

AMBER WAS PACING again when the knock came at the door. She had been expecting the knock at any time for three days, and had been starting to fear it might not come. She knew after sending the email that her tactic would probably not bear immediate fruit, certainly not on the first day. But this morning, on day five, she had awoken from perhaps two hours' sleep and started to doubt herself.

When the knock came, relief flooded Amber's mind. She couldn't quite tell if her blood pressure had been high, and was now plummeting, or if it had been low and now it spiked. She took a deep breath to steady her nerves and stepped to the door.

The knock sounded again, louder, before she reached the knob. Whoever had been sent to collect her was impatient; she took this as a good sign.

"Ms. Olsen."

Owen Spirit wasn't smiling this time. In fact, Amber could swear that the lawyer was wearing disdain as a cologne; he positively reeked of it. The man slouched there in a ten-thousand-dollar cashmere suit with his hands thrust deep in the pants pockets like a sulking child.

"Mr. Spirit," was Amber's response.

The man raised his eyebrows over heavy-lidded eyes. "You got Cameron Task's attention with that email stunt of yours."

"It's no stunt," Amber said, forging as much steel into her voice as she could muster. "That article goes out at five o'clock tonight, unless I stop it from doing so."

"Save the threats for Task, alright? You wanted to see your friend; I'm here to take you to see him."

"Not just Ashe," Amber's eyes narrowed to fine slits. "I want to see Fry as well. That was made clear in my email."

Spirit released an exasperated sigh. The corners of his mouth tightened, drawing his lips into a thin, bloodless line. "Ms. Cieślak will be there as well," he said. His head tilted back toward the way he'd come. "Can we do this?" he asked.

☙ • ❧

"WHAT HAVE YOU done to him?" Amber shrieked.

Amber had been escorted to the headquarters building of Task Life Sciences International. During the long elevator ride, she had reminded Owen Spirit of the impending deadline for the automated release of her article. The lawyer had again deferred talking with her about it, telling her again to save her threats for Cameron Task. Having little else to discuss, Amber had pressed her point. Her demands had been simple, and she reiterated them as much for the sake of her own resolve as the lawyer's understanding; she insisted on seeing Ashe and making sure he was getting good care, and ensuring Fry was safe. She insisted on Ashe's immediate release and transport to a proper hospital. Amber knew she played a risky game with a powerful man. But she had gambled that Task would not want her article about the recent Ashe incident coming to light. It appeared now that her gamble had paid off.

Now she was here.

On the surface, the room resembled a very expensive private hospital room. Medical equipment, most of it unrecognizable to Amber, occupied every free corner, nook, and cranny in the room. LCD panels displayed wavering fields of brightly colored, indecipherable statistics in a continuous display of gibberish. Machines were wired together, strung to the wall, and connected to the figure lying on the chrome and cloth hospital bed. The visual effect was not unlike a helpless insect trapped in the web of some colossal and chaotic spider.

Ashe lay at the center of that web, unconscious on the bed. They had evidently cleaned the old man up, but there the compassionate care had ended. He was naked, save a pair of white boxers. The gashes, cuts, and abrasions received from the woodchipper were not bandaged, but still exposed. These wounds had been cleaned and some sort of salve applied, but no more. Pins and electrodes protruded from his flesh all over his body, making him look like some sort of human pincushion. From each of these needle-like metal spikes, thin wires fed data to the army of beeping machines.

Impossible to miss was the forty-gallon metal drum on a rolling rack to one side of Ashe's bed. It occupied the space where an IV-drip bag and rack would normally be expected. A clear hose led upward from the drum to an elevated pump mechanism which appeared to have been hastily secured to the wall with a metal strap and a half-dozen screws. Below this pump a more typical clear IV bag hung on what appeared to be a scavenged coat hook. Amber figured the bag was a reservoir for when they needed to change the drum. A thick flexible hose ran from the bag and into his left arm.

It became clear at once to Amber that Ashe was not a patient here, but a lab rat. The old man had a feeding tube down his throat, and he appeared to be in a medically induced coma, no doubt maintained by the IV line rapidly dripping into his right arm. Other tubes were visible as well, tending to waste removal and obviating the need for Ashe to do anything but lay there in the role of test subject.

Most of the old scars on Ashe's neck, arms and hands had grown familiar to Amber during the time she knew him. Seeing him like this, she was shocked to realize that his entire body was covered in a vast network of scar tissue. Old injuries were punctuated heavily with more recent wounds, inflicted both before and after his arrival here.

Cameron Task stood on the opposite side of the bed as Amber and Spirit arrived. Frymet was in the corner with a clipboard, looking anywhere but in Amber's direction. On a dolly to Task's right was a stainless-steel tray filled with all manner of surgical equipment, some familiar to Amber and much of it foreign. On this tray was also a cordless drill with a long-shafted bit. The drill bit was red with fresh blood.

Task's blue latex-gloved hands placed a sample into a test tube. Amber guessed that the sample had just been taken from high on Ashe's hip using the drill. It wasn't much of a guess, since a fresh hole above the waistline of Ashe's boxers oozed dark crimson and stained the bedsheet. Amber's stomach heaved and she tasted the bitter tang of bile at the back of her throat.

"Ms. Olsen! Welcome." Cameron Task smiled at the new arrivals. "Your friend here is remarkable. Do you know he doesn't have a direct match to any known blood type? And yet, he is the definition of a universal donor. That in itself would merit study. But his tissue and bone samples tell the most amazing story. This is exactly why I have spent twenty years searching for him, but I had no idea he was going to be this much of a treasure trove."

Amber lurched toward Ashe, but Spirit restrained her with a firm grip on her upper arm. With a placating gesture, she stopped struggling against the lawyer, and he released her.

"The rate at which his body heals is unbelievable. Well, it would be if I weren't seeing it and documenting it myself. Significantly faster than the baseline for a healthy teenager, with a correspondingly higher cost in caloric intake. Hence the feeding tube." Task gestured at the long tube inserted down Ashe's throat and secured to his face with medical tape. "Your friend is a hungry little boy," he smiled.

"It's caused us some difficulty, to be sure," Task chuckled. "He metabolizes anesthetics faster than we could administer them at first. But we've adapted, as you see." He waved a red-smeared blue hand at the drum of liquid beside Ashe's bed.

"And even then, his healing rate is accelerating. The curve started out very shallow but continues to increase. I suspect the chronic low-level radiation the subject exposed himself to may have been suppressing the healing rate, but that will have to be examined further before I can make a conclusion."

Task continued, "I haven't looked into actually breaking bones yet, or amputations, but I have dated his bone growth using four different methods and the results are consistent. Impossible, but consistent. The subject's hip and most of his skull register over two thousand years old. Not all the skull, though. Other areas of bone are newer, but inconsistently so."

None of this made sense to Amber. Task was smart, but he seemed to be completely convinced of what he was saying. Two thousand years? How could he believe nonsense like that? "What are you talking about?" Amber snapped. "That's ridiculous."

Task appeared to not even notice Amber's interruption. He continued. "His right hand and forearm are somewhere in the vicinity of a hundred and fifty years old. One of his legs is around four hundred to four hundred and fifty years old."

Four hundred years? Something sparked in Amber's memory. "Which leg?" she asked.

Task's eyes widened, and he looked in Amber's direction. "His left. The entire left femur below the trochanteric crest dates back four hundred or so years, while the head and neck of the joint is over two millennia old, like the hip itself. The lower legs are a different story though. Both lower legs read as only a little over a hundred years old."

Cameron Task pulled a computer screen closer on an articulated arm. He tapped the screen a few times and pulled up a cascade of numbers and charts. He seemed to think the proof provided by the display was self-evident, though it meant nothing to Amber. He went on, continuing to narrate a laundry list of injuries, many of which sounded strangely familiar to Amber. "The subject's ribs range throughout the centuries and are consistent in morphology with a long history of knife, bullet, and more recently, shrapnel wounds."

Task gestured at another display. This one showed images of bits and shards of metal, each having a numbered tag attached by a thin wire. "We extracted fragments of shrapnel and other foreign materials that we've been able to place at almost every major conflict as far back as the Napoleonic era. There were a few we were unable to readily place."

"It appears the most recent major trauma suffered by the subject was the loss of almost a third of his skull, his entire left scapula and most of his left humerus. The humerus itself is notable; at the time of the injury, there must have been barely enough bone to hold the lower arm in place. But the humerus is now a fantastic concretion of ancient and new growth. This trauma appears to have taken place in the late nineteen-sixties or early seventies. Which got us thinking."

Task appeared to suddenly remember the sample vial he had been holding. He set it down on the stainless-steel tray.

"We found heavily redacted records of a marine from Vietnam with similar injuries. Declared dead overseas with the rest of his unit, discovered alive but incoherent upon his casket's arrival in the States. Cared for at Walter Reed hospital, but eventually declared dead five months later.

"Frymet herself discovered those records, not long after the second time the subject flatlined from our investigations." Task gestured at Frymet. Amber glanced at her friend, who looked down at her clipboard.

Task appeared oblivious to the exchange between the two girls. He stepped around the foot of the bed, brushing past Fry and Amber. He sidled to the small sink. Doffing his blue gloves, he dropped them into a red trash can and continued. "The third time the subject coded, I kept them from resuscitating him and we discovered that he doesn't need to be brought back; he just... restarts after a while. Reboots. The period of cerebral inactivity appears to vary in duration with the extent of the subject's injuries, although we're still working to determine the exact correlation—"

"Subject?" Amber exploded in fury. "Stop using that word! He has a name!"

"That's just the thing; he doesn't. Fry only located the records by cataloging, dating, and cross-indexing his very extensive list of injuries. Rather genius work, actually," Task stated, smiling at Frymet.

Fry's face clouded over; she seemed sickened by having to play a part in this.

Task went on. "Every piece of identifying information in the records she found had been redacted since 1969. Even information regarding the names of the dead from his unit. They were simply buried without ceremony or name in Arlington National Cemetery."

"IF YOU THINK you're going to get away with this, you're insane! Maybe you have the police in your pocket right now, but once my article goes out and people find out what you've been doing here—"

Amber lunged for Cameron Task. Spirit was fast, but not quite fast enough. He grabbed Amber to restrain her, but not until after her nails had raked across Task's cheek.

Cameron Task glared at Amber as his lawyer pulled her back. Task grabbed a napkin and pressed it to his face to catch the small drops of blood produced by Amber's clawing attack.

"Yes," he said. "Your article." Ice dripped from the man's words.

"That's right," snapped Amber. "My article. The one that's going out tonight since I'm here and can't stop it."

"You set up a Deadman's switch." It was a statement, not a question.

"I did." Amber had not known what her trick had been called, but she was not about to let Task know that.

Task grinned. "I have to hand it to you, Ms. Olsen. You ran me on quite a little goose chase. I checked every server on the west coast after I bought your email provider and purged their archives. My people checked every stored bit in seventeen data centers and found nothing. They hit every forum on the dark web; nothing there either. I even personally checked data centers in China and Russia, thinking you might have somehow gotten truly creative."

Task shook his head. "I have to give you credit for using my own technical prowess and preconceptions against me. I never would have thought you would simply have the only copy timed to go out in a scheduled email right here on your laptop..." Task reached down to the counter next to a second power drill and held up what had formerly been a portable computer. Amber had not previously noticed it there on the countertop, but she now recognized it from the eclectic collection of stickers festooning its clamshell top and bottom. The lower portion of the machine was disassembled, with a hard drive hanging by a ribbon cable. The drive and other components she couldn't name had been perforated repeatedly by the power drill.

Amber's heart sank.

Cameron Task looked at her face. Slowly, a look of pure delight came over the man. "You weren't just being cagey," he laughed out loud. "You just never calculated that I made my first millions in computer technology and employ the largest group of security experts and white- and gray-hat hackers outside the NSA. Did you not realize that many of my people used to *be* NSA?

"You kept me spinning for the better part of a week, all because I failed to consider you might take such an obvious and low-tech approach simply out of ignorance. You underestimated me, but it paid off because I overestimated you. Bravo," Cameron Task applauded in sheer delight. "I'm sure as a writer, you can appreciate the irony."

"Laugh all you want!" Amber snarled. "You're not going to get away with this. I will eventually get word out, and once..."

"No, miss, that's where you're wrong," Task interrupted. "You're not going to be able to write about any of it. Do you think I got where I am by being muscled by puny people like you? What great man in history ever changed the world without obstacle?" The man touched his face and regarded his own blood on his hand without apparent emotion. He gestured toward Ashe with a red-smeared finger. "No, I'll keep picking that lock until I open every last one of its secrets, and then we'll see what mankind can achieve once the bonds of death are loosed."

Task turned to Owen Spirit. "Take Ms. Olsen and lock her up. One of the empty secure rooms will do fine for now. Her too," he said, indicating Frymet. "She's done good work, but her affinity for this one," he indicated Amber, "makes her a liability."

Cameron Task stepped toward Amber and Spirit, intending to exit the room. Amber launched a violent kick at the man as he passed. This action caused Owen Spirit to lose his grip on her and he stumbled off balance.

Amber fell to the floor and crab-walked backward towards Ashe's bed as Task stepped out of the room.

Spirit righted himself and brushed off his suit. He reached out to grab Frymet and then took a forceful step to grab Amber's ankle. He yanked her away from under the web of wires, lifted her from the floor and exited the room with the two girls.

He failed to notice Amber slipping the IV tube from Ashe's arm as she was pulled away. Unnoticed, the disconnected cannula dribbled a steady stream of anesthetic onto the floor.

Chapter 22 : ROUND TWO

THUD. THUD THUD. Thud. Thudthudthudthud.

Amber slid down to the floor and rubbed her foot, newly sore from kicking the locked door. "What kind of a place is this, anyway?" she asked no one in particular. "I mean, who armor-plates the door to an office?"

Frymet had not moved since the two of them had been locked in two hours earlier. She had slid to the floor in a back corner of the empty office and barely reacted to Amber's three loops around the small room seeking some means of escape.

The total yield of Amber's searches had been meager at best: a disconnected phone cable box, a paper cup with tarry black sludge in the bottom, two paper clips, and a metal trashcan containing three facsimile cover sheets, crumpled up. Amber thought it a curious anachronism that the papers said "facsimile" rather than "fax." *Who sent faxes anymore?*

Amber sighed. If she were Ashe, she could engineer some way out of the room with that collection of useless trash, but her best efforts amounted to a couple unsuccessful attempts to pick the lock with the paper clips. She'd seen Ashe do some amazing things with an alarming lack of tools, but this problem was beyond her abilities to solve.

Amber scrubbed roughly at her face. "Two thousand years?" she asked Frymet. She was mildly surprised when her friend looked up.

"Hard to believe, isn't it?" Fry mumbled.

"It's impossible to believe," Amber replied, glad to have finally engaged her friend in conversation. "It's *not* possible, is it? It's not possible. I mean... Are you sure the numbers were right? Your tests?"

Frymet gave Amber a blank look. "Have you ever known me to screw up a calculation?"

"No, but—"

"Multiply that by a thousand, and you've got Cameron Task. The man is a machine when it comes to detail. He re-ran every test sample after I'd done them three times already myself, always with the same result. When Task says two thousand years, he means two thousand years. Did you ever have any idea?"

"Me? No," said Amber. "I mean, I dunno. Ashe would tell me these crazy stories like they actually happened, but I figured he was just being creative."

Frymet's eyes glazed over; her face took on a distant look. "This is exactly the break that Task needed. Exactly when he needed it. It's pretty remarkable."

Amber was taken aback. "Are you kidding me, Fry? Are you excited about this?" She looked at her friend, sitting cross-legged on the floor in her white lab coat. Her Task Industries lanyard hung almost to the floor between her legs. Amber squinted at Fry. "You are excited about this!" she exclaimed.

"No, excited is the wrong word," Frymet assured her. "It is amazing, though, the way it's worked out for Mr. Task, and the timing and all of it. How? I mean..."

"How? How? How could 'Mr. Task have gotten so lucky, unless it was meant to be, right? Is that what you're trying to say?" Amber could feel heat starting to flush into her cheeks.

"No, that's not what I mean. I—"

"What you are is confused, Fry! You need to back it up a bit and realize Task is not the good guy here. How could you help him cut Ashe up into little chunks like that?"

"Little chunks? You're exaggerating. He—"

"I am *not* exaggerating! I saw what you'd done to him!"

"Hey! I never touched him, let alone took any samples. Mr. Task would never let me. I just did the research."

Amber rose to her feet and bent forward. Bending toward Frymet, she snapped in a mocking voice, "Right! 'I never threw anybody in an oven, I was just a guard. I only did what they ordered.'"

Amber kicked the wall repeatedly in rage, stopping only when she had run out of breath. She dropped again to the floor, panting.

"That's not fair," said Frymet in a low voice. Her face was darkened by a scowl.

"It is totally fair! You've always thought Task was some amazing visionary. Now you've completely gone over to his side."

"His side?" exclaimed Frymet, "You know he's going to kill us, right?"

Amber sneered. "He can't do that."

"Can't he? The resources that man's got? He can do anything he wants! And he will, because all he sees, all he cares about, is the bigger goal."

"Right, I forgot. The salvation of all mankind. Anything is okay in the name of the greater good, huh?"

"That's not what I'm saying."

"That *is* what you're saying. And you went along with it! Helping him research. Standing by while he carved Ashe like a Thanksgiving turkey."

Frymet glared at Amber. "Well, I found out that your Ashe may not have been the saint you think he was."

"What do you mean?"

"I've seen the scars all over his body. He is absolutely covered with them."

Amber waved a dismissive hand. "Yeah, so? I've seen 'em, too. He's fought in wars; you found that out, right? More wars than we can probably count, if your ridiculous claims about his age are true."

"Yeah, but what about since those wars? Between them? What stories did he tell you about that?"

Amber thought back. "I don't think it ever came up, why?"

"That weird blood of his. I found occasional records of it in several big cities since the nineteen-seventies. Most recently here in the late nineties."

"Yeah, okay. And?"

"And those references came up mostly in police files related to several unsolved homicides. Killings that cut a swath across the country from the east coast all the way here. Authorities never managed to connect the dots; they disregarded Ashe's blood as real evidence because they couldn't figure it out. No blood type, then later, DNA markers that made no sense. They typically disregarded the results as bad samples or test errors," Fry stated. "That, and they weren't highly motivated to solve the crimes."

"What? Why not? What do you mean, not motivated?"

"You've read about the Pharmacist? The guy from the eighties, right?"

"No. You know me and reading. That's what I have you for. Enlighten me."

"The 'pusher killer.' His victims were universally criminals. All of them. The murders started with petty drug dealers in Virginia, but things escalated as the killing spree moved west. By the time it reached here, it was an all-out war. The cops, in general, never even paid attention. They just let it all happen because the results served their purpose. They never bothered to find out who was doing it. I think it was Ashe."

"Go, Ashe," mused Amber. "And he won the war?"

"What? That's how you justify war? By who wins?" Fry snapped. "Who's rationalizing now?"

Amber grabbed the rim of the metal trash can from the floor and slammed it repeatedly against the wall. She finally stopped, her ears ringing in the sudden silence. She rubbed her tingling fingers.

Taking a deep breath, Amber leaned back to rest her head and shoulders against the wall. She gazed up at the tiny perforations in the white ceiling tiles. There were so many of them. Amber's brows creased and she wondered if the pattern was the same on every individual tile, or if each tile was unique. One hole, near one long edge of its tile and slightly larger than the rest, caught her attention. It looked lonely somehow, separated from its smaller, less significant neighbors. She wasn't sure if the hole represented Ashe or Task. "So, you're saying Ashe was some kind of vigilante?"

"Vigilante?" Fry's face contorted. "That's the word you pick? Like he was Batman or something? Your friend Ashe killed people, Amber. A lot of them!"

"Yeah. You said they were drug dealers and criminals."

"Oh, so it's okay for Ashe to brutally murder half a drug cartel for the greater good instead of seeking justice through legal channels, but when Task studies one man to cure disease and save humanity, that's different isn't it? Are you even thinking of the scales here?"

"That's how you justify human experimentation? The scale of it?"

Amber shot to her feet with the trash can. She began beating it against the air vent in the wall near the ceiling to the left of the door. "Let us out of here!" she shouted at the top of her lungs. She was still pounding at the vent when the door to the room opened.

The smirking face of Owen Spirit greeted the girls. "Put that thing down, will ya? You are one noisy little girl," the smug lawyer said to Amber. "Well, come on, then. You got the man's attention."

"Where are we going?" demanded Amber. She dropped the mangled bin to the floor with a clatter as Frymet clambered to her feet.

"To the principal's office, of course," came the reply.

ᕤ • ᕦ

"IS THAT SUPPOSED to impress me?" asked Amber. "Showing off your money?"

She stared at the elephant in the room. Stacked on a conference table in Cameron Task's office sat a mountain of cash. The bills, in twenty or so tightly bound bundles, whispered a hushed challenge to Amber's integrity.

She stood just inside the door, her left arm held in the tight grip of Owen Spirit's right hand. Frymet was similarly held on the lawyer's left. Amber's focus slipped away from the pile of money and made a circuit of the office.

Amber suspected that the interior decorator responsible for Task's office earned more for the job than she would make in five years as a waitress. The cool air in the room carried a subtle blend of well-conditioned leather and exotic hardwood. A pungent scent of coffee cut through the mix, catching Amber's attention. She could tell instantly that it wasn't just some cheap roast picked up from the local grocery on the way to work. The essence of the coffee was an ethereal whisper, a fragrant waltz of exotic origin and meticulous craftsmanship. Its smoky chocolate body entwined itself with the fruity essence of cherry and rich overtones that Amber had never encountered. Amber's eyes followed her nose to a monolithic espresso machine. The machine sat like some pagan chrome idol atop a credenza near the door. Natural light reflected off its surfaces as it filtered through floor-to-ceiling windows and bathed the room in a golden glow.

Amber shook her head, angry at herself for becoming distracted. She really should have gotten more sleep last night.

The furniture, crafted from rich, dark woods, boasted clean lines and promised comfort. Plush leather chairs, arranged around the sleek glass-and-steel conference table piled high with money, hinted at years of world-changing negotiations.

The walls were adorned with a small but significant collection of original artworks. Paintings, tastefully chosen and expertly arranged, provided an air of cultured refinement to the space. Task, or his decorator, had an appreciation for art that surpassed simple decoration.

Strategically placed spotlights highlighted the paintings, adding a glow to otherwise dark corners of the room and accentuating the interplay of textures and colors. The overall effect was one of curated elegance, a deliberate selection that mirrored Cameron Task's meticulous approach to life.

Task's mahogany desk, expansive and uncluttered, stood confidently as the clear centerpiece of the office. A closed silver laptop computer spoke to the integration of technology into the traditional workspace. Aside from the laptop, the desk's surface was empty; it was all business and needed no artifacts to convey its owner's importance.

The view from the windows revealed a skyline that bowed to the power and influence of the man standing behind the desk. The city lay at the feet of Cameron Task, a reminder of the vast empire he had built. The office was not just a place of work; it was a reflection of Task himself: a sophisticated, self-proclaimed advocate of life. But Amber knew that advocacy fell within parameters that Task alone understood.

Cameron Task stood behind the massive desk with a small porcelain cup of espresso. The billionaire blinked at Amber's response to his offer of opulence and compromise. "Well," the man smiled, "it is an impressive sum. But I have to stress: it's not my money, it's yours."

Amber raised her eyebrows in mock surprise. "Oh?" she asked.

"Must I explain the obvious? This is my offer for you to walk away. That will be enough to keep you in that rent-controlled apartment of yours for the rest of your life. Or, if you're more the type, you can find a cabin by a lake in the mountains where you can write in peace and seclusion forever."

"Just no writing about what's going on here."

"Of course not," said Task. "You'll sign a standard agreement—"

"Well, I don't agree. How's that?"

"Very well, five times that amount. But now we're talking a check. There would be taxes—"

Amber interrupted, "Go up to fifty times that amount and you can still stuff it up your butt!"

Task sighed. "What is your price then?"

"Must I explain the obvious?" Amber mocked. "Ashe gets out of here and to a proper hospital."

"Let's not insult each other. That is non-negotiable and you know it. I have waited for that man for over twenty years, and now that I have him, I am not giving him up."

"Twenty years? What are you talking about?"

Task sat down in his leather desk chair. He reached forward and set the espresso cup down on the desk with a faint tap. Leaning back, the billionaire folded his fingers together and raised his eyebrows slightly. To Amber, the man looked like a teacher preparing to give a formal dissertation.

"Let me tell you a little about your friend," said Task. "I graduated in the nineties from Carnegie-Mellon with degrees in both biology and engineering, as you probably know. You no doubt also know how I focused my earliest work in the mid-nineties on establishment of concepts geared at creating 'green' data centers. I saw the direction things were headed and knew the imminent growth of computation was going to outpace our ability to control the environmental impact. Moore's law predicted millions of servers across thousands of data centers within a decade or two, and I predicted the inevitable ecological footprint that came with those servers."

"I thought you were going to tell me about Ashe, not bore me with your amazing achievements," Amber drolled.

Cameron Task smiled and continued as if he hadn't heard her comment. "At first, my efforts were viewed as a gimmick. I garnered enough attention to get rich, of course, but not enough to change the world as I had planned. I started looking at ways to use my data centers that supported my other concerns, such as medical research. Since I owned and operated my own data centers, I had no constraints upon their use other than what suited my purposes.

"I started providing computing power to universities and research hospitals that were doing the type of work that I knew mankind needed to reach its next stage of progress. Genetic sequencing, disease eradication, anything that improved the chances humanity had of continuing, despite its determination to drive itself off the ecological cliff.

"In 1998, I received an unusual request. My microbiology professor from college, an old mentor of mine, approached me. He had been assisting the FBI with a case, and he needed the kind of computational power that I could offer. His problem intrigued me; I had no idea at the time it would change the course of my life, and ultimately the course of all mankind."

Task paused for effect. He took a sip of his coffee. When Amber and the others posed no questions, he continued, vastly enjoying the attention of his captive audience. Amber got the sense she was being told a story Task longed to share in a more public forum.

"The Bureau was trying to track down a serial killer," stated Task. He returned the small cup to his desk. "Someone had started targeting drug dealers, then escalated to distributors, and anyone associated with them. In the early 1970s, these murders were confined to the Washington, DC Metro area, but they spread to the Midwest by the late seventies. Local authorities in many of the affected cities turned a blind eye; criminals of this type killed each other all the time, and it didn't hurt their crime-fighting efforts to just let it happen.

"The killings moved to Chicago but then stopped for a while. Things went dormant throughout the latter half of 1987 and much of 1988. So far, no one had connected the events. But when they resumed in Chicago, the scale of an event in late 1988 drew the attention of the FBI. Based upon similarities to some of the DC area killings and an unusual blood sample found at the scene, the FBI eventually connected several unsolved crimes into a coherent thread.

"Of course, DNA analysis had become fairly common in forensics by this time, but it still was not completely reliable. When samples from this killer were identified, they were typically discounted. The blood was unlike any other blood the FBI—or anyone—had ever seen. They had no way of knowing what to look for, or what to do with the samples. They had no context and determined that the samples were simply corrupted by environmental factors.

"The FBI tracked five more major incidents and dozens of isolated deaths heading westward after that Chicago slaughter at a massive drug turf battle in the port district. The remaining crimes ranged from Chicago all the way here. In early 1997, another anomalous blood sample was recovered at a destroyed methamphetamine lab in New Mexico. It took the FBI a year, but they contacted my professor for assistance due to his track record in helping local police in Pittsburgh with such matters.

"It took them very little time from that point to recognize the need for computing power beyond what they could bring to bear, so my old mentor suggested me as a resource."

Task reached for and finished his tiny cup of exotic, over-powered coffee. He stood up and walked to the espresso machine, setting the cup down. He turned back to Amber, closer now to her and the others.

"What I saw in those samples was revelatory. I had no way of replicating it, no chance of understanding it, but the regenerative powers of that blood were superhuman. Analysis of those early samples spawned ideas that pushed my thinking forward decades. Centuries. What could be nothing but a dream before suddenly looked possible. That blood laid out before me humanity's roadmap to life without disease. To life without the dishonor of old age. Without the specter of death. That blood promised solutions that teased us all from beyond the stars. It all became possible for me in that moment.

"Anyone could have seen it, but only I did. Only I had the vision to know where that blood could take us. But I needed more of that blood. Would I help the FBI find the killer? Yes. Without hesitation. They wanted to find him, but I *needed* to. I needed the subject himself."

Task walked back toward his desk and turned to face Amber and the others. He leaned back against the edge of the desk and folded his arms. His face became a mask of remembered disappointment.

"And then the killings stopped," Task said, frowning. "The vigilante appeared to drop off the face of the earth."

"Why are you doing this?" asked Amber. "This is going beyond you just wanting to improve humanity, isn't it? This is a vendetta."

"I suppose so. I don't deny it. Do you think that it's mere coincidence that I have this lab here, fully equipped with exactly everything I need to examine this man and mine his body for its secrets? I have identical labs set up in every major population center across the country, and several in foreign capitals as well. Nothing was left to chance. I knew he would resurface; I just didn't know where. It was just a matter of time.

"Really, I owe you a debt of gratitude. Do you know how many millions of dollars I have spent searching for your friend and working with law enforcement agencies across the country? For over two decades? How much money and effort I poured into the hunt for that man? And you bring me more than a half-liter of blood, unasked. And a woodchipper, positively brimming with tissue samples! A woodchipper. You do know how to get my attention. That would have been enough, really, but you gave me the best gift of all. You delivered the subject himself, wrapped up in a neat little package. All free of charge."

Amber felt sick at her stomach. Her face blanched and she wavered on her feet. Owen Briggs, thinking she was fighting against him, tightened his grip on her arm and pulled her upright. She wobbled, overcompensating her balance.

Task smiled widely at her discomfiture. "And not just me. Think of all the good that this man will do for the world. Think of the good he's already done, simply by eluding my grasp for twenty-five years. Look at all we've learned. Look at all we've achieved simply from my exposure to the trigger of his existence. And the advances in forensic science! Do you know how many serial killers have been apprehended because of my search for that man in there? How many lives were saved because I developed tools to find him that the authorities could use to find others?" Task pointed out from his office in the direction of Ashe's room.

"When I first learned of this man, when my professor first showed me that sample of blood, it changed the course of my life. It changed the course of history. It made me into the man I became. Further, the science to locate him, to track him, didn't exist. I had to invent it, create it all, in the service of my hunt for that man. The world has reaped vast benefit from my efforts, all because of him. And now, your friend can fulfill his destiny by finally allowing me to reach for the bigger goal."

Amber's lips curled involuntarily. "You are stark raving mad. This is the stupidest thing I've ever heard. You're an idiot," she told Cameron Task.

Something flipped in Task's demeanor. He became suddenly enraged, his face turning crimson. Veins popped from his forehead and bruised neck. "Am I?" he shouted at Amber. He gestured toward his office door. "Am I? That man in there hides mysteries that, when unlocked, will advance mankind into the next age. I will unlock them! Me! Don't you want to help with that? Don't you want to be part of something greater than yourself?"

"No, Mister Task!" Frymet's explosion startled everyone in the room, but no one more than Amber. "Enough is enough! We're done helping you. *I'm* done helping you!"

Frymet struggled against Spirit's grip. Her unexpected outburst caused the lawyer to twist and squeeze the small girl's arm to maintain control.

"I'm truly sorry you feel that way, Ms. Cieślak," said Task. "But you're wrong; you can still help me. Just in a different capacity." Task reached down and opened a side drawer of his desk. He produced a large, nickel-plated automatic pistol.

Without even a pause to consider his action, Task shot Frymet through the center of her left thigh. Amber's ears rang from the assault of the pistol shot on her hearing.

Fry's leg crumpled beneath her like a broken twig. She cried out in pain. Amber twisted free of the suddenly distracted Spirit and dove to her friend's side.

Owen Spirit shouted at his boss. "Whoa! Cameron, what are you doing! You are *not* doing this again!"

Cameron Task looked confused. "Not doing this again? This isn't at all like last time. *She*..." Task indicated Frymet with an off-handed wave of the gun, "...has signed the agreement. And *she* will be remembered by history for helping me perform the first direct transfusion test."

"Okay, you *are* insane!" said Spirit, eyes as round as saucers. "We are way beyond the point where even I can help you. This is over."

Owen Spirit turned. He took two long strides toward the door of Task's office, producing a cell phone from an inner jacket pocket. He had punched the nine button on his digital keypad and the first of two ones when he stopped dialing. The lawyer did not see Task pull the trigger behind him. Neither did he hear the shot or feel the bullet enter his back and burst through the front of his chest.

Owen Spirit's body dropped face-first to the floor like a puppet whose strings had been cut. His cell phone clattered into the hallway.

"Well, if you can't help me anymore, then perhaps it is over," stated Cameron Task. He pointed the gun at Amber.

"Now, Ms. Olsen—"

Task was interrupted by the hurtling silvery-red streak that flew into the office and across his desk. He crashed to the floor and against the floor-to-ceiling window under the thrashing form of Ashe.

Amber kept pressure on Fry's leg wound, but her attention was fixated on the scene before her. If Ashe had been ferocious before in the cave, he was now positively feral. The old man's stance was primal, a coiled readiness learned in countless deadly battles. Grizzled hair sprayed from his head in wild tufts, framing a snarling visage etched with the scars of age-old skirmishes and recent experimentation at the hands of the man below him.

Amber would scarcely recognize Ashe in different circumstances. The ferocity in his eyes, those windows to a soul forged in the crucible of conflict... It burned with wild intensity. Amber recognized nothing human behind those eyes.

Ashe bled from dozens of small punctures left behind all over his body by the needles, electrodes and probes. He must have ripped them all out by force once he recovered from the anesthetic drip that Amber had managed to remove. The old man's skin glistened red in the subtle artistic lighting of Task's office. He resembled an old Roman statue of Mars carved from red Alabaster she had seen in an art museum last fall.

Thick, rope-like muscles coiled under the old man's freshly bleeding skin, poised to unleash lethal fury. Fingers distended like claws arced out as extensions of Ashe's raging spirit, an indication that the beast within him had taken control.

Task struggled to his feet and Ashe danced back with a fluidity of movement that belied any stiffness brought on by age. His shoulders were scarred by the passage of time but retained the sinewy strength of a wild animal. A dripping snarl contorted his lips in a mask of rage and defiance.

Cameron Task leaned back against his heavy desk. Ashe circled him warily.

The pistol in Task's hand barked loudly and Ashe roared in pain and fury as the round tore through his heaving chest. Task fired again. This bullet passed through Ashe's right shoulder, spinning him about and dropping the old man to the floor. As he fell, Amber observed that the bullet had punched through the huge plate glass window after exiting Ashe's body, leaving a spider-webbed hole trimmed in white. Wind, rushing up the tall building, whistled through the new hole in the window.

With effort, Ashe pushed himself back up to his feet. He stood coiled on his haunches in determined readiness to spring at his adversary.

"Amazing!" exclaimed Cameron Task. "Two forty-five caliber rounds at close range, after the trauma you've already endured, and you're still standing. We are going to change the world, my friend."

In response, Ashe coughed and spat a mouthful of blood on the floor. His teeth were painted red.

"Still," continued Task, "We're not done with our work. Why don't you just die so I can sedate you and get back to it?" Task fired the gun repeatedly, steadily, the loud reports assaulting Amber's ears. With each shot, gore burst from Ashe's body and a fresh hole appeared in the glass behind him.

Cameron Task smiled broadly. "Old man, you are phenomenal! What does it take to put you down?" he marveled.

"M... More..." Ashe's voice was faint. Amber could clearly hear gurgling in his throat and wet bubbling sounds from his perforated lungs as the old man drew breath in an effort to speak.

"More?" Task fired again, only too happy to oblige. "More?!" And again. Ashe's body jerked with each fresh impact.

Finally, the slide on Task's big automatic locked open. Smoke drifted upward from the exposed tube of the gun's barrel.

Ashe burst forward. One fist shot out to wrap around Task's gun hand. The other hand locked on the billionaire's neck like a steel clamp. The old man bared his teeth; from her angle, Amber could not tell if he was snarling or smiling. Or both.

"More than you'll ever know," Ashe growled. He raised a foot and placed it against the massive desk. With a mighty shove, Ashe flew backward against the window, pulling Task along with him. The fractured glass, compromised by a half dozen bullet holes, gave way in a burst of sparkling shards and the two combatants sailed outward into the night air.

Amber rushed to the window. Glass crunched beneath her sneakers as she steadied herself against the frame. She peered out the window after the two men in time to see the last couple seconds of their earthward plunge. She watched as Ashe pushed Task away from him in mid-air. This action moved the old man toward the building as he fell, and Task farther away from it. Ashe coiled both legs under him and then kicked off the building at the last moment. He sailed outward away from the building and into the verdant canopy of a mature Oak tree planted in the building's courtyard. A cloud of leaves was all that marked the old man's passage, eighty floors below.

Amber continued watching as Cameron Task became a red splotch on the paved courtyard.

Chapter 23 : RAIN

THE CITY STREET pulsed with energy as the morning sun pierced the dissipating heat of lingering summer. A gentle breeze carried with it a cool hint of moisture, promising relief after weeks of unrelenting drought. A welcome departure from the stifling heat wave, the breeze swept through the crowd gathered in front of an electronics store.

The storefront's large display window showcased a group of high-definition televisions in various sizes. Their screens were tuned to three news networks, each reporting different aspects of the same drama. Muted reflections of the surrounding cityscape mixed with those of the passers-by and danced across the glass of the window, adding a surreal quality to the scene.

The voice of one channel's news anchor, amplified by the store's speakers, was audible on the street. The man narrated the shocking demise of Cameron Task, once-mighty genius entrepreneur and businessman. Task's charismatic smile, shown on a few of the screens, stood in stark contrast to the dark nature of the unfolding story. The scrolling headline on the central screen declared in bold letters: "Tragic Death of Visionary Tech Mogul - Suspected Suicide."

A diverse crowd had gathered, pulled together by an invisible thread of curiosity in the fabric of the day. The members each reacted in predictable ways to the news with a mixture of disbelief and somber reflection. Conversations among those gathered were hushed; expressions of shock were incongruous with the promise of changing weather. The air was pregnant with the scent of imminent rain, a much-needed change from the oppressive heat that had gripped the city for weeks.

Additional pedestrians, drawn by the magnetic pull of a crowd and the unfolding tragedy, slowed their pace and joined the assembly. The store's entrance became a gathering point, a communal space wherein the city's pulse became synchronized with the rhythm of the news. The atmosphere was charged with a sense of shared mourning as the crowd watched the story unfold. The breeze shifted slightly, bearing an imminent cleansing rain.

The large center screen displayed footage of the night scene in front of the Task Life Science division headquarters over a week ago. Flashing police lights illuminated the courtyard of the building, where Task had fallen to his death from his skyscraper window. The scene, also captured in snippets on other screens, added a chilling layer to the news story. Red and blue light from the screens flickered across the faces of the crowd as they absorbed the grim reality of the billionaire's tragic end.

A speaker carried the news anchor's voice to those gathered.

"No additional information this morning from authorities regarding the death of famed multibillionaire Cameron Task early last week. Police have issued a statement that they believe Task shot out his 88th floor office window with a handgun found on the scene before leaping through the window to his death. There is some speculation that a second jumper was involved due to blood recovered at the scene, but, again, this is simply speculation as no other body was found and no eyewitnesses have come forth. Several of the humanitarian organizations and charities funded or headed by Task have issued press releases..."

The atmosphere changed with the first droplets of rain. The air, once pregnant with the scent of imminent rain, now delivered the cool relief of a long-awaited summer shower. The rain danced a transient ballet across the surface of the large display window, blurring the images of the somber news story.

Umbrellas sprouted like colorful mushrooms among the dispersing crowd, shielding onlookers from the gentle arrival of the rain. Some sought refuge under awnings or pulled out magazines and newspapers, fashioning makeshift shields to protect themselves from the shower.

The collective murmurs of the crowd faded into the rhythmic symphony of rain meeting pavement, creating a soothing backdrop that contrasted with the nature of the news. The communal space began to fracture as individuals, seeking refuge from the rain, each resumed their interrupted journeys.

A small child, no more than six years old, tugged at the sleeve of his mother. She had opened a vibrant red umbrella to shield them both from the rain. The child's eyes sparkled with a mixture of curiosity and excitement as he gazed up at the falling droplets. The mother, holding the umbrella with one hand, reached down to grasp her child's small hand with the other.

Amidst the dispersing crowd, the pair moved forward, the child's tiny steps quickening to keep pace with his mother. He giggled with delight, seemingly unaffected by the news that had transfixed the earlier assembly. As the small family unit navigated the now rain-soaked street, the child's laughter echoed, a beacon of innocent hope.

The crowd thinned rapidly to reveal an old man still regarding the store window. He was heavily bandaged under thrift-store clothes and had one arm in a sling anchored around his neck and shoulder. He stood precariously balanced on a pair of mismatched crutches, one wood and one dented gray metal. Despite the crutches, the man struggled slightly for balance due to the compromised arm.

In passing, the young boy accidentally bumped the old man. This caused the child, after a few steps, to accidentally drop the red ball he was carrying. The rain had made the ball too slippery for the boy's inexperienced young fingers.

The ball bounced on the pavement in arcs of diminishing height. It bumped against the foot of the old man, who bent to pick it up, steadying himself with his crutches. Straightening back up, the man's face contorted as white-hot agony seared his side. He pulled his good arm in tight against his fractured ribs, which had started to heal after nearly two weeks but remained very tender. He handed the ball back to the young boy, who accepted it with a smile.

As his pain subsided, a reflection in the store window caught the old man's attention. A young red-haired girl pushed a smaller girl in a wheelchair towards the doorway of the apartment building across the street. The two were laughing as they rushed to find shelter from the sudden rain. The girl in the wheelchair had her entire leg enclosed in a cast, and this protruded straight out from the seat, causing the pair to get stuck in the doorway. The pair tried several times to navigate the portal, giggling with each awkward failure.

A young man in blue jeans and a gray t-shirt paused in his own quest for shelter long enough to reach out and hold the door open for the two girls. Ashe watched in the reflection as Amber and her friend accepted the young man's assistance and conquered the doorway to vanish into the apartment building.

The old man glanced around himself on the empty street. Rivulets of rainwater coursed down his back, seeping through his clothing to wet his bandages. Alone now in front of the store, he turned his face to the sky and allowed the heavy drops of rain to run down his face.

The old man couldn't remember the last time he'd lived.

Epilogue: FIAT

1969

The ceiling didn't look familiar to Ashe. He'd awakened staring at so many different ceilings that he could never count them all, yet he had learned he could easily group them into distinct categories. Hospital ceilings were one of the easiest categories to call out, of course, although that particular class had probably seen the most change of them all over the years.

The lighting was always a dead giveaway. Sure, the pervasive smell of antiseptics didn't hurt the process of identification. But the nose wasn't always his most reliable tool when he woke up like this, and he'd come to rely first and foremost on his eyes. His eyes traced the lines of pendant T-rail used to support the dingy white asbestos tiles. Following a line to the wall and from there to the corner—all while not moving his head (that was a lesson well and early-learned)—Ashe saw no trace of cobwebs or other dirt. That seemed strange, but he was unsure why. His eyes flicked to the light hanging over the bed.

Bed? That seemed strange also. He pondered for a moment why it would seem strange to awake in a bed. People had been waking up in beds for millennia, hadn't they? He was himself not completely a stranger to the process. But it didn't feel right. Why? Don't waste time on that right now. Location first, then situation. The latter typically presented itself as he worked out the former. Back to the light.

The light was turned off at the moment, and it plainly confirmed his earlier hospital hypothesis. Yet, the design was unexpected. It wasn't the type he would expect to find in... where was he? Where had he been, rather?

Not getting past that question. Seems like things were clarifying more slowly than usual. Ashe doubled down on his routine. Control the breathing; let things crystallize on their own. Never worked if you tried to force it.

What was the last thing he remembered? That simpering, greasy-haired thug with his idiotic little whiskbroom mustache and his rank kraut breath. Smiling in Ashe's face like it was Christmas morning and Ashe was the present to unwrap. As if him and his jackbooted sycophants celebrated such a holy day. Bleeding him dry day in and day out, draining him over and…

No; that wasn't right. The details were clear and real. They always were; things never faded for Ashe the way he'd learned they did for everyone else. Those memories were vivid, but things were scrambled. The layering was wrong.

So go through the layers.

President Truman… No, that wasn't right, either. That was for the Big One. Wasn't Truman; it was Churchill. Churchill was in charge when he sent him to… when he met… in the trenches. Not, not the trenches. Landing craft? Suvla? Oh, God - Suvla Bay.

Ashe wriggled his toes, feeling them move against the cotton sheet. But that wasn't dependable, was it? It had to be ghost pain. How many times had it been ghost pain? Sometimes that pain lasted long after things grew back. Stuff would just… hurt. For no good reason. He raised his head to look, catching a glimpse of what was probably the correct number of toes on each foot before his world exploded.

His head! Ashe gasped for breath. Head pain was normal; its intensity this time was not. There was always a headache. It typically faded after he was finally able to eat. That had been quite a while after Krasny, hadn't it? Nothing for quite a while after that one. And he wasn't about to eat the goat. If he'd eaten the goat, he'd have had no one to talk to on the long walk. So, yeah, long-lasting headaches weren't anything new. But the intensity of this one was beyond any he'd had before.

And he'd had a lot.

Angry waves of nausea washed over Ashe, wracking him to his core. His gut heaved in protest to the pain and in so doing, set off fresh agonies he had not yet catalogued. He fought to turn his head to the side as quickly as possible; retching upward while lying on his back was one of the more unpleasant ways to wake up he'd been unfortunate enough to find. The muscles in his neck were only partially responsive, but it turned out not to matter too greatly; it was just dry heaves. Clearly, he'd been empty for a while.

The room spun about Ashe and his entire head throbbed in time to the insistent pounding of his suddenly fast-beating heart. The surge of nausea subsided at last, and Ashe managed to gain control of his breathing.

Okay, so... not Suvla; he had feet. Let's just presume they're intact for now.

Churchill. What about him? Asia. In all his years, how had Ashe never found his way to Asia? Well, Asia Minor, he remembered, sure. Suvla Bay was in Turkey. So was Constantinople. Building the walls after Adrianople. Those were good walls. Later, helping rebuild the Magna Ecclesia. Then a century later, those good walls, built to keep evil out, proved useless against evil from within. The Blues and Greens brought Nika rioting down upon the city and Ashe was called back into active duty to help retake the city and kill neighbors and friends. And he stood weeping as the Great Church burned. Constantinople was in Turkey; Turkey was in Asia. So, maybe that counted. He'd been to Asia. He'd been there. Nika. Leaving the world of war and joining the Stoudites. That was when he put pen to paper to scribe the words of prophets. That was when... when God punished him for it all... All of it. By the darkness and the cold and the drought and the death...

No. He didn't want to remember that. Back to Churchill. Churchill sent him to Asia...

No, no, no. That made no sense. Why was it so hard this time? Prime Minister Churchill...

Prime Minister? No, President, not Prime Minister. He'd relocated again, right? Had to keep moving around. Always moving. Back to the States this time.

President... Which one? Run through the list. Jackson - not Stonewall; the other one... Other ones... Then Buchanan, and he came home after Lincoln... After Lincoln was... Lincoln made it clear that it was all about slavery, and Ashe had never owned slaves or supported it, so once he acknowledged the corn, he deserted. Ashe had never liked ol' Jubal Early anyway. Walked all the way home to Winchester...

Winchester—the fire! Just like Nika, another fire, and she was just... They had burnt it all down while he was gone. All of it. That fragrant swine Sheridan and his blue bellies... they were as bad as the slavers. Worse. They burnt it all. She was... Lorena was just...

No. Still too far back. Push that down. This was Asia. East Asia, not West... Saigon. Laos. Kennedy! President Kennedy. No - President Kennedy has been shot! His head...

Ashe reached up to feel the back of his head. Wrapped in bandages, but he could still feel the new regrowth there. Sore spot in the forehead, numb in the back.

Not numb inside, though. The world erupted again in a fresh burst of white-hot light and pain took over for several minutes before the agony and nausea abated.

Okay. Don't touch the noggin. Got it.

Wasn't Kennedy. Saw that on the TV. Who was it, then? South from Nottingham, right? Out of Bingham, south to Leicester, west to London... Churchill. No, not London. Lyndon.

Lyndon... Johnson. Lyndon B. Johnson. Asia... Saigon. Laos. The thunder, the ground shaking, his men running...

Oh, God! His men; his unit! They...

Ashe thrashed in his bed, triggering a third round of fireworks in his head. Ignoring the pain, Ashe threw the thin sheets off and struggled to get up, only to have his left shoulder collapse under him like a boiled noodle. Fire raged through Ashe's back and left arm as he dropped prone on the bed.

Through the pounding in his ears, Ashe heard the faint sounds of staff bursting into the room. He had screwed shut his eyes with the onslaught of pain and now opened them to see a woman in a blue and white striped uniform and a square-cornered white nurse's cap rush to his bedside.

"Lay it flat, marine," the nurse chided forcefully with a distinct New Jersey accent. "Me and Doctor Lockbridge are the only ones who get to decide if and when you're out of that bed."

Okay, thought Ashe, mystery solved. I'm back in the States.

∽ • ∽

"I SAID, WHERE am I?"

The nurse glared back at him, matching him easily for attitude. "And I said you can save all your questions for Doctor Lockbridge. Now lie still and let me get your vitals."

"Doctor Lockbridge," Ashe repeated, allowing the woman to loop a blood pressure cuff about his right arm.

The first thing Ashe noticed was the sound. Measured footsteps, deliberate, like the slow ticking of a metronome. After the first few faintly audible reports, he noticed the nurse's pumping to inflate the cuff had fallen into a regular double-time cadence with the steps. They echoed down the hospital hallway, growing closer. Whoever this was, they weren't in a hurry. That alone made Ashe straighten slightly in his hospital bed, despite the sharp head pain and persistent ache in his shoulder, back, and left arm. The world Ashe dwelt in didn't leave much room for calm men. Not recently.

When the man finally appeared in the doorway, Ashe had to blink. He wasn't what Ashe had been expecting at all, no stern-faced surgeon or no-nonsense military doctor. This man looked like he'd stepped out of another century, another life. Mid-sixties, maybe, though his upright posture and the quiet confidence in his expression made him seem younger. His hair was silver, combed neatly back, and his tan complexion spoke of someone who still spent time outdoors. He wore a dove gray three-piece suit under his white coat, complete with a pocket watch chain that gleamed faintly in the morning sun spilling through the blinds. A pair of rimless glasses perched on his nose, and his smile, quick but genuine, gave off a disarming warmth that didn't seem to fit the clinical surroundings.

"Good morning, Staff Sergeant... O'Reilly," the man said, consulting his chart as he stepped into the room. His voice was smooth and southern, not thick or lazy, but polished, like the accent of a man who'd spent years learning to read rooms and put people at ease. "I'm Dr.

Lockbridge, and from the look of you, I'd say you're not one for lying still, are you?"

Ashe studied him as he pulled a chair over and set down a red-rimmed folder. His movements were economical but unhurried, the kind of precision Ashe recognized from his time in the field. Lockbridge wasn't just a doctor, he was the kind of operator who knew exactly what he was doing and didn't feel any need to announce it.

"You've had better days, my friend," he smiled.

"Had worse, too. I'll survive," Ashe replied, watching the man closely. His instincts told him this doctor wasn't some small-town charmer playing at being a professional. There was something deeper there: a steel frame concealed by southern hospitality.

Lockbridge smiled again, now with just a hint of something sharper. "Oh, I've no doubt about that. But let's make sure you do it properly. Men like you don't do anybody any good in pieces."

With that, he reached into his pockets, producing a stethoscope and a small notebook, both tools of his trade that seemed both anachronistic and strangely benign in the complicated, death-filled world Ashe had lived in for so long. Ashe thought the man seemed a better fit in a General Store or a country courtroom than a hospital ward. Still, he'd long since learned that relying on such generalized first impressions could be foolish. Disastrously so, on more than one occasion. But there was a steadiness to Lockbridge: an air of competence, even inevitability that made Ashe wonder if this was a man who could handle just about anything, whether it was in a brightly lit operating room or somewhere much darker.

"Where am I?"

"See," replied the doctor. "Asking' is a fair sight easier than tryin' to get all your busted parts workin' afore they want to, isn't it?"

Ashe looked at the man.

"And you sure do have a lot of busted parts, young man."

Ashe grunted in reply, refusing to be baited into a discussion of who was older.

"You're at Walter Reed, Staff Sergeant," stated Lockbridge. "You flew in to Dover, but they didn't have room at the NNMC for you, so we got you." The doctor gave a slight nod to the nurse, who exited without a word, closing the door behind her.

"Dover?" asked Ashe, confused. "Not Andrews?"

"Dover," Lockbridge repeated. His smile faded slightly but took on even more empathy. "Dover, by way of Clark. But we'll talk about that later, I do imagine."

He picked up the red-trimmed folder again, paging through the papers contained within. "This is also one of the hospitals nearest your home, isn't it?"

"I guess so." Ashe was suddenly on guard. "Hard to even tell where home is any more."

"I imagine that's true. Five tours of duty later, I wouldn't be surprised at that one bit. What I would be surprised at is if your mail actually got delivered to…" Lockbridge made a show of reading from the folder, angling his glasses just so to see the address properly. "10 First Street Southeast, right here in Washington, DC."

If Ashe were to be honest with himself, he was surprised his ruse had lasted as long as it had. "I like to read." Ashe closed his eyes against the insistent throbbing in his head.

"Well, who doesn't?" Asked Lockbridge in a delighted tone. "Nothing I love more than to settle down with some Erle Stanley Gardner or maybe some classic like Faulkner or Twain and some iced tea. Or, of course, the Good Book, of a morning. But I don't think I'd long get away claimin' to reside at the Library of Congress on my enlistment papers."

"Just shows not everybody likes to read," quipped Ashe, eyes still closed.

Lockbridge laughed at that, a sparkle in his eye. "That it does, Staff Sergeant, that it does. I wanted to ask… is Ashe O'Reilly really your name? You don't appear to be Irish."

Ashe's eyes opened and he fixed them on the doctor. "O'Reilly is an Americanization of my family name," he replied.

"Oh?" The doctor appeared fascinated. "What's your family name?"

"Doesn't matter. It's O'Reilly now."

"Now? Or *for* now?"

Doctor Lockbridge's tone and expression were no less genuinely cordial than they had been from the start, but Ashe was starting to get the clear sense that the man's line of questioning was anything but casual.

"What are you getting at, Doc?"

"Your friends have been in several times trying to see if you're up for a talk. I've nearly had to beat them off with a stick."

Ashe shot upright, at least as much as he was physically able. He ignored the pain, a skill he had grown very good at across the ages. "My friends? The guys in my unit? Where—"

"No." The doctor's smile faded at once; his expression was now one of authentic compassion. "I'm sorry. Not the soldiers from your unit. Your... other friends."

Ashe was confused. Seemed to be the day for it. "'Other' friends?"

"Other. As in Government Agency."

Ashe rolled his eyes. "OGA? Those yahoos? Great. Feel free to beat them with a stick. What do they want with me?"

It was Lockbridge's turn to look confused. "I know you jarheads are all a fair sight younger than I am, but you are older than most I get through here. I just made the assumption that a man of your years shipped home from Vietnam was with those yahoos."

Don't try to count my years, doc; you'll hurt yourself.
"No, doc." Ashe shook his head, instantly regretting the

motion. "I been nowhere near that game for a long time. All I am is a fighter."

"And a fairly accomplished one. The scars speak for themselves," the doctor mused, his face conveying equal parts wonder and sympathy. He paged through Ashe's folder. "This was your fifth tour?" he repeated. "Each one a voluntary re-enlistment?"

"Yeah. We all find a niche we're good at filling, right? What about you, doc? You got some juice, being able to run off OGA goons and still be privy to my personnel file."

"Yes, well. As you say, we all do find our niche, don't we?"

Ashe thought about this for a moment. He glanced sideways at the doctor. "So, I guess you'll be calling said goons so I can give my AAR? Not a lot for me to recount, actually. May as well get it over with."

Doctor Lockbridge pulled the chair over to Ashe's bed to sit closer. "No, I don't think I'll be calling them any time soon. Your care is paramount. In my book, any patient running a long-term fever of a hundred and eight is not to be disturbed. And one who comes out of that fever? Well, he deserves a break, anyway you read that book."

Ashe raised his eyebrows. The pain hit hard, and he lowered them. "You've got a book that covers patients running a fever of a hundred and eight?"

The smile came back. "No. No, I don't."

Ashe closed his eyes with a sigh. "So, I'm a guinea pig." It was familiar territory, but at least this guy was polite about it.

The doctor's reply came as a surprise to Ashe.

"No, not as far as I'm concerned. I have to admit I'm very curious. Almost painfully so, but you're my patient, first and foremost. All I am focused on is getting you well. Making you whole again. Although your body seems able to do that with or without me. You are pretty amazing, Ashe O'Reilly. You shouldn't be alive."

Ashe's face fell and he glanced away. "I really shouldn't."

Sensing the dark current in Ashe's demeanor, Lockbridge tried to change the course of the conversation. "You're apparently also immune to infection."

"So I've been told."

"Once I realized that the febrile state was—"

"Look, doc, this is great and all, but it's starting to sound a little guinea piggy to me. What happened to my men?"

Doctor Lockbridge stood and laid a long-fingered hand gently on Ashe's uninjured shoulder. His voice was deep with emotion. "You all came together into Dover. You were the only one capable of leaving in an ambulance. I'm so sorry, son."

Fresh pain flooded over Ashe, little of it physical. "I need to see them. I need to go to them." He struggled to work his feet towards the edge of the bed.

"No, son. Not now. It's been four months; their remains have all been shipped to their homes."

"Four months? I need to see their families! They were my responsibility!"

Ashe rose up on his right elbow. Searing agony overtook him, and he could not resist a sharp gasp. He relented to the gentle, calming pressure of Lockbridge's hand.

"Rest up, leatherneck. There will be time for grieving, to be sure. For paying respects and giving condolences. But first, you rest. We're gonna get you well."

Ashe was unsure if it was the man's peaceful confidence, his soothing drawl, or Ashe's own current lack of physical strength, but he gave in to the inevitable. One had to trust the process, and Rome wasn't built in a day. This, he knew for a fact.

"Okay, doc. You win. Can I get something to eat? I'm starving."

Doctor Lockbridge laughed aloud, delighted by the question. "Yes, I'm sure you are, Staff Sergeant! I'll see if I can't scare something up."

"And maybe a gallon or two of water."

Lockbridge smiled. "IV drip isn't doing it for you, then, is it?"

"No," Ashe said, He closed his eyes. "No, it is not."

❧ • ❧

IT HAD TAKEN considerable effort, but Ashe finally convinced Dr. Lockbridge to take off most of the bandages. The doctor had been his near-constant companion during the past two weeks. During that time, Ashe had come to believe that, for the first and only time he could remember, he had encountered someone who was interested in his healing progress purely for Ashe's own sake, not his own. Naturally, it was constantly evident that Lockbridge was intrigued with the speed at which Ashe was recovering, nearly out of his mind with curiosity at times. That was a common thing, of course. As far back as Plinius Secundus, so many academics had tried to pick Ashe apart that he had long since taken to isolation rather than hospitalization to endure the painful recovery regimen handed down by the ageless parade of his injuries.

But Lockbridge was something different entirely. What Ashe had initially pegged as a patina of country doctor charm was instead a core tenet of the man's personality. With this man, the patient's health was not the main thing, it was the only thing. So much so that the doctor had cleared his entire log of patients to tend solely to Ashe during his isolation. Lockbridge had ensured Ashe was fully isolated upon his arrival at Walter Reed, long before Ashe had regained consciousness. He would typically shrug off discussing that decision when Ashe would ask, instead redirecting the conversation in any one of a hundred different directions.

Every conceivable topic seemed to find its way into their discussions over the two weeks since Ashe had rejoined the living. Nearly every topic, anyway. Certain things were off-limits by an unspoken agreement between the two men. What had happened in Vietnam, of course. No doctor worth his salt would force a patient to relive trauma during his recovery. At first, Ashe figured that was because of the doctor's suspicion of Ashe's probable ties to covert operations. However, Ashe had come to understand that Lockbridge had accepted Ashe's denial of direct involvement in that shadow world and had, as a result, become even more protective of his patient against any intrusions by CIA inquisitors.

Lockbridge would similarly dodge discussions of the events that landed Ashe at Water Reed after being shipped stateside in a pine overcoat. Ashe knew he would get those details eventually but was satisfied to table the topic for now while he pulled himself together under Lockbridge's watchful eyes.

"Nonne putas tempus illud esse ad has fascias tollendas?" asked Ashe for what seemed like the hundredth time, in as many languages as he and the doctor shared. Lockbridge noted that Ashe had done a great deal of mumbling in his fever delirium, and little of it had been in English. Nurse Toffee had at first thought Ashe to be one of those Pentecostalists, speaking in tongues, but Lockbridge had quickly identified smatterings of French, Spanish, Russian, and German among other languages that evaded him. He had asked Ashe about it early on, and had, at least on the surface, accepted Ashe's claim to have traveled extensively in the years before Uncle Sam sent him to Southeast Asia. Ashe told Lockbridge that he was just good with picking up languages and backed this up by rattling off every word he knew in Vietnamese all threaded together. It probably amounted to something like "I want to eat whatever the polar bear is having, and am very thirsty, so I will need to find the bathroom as soon as possible. Please don't shoot me or steal my pants while I am gone," but the doctor did not know enough of that particular language to call Ashe's bluff.

On the other hand, Lockbridge was nearly fluent in French and German, and he would often hold entire discussions with Ashe in those languages. But most of all, the doctor was ecstatic to find someone functional in Latin, having developed a love for that classic language in medical school but having failed for the decades since to find opportunities to speak it with anyone.

The doctor smiled at Ashe's repeated request to get his bandages off. ˙

"Minime, non puto," replied Lockbridge with a shake of his head. "Propter magnitudinem vulnerum tuorum, nulla via est ut cutis tua sine protectione harum fasciarum iam functionem habeat."

Sensing an advantage, Ashe switched to English. "Given the extent of my injuries, my skin can't hack it on its own? Who are you to call a Marine thin-skinned, Dogface?"

Despite Ashe's head being almost fully wrapped in a fabric cocoon, Lockbridge could easily discern the smile hidden under the bandages. He returned the expression with a grin of his own. "How about we compromise? Let's start with changing the dressing on your abdomen."

Lockbridge directed Nurse Toffee to retrieve fresh bandages and set to gingerly removing the wrappings from Ashe's torso. Layer by layer, he unwound the gauze to finally expose the core dressing, stained dark red in a jagged line running from Ashe's ribs to his groin. He pulled gently at this lowest layer, finding it at least partially adhered to Ashe's skin.

"Nurse Toffee, please also grab a sterile wash bottle. We have some adhesion here, and I don't want to re-open those stitches."

The woman laid the new bandages on a stainless steel tray and wheeled it over within the doctor's reach before slipping out the door.

"What's the holdup, doc?"

"Well, you've been showing no overt signs of infection, and your outer bandages never expressed saturation, so I decided to let your dressings stay in place as long as possible to prevent any fresh trauma or re-opening of the wound. The inner pad has clung to your skin, though, so I'm starting to question the wisdom of that decision."

"Nah, it's fine," Ashe said. Before Lockbridge could react, Ashe reached across his body with his unwrapped arm to grab a loose edge of the large gauze pad. A single rapid pull freed the fabric from his stomach, leaving numerous frayed threads behind.

"No!" shouted the doctor. He grabbed frantically at the pile of bandages laid on the tray by his nurse and struggled to rip open a new pad as rapidly as his aged hands would allow.

Norse Toffee, alerted by Lockbridge's exclamation, flew back into the room to find the doctor staring on in disbelief as Ashe took hold of several remnants of gauze that had been encapsulated by his skin as it healed. As he tore each cluster of fabric away, it opened a small tear in his skin which glistened with fresh droplets of blood.

Neither doctor nor nurse found words to say or actions to undertake during Ashe's self-administered regimen. He was working at what remained of the stitches now and pulled a long thread of catgut from his stomach by yanking on a protruding knot. "Man! That itches like crazy!" Ashe mumbled, raking his fingernails vigorously up and down along the bright pink, foot-long sutured scar traversing his abdomen.

"Stop!" Doctor Lockbridge, finally recovered his ability to speak, though he struggled with finding words that made any sense.

Ashe looked up at him. "What's the matter, doc?"

"Four months ago, you were functionally dead." The doctor looked at Ashe as if that statement should explain everything. Ashe stared back, waiting for the other shoe to drop.

"And?" prompted Ashe when the second piece of footwear failed to make a showing.

"And there's no possible way you could have healed to this level in this span of time. I saw you four months ago, and I saw you two weeks ago, when this set of bandages went on. We've been..." Lockbridge paused, looking past Ashe to pin Nurse Toffee with a meaningful gaze.

"We've been waiting for you to die," Nurse Toffee finished the doctor's statement in a flat voice.

"Huh! Yeah, you and me both, darlin'. Guess we're gonna have to keep waiting on that one."

☙ • ❧

ASHE STEPPED OUT of his Ford Bronco, swinging the door shut behind him as he stepped onto the sidewalk. He paused momentarily, facing away from the house. This afforded him a moment to both scratch at a random thread of gauze still trying to work its way out of the skin under his ribs and to gather his thoughts for the task ahead.

If Doctor Lockbridge and Nurse Toffee had been amazed by the progress of his abdomen, they were both stricken speechless upon removing his shoulder and head bandages. The new bone growth was impossible, they said. Between the tank battle in Vietnam and the "subsequent events" which Ashe had still not cajoled out of the doctor, nearly a third of Ashe's skull had been destroyed. And yet, when Ashe finally consented to an array of tests, the X-Rays showed a near-complete reconstruction of the bone and something the doc had called "cerebral angiography" had presented a picture of the level of vascular regeneration that he could not explain.

As inexplicable as that was, the healing of Ashe's back and shoulder was unprecedented in all of recorded medical science, according to Lockridge. The doctor had explained to Ashe early on that he would never regain the use of his left arm, as the shoulder blade had been blown off in whatever explosion ended his time overseas. And yet, Dr. Lockbridge watched Ashe six months after the incident, windmilling his left arm (albeit with great pain) thanks to a freshly-grown scapula.

When pressed repeatedly, Ashe had simply told the only real truth he knew: he healed very quickly when he had enough to eat, and plenty of water. Ashe had his own long-held conjecture concerning the root of his abilities, but as always before, he was determined to keep that exclusively to himself.

For his part, Lockbridge had remained resolute in his refusal to discuss the details of Ashe's arrival back in the United States. Ashe was convinced that this was out of spite, but he didn't press. Despite having been carried in prominence by the doctor on the day Ashe regained his faculties, the thick folder with the red trim never made another appearance during their time together. Ashe had broached the subject several times. At first, Lockbridge had been steadfast in his statements that Ashe knowing certain details would be detrimental to his road to recovery. Later, when it became clear that Ashe had sprinted farther down that road than the doctor ever expected to see him crawl, his refusals to share the information became more generalized and finally completely arbitrary, replete with hand-waving and half-hearted quips about classified information.

Ashe eventually let the topic drop and focused on getting out of that bed and Walter Reed faster than humanly possible. He had more pressing obligations.

Doctor Lockbridge had arranged for a new Service A uniform for Ashe, replete with a full set of his service ribbons and badges, presumably using information culled from his personnel file. The doctor had shaken his head slowly when Ashe had asked about a set of utilities to go along with the alpha kit. "You're not going back into combat, Staff Sergeant; you won't need a field uniform any more. They've rolled you out with full honors, but they're asking you to keep it quiet. But I knew you'd want this uniform; you told me you've got some folks to visit."

For all of the frustration that came with being denied the full picture by Lockbridge, it was those visits that fully occupied Ashe's attention at the moment. The men with him that day west of Ben Het had been his responsibility; he owed it to those men to personally convey his condolences to their loved ones.

The first six visits to the families of Ashe's fallen patrol had all followed a bewildering pattern and had done so with a precision that made Ashe's head spin. A pattern repeated in small towns and big cities from Tallahassee to Tacoma.

The pattern went like this: Ashe would step up to the door and stand ramrod-straight. Three knocks on the door, confident but not insistent. The door would open. Here there was some variation in the pattern; in small towns the door generally swung wide in one welcoming motion, and in larger metropolitan areas it would first crack open to the length of a silver or gold chain before closing and reopening to admit Ashe. Tea was offered (lemonade on one occasion), and Ashe would accept politely before the family member would bid him be seated. They would sit together. Ashe was always careful to descend onto the furniture at the same rate as his host out of respect, setting the glass before him on a small table of some sort. Thus far, the pattern was to the letter what Ashe had expected at the onset of his mission.

The remainder of the pattern was a series of events that made sense in the first couple visits, but nuanced variations and answers to cautious questions posed by Ashe quickly painted a picture that troubled him a little bit more with each stop. It turned out in every case that the family had long since received a visit from a man claiming to be the commanding officer of their fallen son, brother, or husband.

That, taken by itself, wasn't anything surprising. Though it seemed to Ashe that he'd only been back stateside for less than a month, he knew from what details Doctor Lockbridge had felt inclined to share that the time since the repatriation of his men's remains had been five times that. It made perfect sense that the U. S. Government, in its clock-like efficiency and ultimate regard for the wellbeing of its citizens, would have long since made the gesture that Ashe was now himself trying to make. Well, perhaps if one looked at it in the light of governmental efficiency and compassion, it might be a bit weird after all, but not unheard of.

So, while it wasn't overly unusual that the CO would have already made this visit, what was strange to Ashe was that none of the families recalled seeing a name tag on the officer's uniform, and none recognized any of the names of Ashe's own command structure when he recounted them. If this man had been a commanding officer of the fallen Marine, he would also have been Ashe's superior as well. Discreet questioning started to form a picture that Ashe didn't like. He didn't like it one bit.

The officer had been young. Younger than Ashe, to be sure. Matty's and Bellows' fathers both asked whether it was all that unusual for officers to be a bit younger than a seasoned old Staff Sergeant like Ashe. It figured it would be those two men; Madison and Bellows were two peas in a pod, despite being raised thousands of miles apart: they always asked questions, but the questions they asked were always the right ones. Matty and Bee. They were good men. All his men were good men, save... Save one.

The problem was simple, although Ashe saw no sense in telling these two fathers or the other families. The problem was, Ashe's company, and thereby, the company of his slain men, had no officers that would in appearance seem significantly younger than Ashe.

The officer had been tall as well, and the broad expanse of his chest was adorned with what Frito's grandmother in Louisiana recalled as enough ribbons and medals to sink a swamp boat. Ashe had smiled knowingly along with the woman. Lots of men lived for showing off everything they'd done.

But it was the conversations themselves that set off alarms when the families recounted them to Ashe. In each and every case, the officer had held his cover in his hands and requested to see the fallen marine's footlocker. In a couple of cases, the deceased's effects had not yet been delivered and the officer had made arrangements to return once the family received them. In the other four cases, the visit had miraculously been timed to the day of the shipment's arrival.

The officer had seemed genuinely penitent for such an intrusion, but he had explained that this was a matter of national security and he needed to review the contents of the locker before the family could do so. He understood the extreme magnitude of his request, but it would be best to get it over with so that the family could grieve, wouldn't you agree? He stressed that their fallen loved one was in no trouble at all; it was just an innocent oversight that had been missed by the company's censors. With all the negative sentiment in the news of late, what good could come of not catching an issue like this? No one wanted their loved one's name read by Walter Cronkite in a certain... context, did they? He then offered recompense for their time and compliance. A modest sum, in cash. So convincing and heartfelt was the man that even the two late shipments were arranged for, and the officer had been able to investigate each of the six lockers so far without oversight from the families.

Six times had this pattern repeated, with only the variations stated. A mysterious young officer appeared and intercepted each marine's personal effects, then vanished without a trace—save a wad of cash—left behind.

Six times had Ashe not felt it right to ask more than glancing questions. These people had lost their precious son, their husband, or brother. Who was Ashe to stomp heavily through their grief in the pursuit of a truth he wasn't sure he should even care about? So, six times, he had asked only the most innocuous of questions. But the six small data sets he gathered had begun to coalesce into an image that turned his stomach. And, he thought, the data might point to someone he thought he'd already dealt with.

Turning toward the house, Ashe strode up to the door and mounted the half-dozen steps to the front porch.

Three knocks on the door, confident but not insistent.

Silence.

Ashe waited patiently. It was a beautiful day. Behind him, he heard a pair of squirrels frolicking and rushing from one tree to another to another, their claws clattering on the cracked cement of the walk.

Three more knocks on the door, confident but not insistent.

A car passed behind Ashe, causing the dog in the yard next door to bark. He didn't remember the dog barking upon his arrival; maybe the animal didn't like sedans.

Three more knocks on the door, not insistent but also no longer confident.

A final respectful pause. Ashe thought kindly of Andrews, the man whose family he was here to visit. Andrews was from the other squad that Ashe had "adopted," so he hadn't known him as well as some of the others. But he was solid and reliable; Ashe did remember that much.

Three final knocks, another, shorter, pause, and Ashe spun crisply on his heel to descend the six steps and head back to his vehicle. Reaching the level of the pavement, Ashe looked over the hood of his Bronco and locked eyes with the neighbor directly across the street from the Andrews residence. The man returned Ashe's gaze unflinchingly, standing stock still in front of his gabled house holding a dilapidated rake and looking for all the world to Ashe like that scrawny bald guy holding a pitchfork in that painting. The only thing breaking that mental image was the prolific bush of a silver-white mustache that appeared to be the only hair above the man's shoulders.

The man held Ashe's gaze until Ashe reached for the door handle to his Bronco, whereupon he raised one eyebrow.

Okay, thought Ashe, you must really want to tell me something if you're gonna show that kind of emotion. I'll play along.

Ashe waited as a wood-paneled station wagon drove by from the left, then strode across the street. Reaching the crumbling gate to the man's fence, Ashe stopped at a safe and respectful distance. The man, moving slowly but with purpose, flipped his rake over and leaned it against a thriving elm tree in his yard. He walked forward and stopped, matching Ashe's distance from the gate, just on the other side.

"Good afternoon, sir," opened Ashe.

"Good enough, marine," replied the man in a western cowboy drawl. A little out of place here in northern Maryland, but Ashe wasn't one to judge folks for moving around.

Ashe sensed from the man that he was about as no-nonsense as they came. He could respect that.

"You served?" asked Ashe.

"I've seen the elephant, yes. Korea."

Ashe nodded. "Thank you for your service."

The man nodded back. "And you for yours."

The words hung in the air during a pause that might have been awkward if the two men weren't trying to size each other up. The man broke the silence, evidently having reached a conclusion.

"She's not there," he said.

"She?"

"Mrs. Andrews."

"Oh, of course. Do you know when she'll be back, then?"

"I do," stated the man flatly, as if Ashe were asking all the wrong questions. Ashe felt that had been happening a lot of late.

"Great. When will Mrs. Andrews be returning?"

"She won't be."

Hadn't expected that, thought Ashe. He started counting slowly to ten, determined to keep himself from sniping back at the man. Around the time Ashe's count reached seven, the man continued.

"She died."

The story finally poured forth, economical in language and to the point, as if the man had given up on Ashe's capacity to elicit the answers from him and decided to explain purely out of mercy.

Mrs. Andrews was a widow, a mother of two sons. Harrison, the older son, had died in Vietnam in 1967. When Ashe explained that Wilson Andrews had served with Ashe and had died as well, the man cut him off. He'd already known of younger son Wilson's demise. When Mrs. Wilson had first heard the news, she had come over to confide in Graham (as Ashe found to be the man's name) and tell him that she was going to visit her spinster sister in Pennsylvania—her only living relation—whereupon the two would grieve Mrs. Andrews' loss. Expecting to be gone about a month, Mrs. Andrews had made arrangements for her mail to be delivered to Graham's address. This was a reciprocal favor the two of them shared when the other was away. Graham was a widower himself and had felt it his obligation to look out for Mrs. Andrews since her husband and his neighbor had passed away.

Something clicked in Ashe's mind, and he could suddenly sense where the man was going. "Mrs. Andrews received another visit a few months back, didn't she?" Ashe asked the man.

"She did."

"Problem was, she wasn't here, right? She was in Pennsylvania."

Graham shook his head.

"No?" Asked Ashe, confused.

"No. Problem was, she was dead."

This turn of events was enough to catch Ashe completely flat-footed. He stared at Graham, dumbfounded.

"Mrs. Andrews and her sister were driving and were side-swiped by a delivery van there in Pennsylvania. They hit a light pole, and both died instantly."

Ashe didn't know what to say. The man continued, obviously trying to get Ashe back on track.

"I didn't trust the other guy," he said.

Ashe blinked. "The other guy?"

"The officer, four months back," explained Graham. "Keep up."

"But you trust me?"

Graham looked Ashe over, slowly, from top to bottom.

"Yup," he replied.

After a moment, he continued, "The guy came up like you did, but wasn't as patient. No respect at all. He didn't get an answer, so he hung around for over an hour. Pounded on the door like he wanted to break it in by the end of it. Finally left in a huff."

The bony man scratched at the stubble on his chin, then continued, "He came back the next day, then the day after that. Louder and less respectful each time. I'd taken to watching him from here in the yard, but I could tell he wasn't the kind I'd like to invite over for a chat like I did you. I didn't like his looks."

Maybe they were getting somewhere, Ashe thought.

"What did he look like?"

Graham almost cracked a smile. "Well," he said, "Big, tall boy. Tall, even to me. Massive shoulders, like a linebacker, short hair, blond, cut like yours. Cornhusker's tan, like a farmer."

They were definitely getting somewhere, Ashe realized. And that place was somewhere he simultaneously expected to arrive at and wanted not to. Either way, it was enough to add some serious weight to his suspicion. He reached into a uniform pocket and fished out a folded, worn photograph. He showed the picture to Graham.

"This is a photo of my unit in 'Nam. It was taken about a year back. Would one of these men happen to be the man you saw?"

"Yup. It's that big bruiser standing right next to you in the picture. On your right."

Ashe's gut clenched into a knot, his suspicions finally confirmed. Wyatt Ming, his former team assistant leader. His AL had never gone by his first name. Most of the team had called him "Wyoming," knowing how much it irked the boy, being son of a beet farmer from Utah. Ming had preferred another name that he appointed himself: "Ming the Merciless."

In trying to live up to that name, Ming had gone down some very dark paths that had led to Ashe beating him near to death's door with his bare hands and then having him thrown in the stockade to await court-martial.

"Huh," grunted Graham, still regarding the photo. "When did your boy get promoted to Major?"

"He didn't," snarled Ashe.

"Huh," repeated Graham. "Guess you can add 'impersonating an officer' to the list of reasons you hate the boy."

Ashe looked up into the man's earnest face. "Am I that transparent?" he asked.

"Yup," answered Graham.

Ashe's eyes narrowed. "You mentioned you were receiving Mrs. Andrews' mail. Do you happen to have Wilson's footlocker, by any chance?"

"I do," said Graham, reaching down for the latch to the gate. "I thought you'd never ask."

ॐ • ॐ

"I NEED TO know what that is," demanded Ashe.

Lockbridge glanced at the cellophane-wrapped brick of white powder that Ashe had dropped on his desk, then up at his former patient.

"Quid nunc? Ita salutas veterem amicum?" asked the doctor with a slow grin.

Ashe sighed audibly. He replied in English, wanting to keep the visit focused as much as possible. "No, I know that's no way to greet an old friend. Problem is, I'm still trying to figure out who my friends are."

"But...?" prompted Lockbridge.

"But... You are certainly the closest thing I have right now." Ashe finally took a seat in one of the two padded chairs facing Lockbridge's desk. "How you been, Doc?"

"Better than you, I imagine. You're dead."

"I'm what?"

"You're dead," Lockbridge repeated. "I guess my ordering that uniform for you got someone's attention across the river. Your 'other' friends descended on this place like a swarm of locusts. Really wanted to talk to you. I see you're not wearing the uniform today, by the way."

"I'm not here on Marine business," replied Ashe. "Sounds like I'm done with that anyway. What did you do about my 'friends'?"

"Only thing I could do, I suppose. I told 'em you had finally succumbed to the grievous nature of your wounds and, out of respect for your service, I had ordered a uniform for you to wear during your departure from this vale of tears."

"And they didn't insist on seeing the body?" Ashe paused before amending, "My body?"

"Oh, they surely did. They were extraordinarily unhappy when they discovered that I had ordered your cremation. I handed over the sacred insignia and ribbons to them, of course. I would never burn those. They didn't seem to care. Not about that, anyhow."

"Oh? What did they care about?"

"Their main guy nearly had a conniption that there was no body left for them to examine. Only ash." Lockbridge paused for effect, a wry smile on his lips.

Ashe smiled back. "Only ash. Good one, doc." *Like I've never heard that one before.*

"They were downright apoplectic. Stormed around here for three days, tearing through every record they could get their hands on, questioning every member of the staff twice, whether they ever saw you or not. Nearly had me written up for my failure to record your cremation in a timely manner. Minor oversight on my part; it's been done now. Want a copy of your death certificate?"

"No, thanks. I'd be tempted to start a collection, and I don't have time for that right now." Ashe looked Doctor Lockbridge earnestly in the eyes and asked, "Are we done dodging the subject yet?"

It was the doctor's turn to sigh loudly. "You know, of course, I'd hoped this day would never come."

"But you knew it would."

"I did." Lockbridge closed his eyes, tilting his head slowly from side to side for a moment in a rocking fashion. His head returned to center, and he opened his eyes slowly. They were fixed on the parcel Ashe had dropped on his desk. "I have a strong suspicion you already know what that is," he said to Ashe.

"I have a strong suspicion. Your reaction confirms it, so thanks."

Suddenly, a curious expression rolled across Dr. Lockbridge's face. Ashe could tell at once that the doctor had long known this conversation was coming, had rehearsed it mentally and even perhaps practiced his part in it, but was now faced with some peculiar aspect of it that changed the context completely.

"Where did you get this?" he asked. Removing a white linen handkerchief from the breast pocket of his suit, Lockbridge unfolded the fabric and laid it on the white brick. Lifting it, he brought it near his face briefly and wafted air toward his nose with his other hand. He set the brick down on his desk and folded the handkerchief again, placing it on a far corner of his desk as if it had been contaminated.

His eyes still on the brick of evil powder, he finally spoke. "It... doesn't smell like formaldehyde."

That one caught Ashe completely off-guard. Seemed to be happening a fair bit lately. "Why would you expect it to smell like formaldehyde?" he asked.

Doctor Lockbridge's eyes narrowed. "If I promise to tell you, can we maybe start with how you came by it?"

"Okay, sure. I went to see the families of my men. Someone else had beaten me to the punch. Not the typical two servicemen charged with informing the next of kin, this came a couple weeks after that initial visit. Single 'officer' for that second visit, and he wormed his way into getting first looks into the personal effects of each one of my men."

Ashe had used the first two fingers of both hands like floppy bunny ears to indicate that his use of the word "officer" was intentionally and ironically false. Lockbridge may or may not have caught the intent, but he let Ashe continue.

"Sheer dumb luck and a flower delivery truck conspired to block his access to one shipment, though." He pointed at the brick of drugs on Lockbridge's desk. "I got to Andrews' box first and found that."

Lockbridge breathed deeply. "And do you think this Andrews was dealing with these drugs? Shipping them home or something?"

Ashe shook his head. "No. No way. I hadn't known him for long, but he was a solid guy. Bit of a milquetoast, but seemed very strait-laced. And absolutely solid under fire. Knew his tanks, too. Better than I did, at least."

"And so you suspect the 'officer' that intercepted the shipments. And you know who he is." Lockbridge repeated the air quotes gesture. He had caught on after all.

"Ain't no suspicion," growled Ashe. "I confirmed it."

Lockbridge again closed his eyes. "Don't tell me; it's best if I don't know."

"Consider yourself left out of it, doc," said Ashe. "Don't you think it's time you stopped leaving me out of things?"

Doctor Lockbridge was rattled. Ashe could see that, but couldn't figure out exactly why. Ashe didn't think he'd done or said anything that implied Lockbridge was culpable in any of this. And he was still convinced the doctor had no part in it. So why the reluctance?

Lockbridge rose from his chair. Retrieving his handkerchief, he lifted the brick of drugs from his desk and carried it over to a bin in the corner marked "Incinerate." Dropping it into the bin, he then lifted the upper portion of the thick black plastic bag and tied it shut before closing the bin's lid on the closed bag.

He then strode slowly over to a filing cabinet in the corner of his office and spun the dial of its lock for a brief moment before opening the bottom drawer. From it he pulled a single red-trimmed manilla folder that Ashe recognized immediately.

Once seated again at his desk, Dr. Lockbridge rested his hands together atop the folder and looked up at Ashe. Having had enough time to compose his thoughts, he spoke.

"To be clear, I intentionally kept things from you, sure. But I'm a doctor. Nothing good would have come of giving any details of this kind to a dying man. Then, when you kept holding on, and getting better, I never shared any of it, because what good would come of it during your recovery?"

Ashe looked at the sheaf of documents under Lockbridge's hands. "That red stripe tells me you weren't the only one keeping secrets from me."

Lockbridge allowed a wry grin before continuing. "No, I was surely not." The grin faded. "They call me up to Dover, sometimes. Chief M.O. is a good friend of mine.

He usually only calls me when something particularly heinous arrives and he wants a second opinion. Don't know why; he's five times smarter than I ever was.

"This time was different. Mason was shaken, and nothing spooks that man. Never has. I didn't understand till I got there. I didn't know what I was expecting, but I wasn't expecting that."

The doctor's face had gone white, almost as white as his silky hair. He slid the folder slowly across his desk toward Ashe, rotating it as it went. Ashe regarded the folder and thought it resembled some frosty, blood-rimmed glacier moving toward him, pushing a wave of cold dread before it.

"They made me swear that I'd never show this to another living soul," stated Lockbridge. "But I guess since you're dead now, there's no reason to keep it from you."

Ashe reached for the folder and opened it. The topmost section was several sheafs of paper grouped with paper clips. Each one of the sheafs was a copy of the personnel file of one of the marines in Ashe's unit, detailing their personal information as well as their service history, honors and awards. The thickest of these stacks was Ashe's own file. This, he skipped past. He had no desire to look at that.

At the bottom of the file was a large envelope, large enough to hold the unfolded report and several 8x10 photos clipped to it that slid out into Ashe's hand. Ashe scanned the report quickly to catch the pertinent details, then returned and re-read it slowly to fill in all the blanks.

The report told the story of a break-in at Dover Air Force Base. Ashe gathered that the incident remained under investigation at the time of this copy of the report. The shipment of caskets carrying Ashe and his unit had been diverted upon landing to a hangar near the outskirts of the base. This was not established procedure, but as yet, no responsible party nor even any record of the flight's arrival had been located. It was only upon the discovery of an open hangar door by a patrol that the events had started to come to light.

What was found inside the hangar was described in the report in exacting clinical detail, and illustrated in harsh, graphic black-and-white by the photographs accompanying the report.

Lockbridge must have seen that Ashe had blanched as well. He spoke at last, breaking the silence, narrating from his perspective as Ashe paged from one photo to the next.

"It was a horror show. I got there within a couple hours of the discovery. Mason had me brought up in a car immediately. He and I were there for an hour or so before the secret squirrels arrived and shut it all down."

Ashe confirmed this with the topmost image. In it, Lockbridge and a slightly shorter man in a white lab coat stood conversing as several airmen strove to secure the area. In that image, one could see several of the interim caskets used to ship remains home. Each one had been pried open with force, several appearing to have been hacked open with an axe. That image only depicted the vaguest hint of the contents of those mishandled boxes. Those details were not spared in the other pictures.

Ashe looked at the images of his men. Although they had apparently been retrieved from where they had fallen on the battlefield and then treated and transferred stateside with dignity, there the respect had ended. Each one of his men, rather than being allowed to rest peacefully in death, had been violated in the same despicable manner. Each of their torsos had been unceremoniously sliced open, not with a scalpel, but with what appeared to have been a jagged knife. Ashe surmised it had been a Ka-Bar; he was familiar with the style of wound. He'd inflicted more than one on enemies. But always in fair combat, never like this.

In each case, the victim (Ashe had stopped thinking of them as simply his fallen comrades, but rather victims of this horrific crime) had been hollowed out. Liver and intestines had been removed before shipment home, and something else had been transported in the cavity instead.

Ashe's right hand involuntarily moved to his abdomen and traced the still pink line through the fabric of his shirt.

"Yeah, you too," said Lockbridge with an air of infinite sadness.

Ashe flipped through the rest of the photos. Where there had been only one of each of his men, there were several images describing Ashe's fate. Ashe looked at himself, frozen there in stark contrast by the flash bulb. MPs were in evidence, stringing up barriers of crime scene tape that Ashe immediately identified as yellow and black rather than the black-and-white of the photo. Ashe's body had been gutted like a fish, exactly as had the rest of his men, but that was where the similarities ended.

Ashe's body was unique, being the only one that showed any evidence of internal organs. Moreover, his body resided in about two inches of a blackish sludge that was not to be seen in any of the other caskets. Other images were detail shots. One showed the top lid of his box that had presumably been removed using the crowbar still shown lying next to it. The inside surface of the lid was deeply scratched and splintered from being assaulted from within. Two other images showed Ashe's hands. Each one was severely bruised and lacerated, and few of the nails on either hand remained intact.

Ashe lifted his eyes for a moment to look at Lockbridge across his desk. The doctor was sitting quietly with his eyes closed, likely reliving the horror of the scene from his own perspective. Ashe returned to the photos.

Two other major differences were shown in the photos of Ashe as compared to the others. Nearing the bottom of the stack, the next image was of three plastic-wrapped bricks that were probably initially identical to the one he'd brought in here to discuss with Lockbridge.

None of the other photos had shown the bricks; Ashe had guessed that whoever—strike that; he knew it had been Ming—had opened up the caskets and the bodies inside had done so to retrieve the drugs and had taken them away. The three packages in Ashe's casket had been permeated by the thick blackish liquid gore and left behind as tainted beyond usefulness.

"We analyzed the bricks that were left behind," spoke Lockbridge quietly. He had noticed which photo Ashe was looking at. "They were changed chemically beyond recognition. Completely degraded by whatever process your body used to either reject or metabolize the stuff. It made no sense at the time. Doesn't make much now."

Ashe glanced down to finish his tour through the pictures. The second to last was curious at first, but Ashe soon understood the tale it told. The photo showed the outside edge of the casket and featured a prominent handprint. The print had been marked there in dark black gore from inside the box—left there *after* the box had been forcibly opened. Left by the hand still resting near it in the photo. Ashe's hand.

The final photo was an oblique shot of Ashe's head. Dead center in his forehead was a circular hole from which a single trickle of black oozed into his left eye. What made the image most memorable wasn't what was shown, but what was missing: an entire third of the back of Ashe's head had been blown off in a jagged exit wound from the high-caliber bullet.

"None of it made a lick of sense to any of us. What it looked like was, you had survived your last battle somehow. Then you'd been hollowed out and used as a drug container, shipped to America with your unit, only to survive the trip and then try to attack whoever perpetrated this abomination, whereupon he shot you in the head at point-blank range with a .45. That's what it seemed like. But that's impossible.

"But since then," the doctor continued, with a type of reverence, "I've seen you do the impossible. Any of the wounds you had in Vietnam or since, or even many before, based on your scars should have been fatal by themselves. But somehow, you still had a heartbeat and respiratory function. Faint, sure, but it was there. Took some doing, but Mason and I got you out of there before your 'other' friends descended on the base to stitch up the scene."

Ashe looked at the doctor, then back to the photos of his men.

"I have seen you do the impossible, Ashe. The impossible. The bone regrowth... No., regeneration. That's not possible. You had your organs excavated, and they grew back. The head wound..."

Doctor Lockbridge shook his head in wonder before concluding, "You shouldn't be alive, Ashe."

"I really shouldn't," Ashe growled in reply, burning the grisly images of fallen heroes into his memory. "Good thing I'm not."

 ৯ • ৶

THERE HAD BEEN one more visit to make, this one in New York City. One more time to don the uniform Lockbridge had provided before he hung it up forever.

Lance Corporal Alexander Chisholm had missed the unit's terminal engagement at Ben Het by way of being in the wrong place at the wrong time. Ashe had saved visiting Chisholm's folks for last because he was still trying to get some level of understanding of Al's death himself. Everything he had learned from his recent return visit to Walter Reed helped clarify a lot of it. Not necessarily why it had all happened, but certainly what he was going to do about it.

Chisholm had had the particular misfortune of coming up through Boot Camp at Harris Island, South Carolina right alongside Wyatt Ming. Ming had left home in Utah on his eighteenth birthday and had never looked back, not even when his parents both died in an apparent murder-suicide shortly thereafter. Ming had taken up temporary residence in Southern Georgia when the selective service caught up with him and as a result, he had landed at Paris Island rather than at the MCRD in San Diego. That was misfortune number one in the events leading to Alex Chisholm's demise.

The second such misfortune was being assigned the bottom rack under his bunkmate and eventual pet project, Wyoming. Chisholm himself coined the nickname that Wyatt Ming learned to hate. To Chisholm, any place west of Hoboken was cowboy country, and Wyatt Ming's name was just naturally going to be "Wyoming" to someone as good-natured and jocular as Chisholm, who'd never left New York City until Boot Camp and was proud of that fact. Chisholm saw at once that Wyoming was a bit of a hard case, and to someone like Al, that was about the same as getting a tattoo on your forehead that said, "fix me."

Ming and Chisholm were inseparable in Boot Camp, and Chisholm pulled a few strings to ensure they posted together. Ming was purely fueled by his anger at the world, and that fuel propelled him to the ranks of the Recon Marines. Chisholm went along for the ride, partly because he'd wanted to make a difference, and partly because he couldn't let his experiment, Wyoming, get away. Like Ming, Chisholm had excelled in all the specialized training, but through the more conventional route of being physically and mentally tough and adaptable, and committed to excellence in everything he did.

For his part, Ashe had come to understand that Wyatt Ming had not resented the friendship, despite his taciturn nature. To Ming, it was just another thing to endure. Chisholm once had told Ashe that he was convinced Ming was lightening up a bit toward the end of training.

Everything changed when the pair arrived in-country. Ming changed almost at once, as if connected to a light switch. The day Ming arrived as a fresh E-1, Ashe had pegged him at once as trouble. His bitterness may as well have been a service patch on his sleeve, so obviously did he wear it. But within a few short days, Ming had brightened immensely. Maybe Ashe should have heard the warning bells at that point, but he was just grateful that he wouldn't have to break the boy like some angry wild horse. By the time they returned from their first live-fire mission, Ming was positively ebullient.

Chisholm took Ming's shift in mood as a personal victory. He and Ming were inseparable. On leave, Chisholm acted as a moderating influence that Ashe was glad for Ming to have. In battle, Chisholm treated his support for Ming to be a holy duty, second only to defending the ideals of democracy. Ashe had seen so many good men sour that he was relieved to have the two men a part of his unit.

There was no animus or rivalry between the two friends, even as they both advanced in rank. Ming made Corporal first, largely buoyed up by help from Chisholm.

The third misfortune in Chisholm's sad story was Billings falling sick the night before a big sortie. Billings was Ashe's Assistant Lead at the time, and Ming now held the highest rank among the remainder of the team. Ashe decided to try Ming out as AL, though he hated the idea of moving the large farm boy up from his position as slack man. Ming was a natural with the big, heavy M60 machine gun they'd affectionately named "Porky."

But Eddie was pretty stout, so Ashe had made Ming the AL and handed Eddie the pig.

If Ming had brightened once he entered combat, he practically glowed after tasting command, even in such a small dose. Ming grew more and more intense as the weeks grew into months. Eventually, after seven months in-country, Ming and Chisholm earned their first leave.

Earning leave at the same time as Ming was the fourth and final misfortune that befell Chisholm.

By this time, the two young men had started to drift apart somewhat, though they both remained consummate professionals in the field. At the time, there were no foreign leaves approved, so the pair headed to Saigon. Ashe had company business in Saigon, so it was decided that he would accompany the two of them to Saigon, and return the next day, while they remained for the rest of their week.

Separating upon arrival, Ashe bid the two men farewell and reminded them of the wrath that would befall them should they overstay their time in the city. Ming and Chisholm saluted and turned smartly, eager to start enjoying their R&R.

Later that night, Ashe was walking through the entertainment district in search of a suitable eatery. Hearing a commotion, he turned down Bourbon Street toward the source of the noise. As soon as the first gunshot rang out, Ashe broke into a dead run. He was unable to reach the scene before two more shots split the already broken night.

Undaunted by any danger, Ashe took in the scene all at once. Two MPs were lying on the ground, fresh holes in their chests. The white helmet had fallen off the nearer MP and was spinning slowly in a wobbly circle like a turtle stranded upside-down on its shell. Onlookers, both American and Vietnamese, stood around or darted for cover.

Two men and a woman were there at the center of the scene, just outside a bar. The large plate-glass window of the bar had been shattered, apparently by the first MP, whose left leg was still entangled in the frame. Millions of shards of glass reflected the gaudy rainbow of the neon lights surrounding them: reds and blues, blinking yellows and flashing greens. The lighter colors reflected off the pools of spreading blood from the two fallen military policemen.

Ashe took in that the second MP had died reaching for his sidearm, presumably to stop the assailant who had snatched the first MP's weapon from its now-empty holster. That assailant, a giant of a man, now stood with feet planted wide, smoking pistol in one hand. His other hand held a brutal fist full of hair attached to the young Vietnamese woman shrieking on the ground. Having both hands full seemed to hinder the large man as he tried to shrug off the smaller man who was trying to defend the young woman.

As he turned in the dancing lights, Ashe saw several additional details at once. The large man's face was as familiar as it was predictable; it was Wyatt Ming, his visage twisted into a murderous parody of its former self. His smile was wide and evil; this was the moment his life had been building up to.

The woman's defender was, of course, Alex Chisholm. Whether he was trying to stop Ming from committing additional crimes, was simply defending the woman from Ming's unwelcome affections, or still thought he could somehow "fix" Ming, Ashe never got the opportunity to ask.

Ming took a step backward, placed the already hot muzzle of the gun to Chisholm's forehead, and pulled the trigger.

Ashe blinked.

Back in the present, he regarded the poor couple in front of him. Ashe realized he was likely just reopening old wounds with his visit and was unsure what he hoped to achieve. Chisholm's parents looked so small on the red velvet couch across from him.

What do you tell someone about their lost loved one? Their fallen son? Do you tell them that you wanted to avenge their son's death? That you tried? That it took eight more MPs to finally stem your rage-filled fit of retribution and pull you from Ming's badly broken body? That you had personally unleashed two thousand years of military training on a man twice your size that didn't stand a chance against your holy fury? No, there was nothing holy in it, and you knew that better than anyone on this planet. What, exactly, do you tell them?

Ashe reached for the glass on the table. Of all the families, this was the first one to offer him a glass of water. He drank it, careful to leave about a third of it in the glass so as not to make Chisholm's mother feel like she needed to offer him a refill. He set the glass down gently.

"I'm so sorry for your loss," he said. "Alex was a good Marine. He was a good man."

❧ • ☙

AROUND THE CORNER from the Chisholm's apartment building, Ashe walked into a local club. He liked the name of the place: "The Bitter End." Seemed appropriate. It was the type of place that focused on coffee and atmosphere but shifted to beer and music once it got dark. Ashe thought he was in the mood for some music. He grabbed a table in the back after filling a drink order from the bar. He wanted to sulk for a while as he tried to figure out what to do next.

By nine o'clock, the place was pretty full. The low hum of conversation and clinking glassware blended with the smoke that had grown thick and hung in the air. Ashe had not relinquished his table, which was now almost full of empty glasses.

The place was packed now, the air heavy with the smell of cheap beer and sweat from the late summer heat. The tables were largely occupied, and the spaces between were starting to fill with late arrivals. The band on stage was tuning their instruments, their sound a blur of distorted notes rising above the chatter. A short woman dressed in flowy pants doffed a striped jacket with a fur collar, strange, in August, and threw it without ceremony into a corner before weaving her way to the microphone. Ashe could tell she was already more than a little drunk.

"Mind if I sit?"

Ashe looked up from his drink. The man was relatively short, at most, an inch or so taller than Ashe. His hair was dark and wavy; only the slightest care had been taken to keep it in line. Dressed in unassuming clothes like he was, the man was someone you'd probably not notice passing on the street.

Ashe blinked, his hand moving toward the worn rim of his glass. He hadn't expected company, but he wasn't particularly bothered. The man didn't seem like trouble. He didn't seem like anything, really, just a guy. And Ashe was good at not caring. He shrugged.

The man sat down across from Ashe but turned halfway in his seat so that he could see the stage clearly without obstructing Ashe's view.

He seemed about to speak when a sharp cry came from the stage. The young woman at the microphone had a voice that could cut through glass. It easily parted the din of the crowd. "Wooo! Hey, y'all! Leonard's here tonight! Hi, Leonard!"

The man across from Ashe smiled in embarrassment and blew out a lungful of smoke. Maybe half the club's patrons applauded, many of them seeming to do so to humor the woman on stage rather than out of any real appreciation for the man at Ashe's table. It wasn't his night; it was hers. Raising his glass in the air in mild acknowledgment was all it took for him to shift the focus back toward the band.

"Hey, Willie!" The singer seemed to have one setting, and it was full volume. "There's a soldier in the back with Leonard. I want you to give him a drink on me, and bring me two of whatever he's having."

The crowd seemed delighted by this, possibly in the hopes that the woman would buy their drinks, too, and cheered raucously. Someone in the crowd shouted to the woman on stage that Ashe was a Marine, so technically not a soldier. She bantered with the heckler briefly while the band continued to ready their instruments. The bartender—Willie, apparently; Ashe had not bothered to find that out—sent a girl over with a fresh round for Ashe in a tall glass and a bottle for his new table partner. The girl smiled broadly at Leonard as Willie himself handed the singer a glass, setting the reserve on the nearest table.

"I don't suppose you've heard her sing before, have you?" the man asked, nodding toward the stage.

Ashe glanced over at her. She had wild, untamed hair, and her posture was something between defiance and exhaustion. She seemed to be using the microphone stand to help her remain upright. She placed the glass to her lips and drank deeply.

And immediately spat the liquid out, spraying half the table nearest the stage area. "Oh my God!" she cried out. "Willie, what is that stuff?"

Willie, undaunted, shouted back at her. "You wanted what the Marine was drinking, so that's what you got. It's water."

"Well, get rid of it!" she replied. Her eyes rolled beneath the large blue-tinted circles of her hippie glasses. "And bring me something decent. Whoever heard of a Marine who don't drink?"

Ashe looked down at the table, suddenly wishing he was anywhere else as the crowd laughed and applauded. The band finally started the opening measures of the first song as the young woman grabbed the beer offered her by Willie and took a deep swig from the chilled bottle.

"Sorry friend, she can be... unapologetic," said the man across from Ashe. "But she is special. It's just, uh, not her war, you know?"

"Yeah, whose war is it? Yours?" Ashe was too full of raw emotions to feel bad for snapping at the man.

"Mine? No, not mine; I'm just passing through. A wandering Canadian."

Ashe looked up from the table. "Huh. So, a pacifist, then?"

The man thought for a moment. "No, I don't think so. I'm skeptical about war, of course. But at the decision-making level, not yours. And I want peace. But pacifist? No. I think too much pacifism might just empower the killers, maybe, you know? I don't think that's appropriate."

"Not a very popular opinion these days, is it?" Asked Ashe.

Leonard laughed. "Many of mine aren't," he declared with an enigmatic half smile.

The female singer's voice burst again from the stage, cutting through the moment like jagged glass. "This one's for my new friend, the tee-totaling marine!"

As she sang her first few lines about awaiting a train in Baton Rouge, Ashe stood up from the table. He tucked his hat beneath his arm and dropped a ten-dollar bill on the table.

"Leaving so soon?" said the man, remaining seated.

"Not soon enough," replied Ashe, striding away.

Back out on the street, Ashe felt the cooling air on his skin and was grateful to take a deep breath of relatively unpolluted air. He walked away from The Bitter End, fully committed to his new path.

By the time Ashe reached the corner to stand and wait for the traffic light, the raw and gritty voice of the woman in the club had reached the chorus. She belted out her own particular definition of freedom over the driving bluesy riff. The thumping of the bassline carried heavily, setting a background like falling artillery in the distance.

Ming was still out there. He'd made it back to America, and whether he had somehow dodged court-martial or not, he was walking free. Wyatt Ming. Ming was going to pay for desecrating the memory of Ashe's men. Ming the Merciless.

In nearly two millennia of combat, Ashe had killed a great many men, but not until this moment did he vow to commit murder in cold blood. Ashe was a dead man himself; more times over than he felt like counting. He decided he liked the singer's definition. He had nothing left to lose.

Fiat justitia ruat caelum.

* * *

ABOUT THE AUTHOR

THE CREATIVE JOURNEY of pHil Rittenhouse has meandered from art to science to technology. Roughly in that order, and sometimes all at once. Once upon a time, pHil was a cartoonist. Of course, he also spent over a decade as a research chemist, so that probably cancels out any credibility he may have gained from cartooning.

As a chemist, he learned to approach the world through experiment and observation—habits that shaped his attention to detail as a storyteller. He also learned that explosions, while educational, are frowned upon in most laboratory settings.

These days, pHil (he insists on capitalizing his name that way for obscure reasons no one fully understands) works in software development at Microsoft, where logic and architecture meet imagination, and where he's spent nearly two decades wrangling SharePoint and Dynamics 365 into submission. The precision of coding and the chaos of creativity somehow coexist comfortably there, which might explain both his career longevity and his fiction.

A lifelong reader with a fondness for history, philosophy, and frequent esoteric rabbit holes, Rittenhouse draws from ancient texts, scientific theory, and forgotten myths to craft stories that blur the boundary between the known and the unknowable. His writing explores how obligation, guilt, and grace echo across time. Sometimes with explosions, but fewer than he'd probably like.

He lives in rural Illinois with his wife, four amazing kids, and a cast of household pets large enough to qualify as a small ecosystem. When not writing or debugging, he can often be found reading late into the night or volunteering at his church—still experimenting, still observing, and still sketching his next idea in the margins.

All statements of fact, opinion, or analysis expressed are those of the author and do not reflect the official positions or views of the US Government. Nothing in the contents should be construed as asserting or implying US Government authentication of information or endorsement of the author's views.